/17

WARPED AMBITION

A JO RISKIN MYSTERY

Connie-

Thanks for coming to my first book signing! I appreciate your support!

I hope you enjoy!

Debbie S. TenBrink

DEBBIE S. TENBRINK

Warped Ambition
A Jo Riskin Mystery

First Print Edition: November 2016

ISBN-13: 978-1-940215-84-6
ISBN-10: 1-940215-84-6

Red Adept Publishing, LLC
104 Bugenfield Court
Garner, NC 27529
http://RedAdeptPublishing.com/

Cover and Formatting: Streetlight Graphics

For John
My foundation, my best friend, my love

CHAPTER 1

MEGAN SAT IN THE BACK of the taxi, snapping and unsnapping the clasp of her purse. She scooted closer to the door, away from the suspicious stain on the seat. She had never been in a taxi and wondered if they all stank. As they neared her destination, she realized she had no idea how much to tip the driver.

The cab jerked to a stop in front of the Old Mission Thrift Store. "You sure you got the right address?" the driver asked. In the rearview mirror, he glanced at the Michael Kors purse perched on her lap.

She gave him a little smile and tried to look confident. "I'm sure."

She checked her phone again. No messages, no missed calls. She wanted someone to talk her out of what she was about to do. Or tell her it was okay. Ashley was the only one who knew, and she couldn't help. *She tried to warn you.*

Her mom would know what to do. She punched in her mom's number then stared at the screen with her thumb hovering over the dial button. But it was too late. Megan would have to explain too much.

She put her phone away and leaned her head against the cool window. Everything had gone wrong so fast. He loved her. Or at least he said he did. *So why am I here all alone?*

You know why. That other part of her brain, the part that had always known she was doing something wrong, taunted her. *You let him convince you nothing could happen. He used you.* Megan squeezed her eyes shut and tried to block out that tiny voice. It was too late for blame.

The driver cleared his throat.

"I'm a little early," she said. "Is it okay if I wait a few more minutes?"

He shrugged and glanced at the meter. "Up to you, kid."

Yeah, it's all up to me. She picked at a tear in the back of the front passenger seat and stared at the building across the street. The Old Mission Thrift Store sign had once been red, white, and blue, but the paint had faded to a faint pink and shades of gray. Boards covered all the windows, and someone had tagged the front wall with bold round letters that spelled out "WidowMaker" in shades of blue and green. The style would have made any art teacher proud, but Megan had heard rumors that gangs tagged only buildings where someone had been killed by one of their members. In her part of town, people didn't paint graffiti on buildings, and they definitely didn't kill each other. But she wasn't in her part of town.

Realizing the fee was adding up, Megan pulled money out of her purse, deciding to tip the driver the same as a waiter. She thanked him and stepped out into the crisp October air. Pushing her balled-up hands into the pockets of her jacket, she crossed the street then walked three blocks to the brick building where she had her appointment. She hadn't given the taxi driver the address because she didn't want anyone, even some guy she would probably never see again, to know what she was about to do.

Two weeks earlier, a nurse, Karen—Megan would never forget the woman's name—had counseled her about her options. Karen's talk about the procedure was clinical, with charts, statistics, and medical terms. Even though Megan's mind had screamed with unanswered questions, she had nodded and mumbled that she understood. Karen softened, her tired eyes full of concern, as she encouraged Megan to take some time to think about it, maybe talk to her parents or school counselor. But Megan was sure, so Karen made an appointment and helped her fill out paperwork for a judicial bypass. The following day, she took that paperwork to the courthouse, where the judge barely looked at it, or her, before he signed it. The whole thing had been almost too easy. Her parents would never have to know. But as she trudged up the street beside the building, trying to build up her courage, she wanted her mom more than anything.

When she rounded the corner of the clinic, she froze, her heart jumping into her throat. Protesters lined the sidewalk. A few stood together, holding rosaries and praying quietly. Others paced back and forth, carrying signs that said things like Abortion Kills. I Regret My Abortion. Babies Murdered Here.

What if one of them says something to me? What will I say? What if someone recognizes me? She looked around desperately, but there was no other way into the building. She would have to go past them. Her head down, her long, dark hair hiding her face, she skirted around them, keeping as much distance as the limited space allowed.

Someone waved a pamphlet in front of her face. "You don't have to do this."

Megan glanced into the kind eyes of the woman and took the pamphlet without looking at it. She shoved the paper into her jacket pocket then sprinted to the door. She stumbled into the office and made a beeline for the receptionist window. When she finished checking in, she grabbed a magazine and scanned the waiting area. The other women scattered around the room glanced in her direction then went back to their own reading material and cell phones. Megan slid into the closest chair and flipped through the pages of the magazine without seeing them. She couldn't concentrate. Her eyes kept wandering to the window, where she could see the protestors. She couldn't stop watching them, even as her eyes swam with tears.

After twenty minutes, someone called her name. She looked up and saw Karen in the doorway that led to the back of the clinic. The knot in her stomach loosened a little at the sight of a familiar face.

Megan stood on trembling legs and followed Karen through the door and down a dreary hallway lined with closed doors. She concentrated on the numbers on each door, ticking them off one by one, trying not to imagine what was happening behind them.

One door at the end of the hall stood open. Megan's heart pounded in her ears. Her vision blurred around the edges. She couldn't see anything but that open door.

They entered a small room with beige walls sparsely decorated with posters and a framed garden print. A doctor's diploma hung beside a white cabinet. Karen closed the door, and Megan stared at the exam table covered in white paper. She averted her eyes from the adjustable lamp and metal stirrups on the end of the table to the safety of the ceiling. Bile rose in her throat.

Karen's voice droned in the background, but through the ringing in her ears, Megan caught only the word "seat," so she perched on the edge of the single chair in the room.

Karen pulled a wheeled stool in front of Megan and settled on the metal seat. The springs squeaked in protest under her ample frame. "You know it's not too late to change your mind. Did you read the materials I gave you?"

"Yes." Megan stared intently at her shoes and rubbed together the hands pressed between her knees.

"And you still want to go through with it?"

Megan met Karen's compassionate gaze. "I don't have a choice. I'm fifteen. My parents don't even know." She lowered her head. "They would kill me."

"You know your parents won't kill you, Megan. You have to make the right decision for you, not them." Karen laid a hand on Megan's knee. "I know this is difficult. I just want to be sure you've thought it through. This is a decision you have to live with for the rest of your life."

Megan shoved her hands into her pockets and felt the crumpled pamphlet. The sound of the protestors' quiet praying rang in her ears. She wanted to cry. She wanted to run home and ask her mom what to do. She wanted to be anywhere but in that depressing room.

She thought about telling Karen how she felt. But Karen

couldn't help her. No one could. She forced strength that she didn't feel into her voice. "It doesn't matter. I have to do this."

Karen smiled sadly. "Okay, then, if you've made up your mind."

After a curt knock at the door, a pretty, young blonde in a white lab coat walked into the room. Karen patted Megan's knee then stood and handed the woman a file.

The young woman glanced at the file then held out her hand. "Megan, I'm Dr. Lipscomb."

In Megan's nightmares, the doctor had always been an old man with cold, accusing eyes and sharp instruments. She shook the doctor's hand and forced a weak smile.

"I know you spoke with Karen a couple of weeks ago, and you were given information to read at home. Do you understand what we're going to do? Do you have any questions for me?"

Megan glanced at Karen, who opened a cabinet door and took out a box of surgical gloves and a tube of gel. The tray on the counter was lined with a syringe, gauze, and metal instruments.

Oh God, are those scissors? Megan looked away and took a deep breath. "I understand."

Dr. Lipscomb nodded. "Okay. Do you have someone here with you?"

"No, but I have someone who will come and get me when… it's done."

The doctor glanced at Karen. Megan ducked her head and started picking at her nail polish. *Yes, I'm alone. Why do you think I'm doing this?*

"We really prefer if you have someone here with you," the doctor said. "If there are any complications—"

"I have all of the paperwork done and emergency numbers and stuff," Megan blurted. "If there are any problems, you can call."

"Well, then, we'll leave you alone for a few minutes to get out of your clothes and into the gown. It ties in the back."

Alone in the room, Megan took off her jacket and tossed it over the chair. A crumpled paper fell to the floor. The bold print of "Life Matters" was all she could see of the pamphlet. Her hands trembled as she picked it up and smoothed out the creases.

The blue eyes of a newborn baby stared back at her. "I Matter" was emblazoned across the bottom. Megan covered her face and sobbed.

I can't do this. She pulled her hands away from her face. Her eyes darted from the stirrups to the instruments to the pamphlet in her hand. She had thought she could bury her beliefs, but she couldn't.

Her breath came in short gasps. She swallowed to keep the bile from rising any higher in her throat. *I have to get out before they come back.*

Megan dropped the pamphlet and grabbed her jacket. She opened the door then peered down the empty hallway. A sign at the end of the hall pointed to the waiting room. She hurried in that direction, scurried past the receptionist desk, then pushed through the front door.

Once outside, she leaned against the cool brick and gulped in the fresh air. The protestors continued their circuit in front of the building. Megan couldn't bear to pass them again. She followed a narrow footpath between the clinic and an adjacent building to the back parking lot.

Behind the clinic, she sat on the ground and sent two text messages:

can u pick me up? we need 2 talk

karen's right. I can't do it. ima have the baby. i'll give ur money back pry tomoro. gotta tell my prnts. will u help?

While she waited for a response, the sun disappeared behind thick, dark clouds that promised rain. He wasn't coming. He probably didn't expect her to need a ride so early. Or maybe he knew what was coming and didn't want to face the reality of her decision. He'd been clear that he wanted her to have the abortion.

She let the tears of fear and frustration fall as she wrapped her arms around her waist and began to walk. The autumn wind cut through her thin jacket. When she got far enough away from the clinic, she would flag down a taxi and go home.

She dreaded telling her parents, but getting it off her chest would be a relief. They would be devastated and disappointed in her, but they would know what to do. They always did. She was tired of dealing with the fear alone. Her secrets would be out in the open, and maybe that was good. It was time to stop hiding.

The humiliation of going back to school, of everyone knowing she was pregnant, would be almost as hard as facing her parents. She was one of the popular girls that others wanted to be. Pregnant, she would be the butt of their jokes.

When a steady rain began to fall, she put her hood over her head and picked up her pace. Someone called her name from the street. She peered through the shower and was relieved to see a familiar car.

Megan trotted over, opened the door, and slid into the passenger seat. As she buckled her seat belt, she said, "Boy, am I glad to see you."

CHAPTER 2

Lieutenant Joellen Riskin leaned her elbow on the windowsill of her Ford Ranger and pushed her hand through her blond hair. She tried to rub the tension out of the back of her neck. She had been summoned to court to give additional testimony in a murder investigation. Delays, objections, motions, and all the other necessary evils of justice had played out before she'd been called to the stand, wasting most of her day.

She was stuck in traffic on I-96, which wasn't unusual in the fall. In Michigan, summer was road-construction season, so in October, crews worked long hours to make sure the roads were finished before winter weather hit. The cold, ice, and salt would undo most of the repairs, so they could start over again in the spring. Jo had no patience for the delay. She wanted to lay on the horn or, at the very least, flip off a construction worker or two. They were just doing their jobs, but it would give her some satisfaction.

I'll never get back to the office by four. She tried to remember the relaxation techniques she'd learned from the holistic practitioner the department had brought in for the detectives. *Start with the toes, tense as hard as you can, then release. Work your way up your body, tensing and releasing, until everything is relaxed.*

It didn't work. *Such bullshit. Does that really work for anyone? I don't need to relax my toes. I need to get out of this damn traffic and back to the office.*

An end to the orange cones brought a break in traffic, and within minutes, Jo arrived at the station.

After striding through the bull pen and ignoring everyone in her path, she plowed into her office. Her partner was sitting in one of the guest chairs, with her feet propped up on Jo's desk.

Lynae looked up from the report in her lap and pushed back a strand of auburn hair that had escaped from its loose, messy bun. "Hey, you're finally back."

Jo eyed Lynae's Troopa boots and the empty coffee cup stuffed full of discarded wrappers. "I'm glad you made yourself at home."

"I'm just helping you out, partner." Lynae nodded toward the television.

Jo grabbed her coffee mug and poured a cup from the half-empty pot on her credenza. "What did I miss?"

Lynae put her feet down, stacked her paperwork into a neat pile, and put it on the corner of Jo's desk. "Not much. You're only a few minutes late."

"Good." Jo flopped into her chair and wrapped her hands around the mug. She anticipated her coffee as much for the warmth as for the taste.

Lynae picked up the remote and turned down the volume on the TV. "What took you so long? Court adjourned an hour ago."

"I got stuck in construction traffic. At least I think we'll get a quick verdict on the Schneider case."

"I don't know how we wouldn't. We wrapped him up like summer sausage, and we got a signed confession. I don't even know why it went to trial."

Jo snorted. "Summer sausage?"

"You know... summer sausage. Packed all tight in the skin?" Lynae motioned with her hands.

"Yeah, I get it. I just never thought of my cases that way." Jo slugged a mouthful of coffee and grimaced at the bitter taste. Disgusted, she set the cup aside.

"Well, you will from now on." She pointed at the cup. "And I made that coffee about four hours ago."

"You couldn't have told me that sooner?" Jo rummaged through her desk. "I need some gum or something to kill that awful taste."

Lynae went to the credenza. "I'm sure I have something in here."

Jo scowled. "And why do you have something in my office?"

Lynae dropped a pack of gum on Jo's desk. "It's the only safe place. You've seen what those vultures in the bull pen do with anything edible."

"Yeah, nothing is sacred out there." Jo pulled out a piece, unwrapped it, and popped it in her mouth. "You're right that the verdict should be a no-brainer. Schneider had a public defender who could barely remember his name without checking his notes. Jack Riley did a good job. I like him. He seems like he knows what he's doing."

Lynae grinned. "He's easy on the eyes too."

"You think? I never really noticed." She decided not to mention the lingering looks or the too-long handshakes she and the handsome assistant prosecutor had shared.

"How could you spend thirty seconds with him and not notice?"

Jo worried her wedding ring around her finger. "Anyway, it was just damn good police work that wrapped that case up. Any third-year law student could have handled it."

"Yeah, we're good. What can we say? So how about catching a drink at Teazers later to celebrate?"

At the end of court days, Jo just wanted to go home and put it away. But when she considered the mounds of paperwork, interview transcripts, and impeccably handled evidence that she had watched the prosecutor dole out to the jury, she felt she owed her team a drink. They had worked hard on that case and deserved a little fun to celebrate its end.

She checked her watch. "I can't leave Mojo waiting too long. You know how impatient that dog is. But I'm game for a couple of drinks. I should be done here by six. See who else can make it. Tell them the first round's on me."

"That always brings them out."

Jo peered at the television. "Show's back on. Now get out of here or be quiet."

"Nice." Lynae snatched her paperwork from Jo's desk and left the office.

Jo settled in to work with *The Ellen DeGeneres Show* playing in the background. She found that having that small amount of time to see some humor and happiness in life gave her a renewed sense of purpose.

At six o'clock, she packed what was left of her paperwork into her shoulder bag and made the short drive to Teazers. The bar was a dive, but the burgers were good, and the drinks were cheap.

She spotted her people the minute she walked in the door. Apparently, she was the only one who had waited until six o'clock to get started.

"I guess I'm a little late to buy the first round," she yelled over the music pumping out of the old-fashioned jukebox.

Isaac Breuker chuckled. "Don't worry, Lieutenant. We started a tab for you."

Jo slid into the chair across from Lynae. A waitress appeared with a Corona and set it in front of her. "Good to see my team has me covered, as usual."

Isaac gestured at the beer. "See? We told her to bring it as soon as you got here. Thanks for letting me celebrate with you, even though the case was wrapped up before I started."

"You're part of the team, Isaac. It doesn't matter when you got here. You'll earn your drinks on the next one." She tipped her beer to tap his bottle in a toast.

Charles Lainard, Isaac's partner, leaned in over Jo's shoulder. "The kid's gonna be handy to have around. Did he tell you he's got a connection in the lab?" He folded his tall, pencil-thin frame into the seat next to her.

Isaac beamed. His pearly teeth flashed in sharp contrast to his dark skin.

Jo raised an eyebrow. "How good of an in?" A good connection in the lab could push results ahead by weeks.

"Pretty solid, I think." He smirked and took a long drink of his beer.

Lynae shoulder-bumped him. "I'm sure the tight shirts don't hurt."

Isaac held out his arms and looked down. "I don't know what you're talking about."

Jo chuckled. "Whatever it is, just keep doing it. We need that connection."

Charles pointed at Isaac. "Speaking of tight shirts, let's see who's at the bar. There must be someone waiting for a handsome man to buy her a drink." He stood and buttoned his charcoal suit.

"Keep an eye on him, Isaac. He tends to forget he's married." Jo didn't care for Charles's cavalier attitude about his marriage.

Charles grinned and grabbed his beer from the table. "Lieutenant, I'm offended. I'm just helping the kid out. There's nothing wrong with being a wing man."

The two men made their way to the bar, with almost every female head, and more than one male one, turning in their wake.

Lynae sighed. "He definitely doesn't need a wing man."

Jo picked at the damp napkin under her beer. "Hey, not to get serious, but your caseload is pretty light right now. I could use some fresh eyes on Mike's file."

Lynae put down her drink. "That's not even our jurisdiction. How do you have the file?"

Jo shrugged. "It doesn't matter. And I don't have the whole file."

"You have to let Madison handle it. He's the primary, and I've heard he's good. Besides, you're too close to it to be objective."

"I can't let it go, Nae, you know that." When the napkin was shredded down to nothing but what was stuck to the bottom of her bottle, Jo reached for the bowl of peanuts. "To Madison, it's just another case, but to me, it's my life."

"Jo, I get that, but I'm sure he will give it plenty of attention."

"I heard it's going to Unsolved. Madison's not even looking at it anymore." She cracked several peanuts and dropped them back into the bowl. She had no appetite, but she had to keep her hands moving. "Never mind. I shouldn't have asked."

"Jo—"

"Seriously, never mind." Jo flagged down the waitress and

motioned for another round. She gave a quick salute to her team when they broke into applause. She turned back to Lynae. "I'm sorry. I'm putting you in a weird spot, and it's not fair. Just forget I asked."

Lynae laid her hand on Jo's. "I'm in."

"You are?"

"You're my partner, and my friend. Of course I'm in."

Jo squeezed Lynae's hand and nodded. She didn't trust her voice.

"But not tonight," Lynae added as appetizers were brought to the tables, and the crowd descended on them like locusts. "Tonight, we celebrate."

Jo sat back and watched as plates were passed, greedy hands were slapped, and mouths were stuffed. Laughter punctuated the conversations as everyone talked at once. Her team was camaraderie at its finest. Lynae was right, tonight was about their victory. There would be time for Mike's case later.

CHAPTER 3

Jo pulled into her garage and killed the engine. She had forgone the greasy bar food in anticipation of taking a run, then she stayed out later than she had planned. It was too dark to run, and her stomach grumbled in protest of the missed meal. She grabbed her bag and got out of the car, mulling over her limited food options. As she headed for the door, she heard Mojo shuffling and whining on the other side. She entered the house, and forty pounds of squirming furball danced around her legs.

She squatted to give Mojo a good scratch and received several slobbery kisses for her effort. "Hi, baby girl. It's good to see you too."

Mojo ran to another room and trotted back with a ball in her mouth. She dropped it at Jo's feet. Her body quivered in anticipation as she looked from Jo to the ball. When Jo picked up the ball and tossed it, Mojo ran after it as if her life depended on it. The sound of her skittering feet and clumsy scampering were the only noises in the big, empty house. Jo wasn't sure which of them appreciated their nightly ritual more.

Her phone rang, and she groaned. She was done being social for the day. Unless it was the station, she would let it go to voice mail. But when she checked the caller ID and saw her mom's number, she smiled and answered, "Hi, Mom."

"Hi, Joellen. How goes the battle?"

Only her mother called her Joellen. Jo had decided in middle school that she hated her name and would go by only Jo. But her mother refused. "It makes you sound like a boy. My son's name is Brian, and my daughter is Joellen." Jo stubbornly stuck to her guns, and from that day forward, she became Jo to everyone except her mom. Over the years, they had developed a grudging truce. Her mom stopped scowling every time Jo introduced herself, and Jo stopped correcting her mother when she called her Joellen.

"I spent the day in court. You know how much I love that."

"Oh yeah, your favorite thing. Are you still testifying in the Schneider trial?"

Jo walked into the kitchen. "Finally finished up on Schneider today. Now we wait for the jury to make the right decision. It should be quick."

"Good. It will be good for you to finally put that to rest."

Jo searched the freezer for something edible she could throw in the microwave. "So what's up, Mom?"

"You're still planning on lunch Sunday, right?"

"I wouldn't miss it. It's the only good meal I get all week."

Her mother laughed. "Well, I want to call your aunt Trudy and ask her to join us. What do you think? She's all alone since your cousin moved to New Orleans. Brian said they would love to see her."

Jo rolled her eyes. *I should have let the call go to voice mail.* "Of course he did."

Her brother was the quintessential perfect son. He never made any waves and always did exactly what was expected of him. He had a beautiful wife who was not only successful but also kept their home looking as though Martha Stewart lived there. They both had steady, safe jobs that brought them a substantial income that allowed for a nice house and a couple of vacations each year. As if that weren't enough, three years ago, they had given birth to the Second Coming.

Jo had taken on the role of wave-maker. Her parents weren't thrilled with her choice to be a detective. They imagined her life was as dangerous as that of the detectives they watched on television. Holidays were often workdays, and vacations were postponed if a case was hot. The only connection Jo had to Martha Stewart was the unread magazines that adorned her coffee table, courtesy of her sister-in-law. Jo had always hoped that she would fill her house with kids so she could decorate with their chaos and clutter.

She had also failed to learn the art of biting her tongue. "Brian doesn't want Aunt Trudy there any more than I do, Mom. He's just too much of a suck-up to say so."

"Oh, I don't think so. He seemed fine with it."

Jo decided on the least boring meal in the freezer and shoved it in the microwave. "Of course he seemed fine with it. He always lets me be the bad cop."

"That's not true, Joellen."

Jo paced the kitchen. "Sure it is. Brian knows I'll open my big mouth and say all the things he's thinking. It's what I do. And Aunt Trudy's son moved to New Orleans to get away from her. Everyone knows she's crazy."

"Joellen! Aunt Trudy is not crazy. She's just a little…"

"She's crazy as a shithouse rat," her dad called out in the background.

"Eddy! You're as bad as your daughter."

Jo snickered. She could picture him sitting in his leather recliner, watching whatever sport ESPN was airing at the moment. He would be dressed in baggy sweatpants and an old T-shirt with a bag of chips in his lap and a beer in his hand. Her mother's cup of decaf and an open novel would be on the end table that separated his recliner from Mom's glider rocker. They had relaxed in the same way for as long as she could remember. Jo had spent a great deal of her childhood watching sports with her dad while her mom was tuned in to the mystery of the week.

Jo grabbed a beer from the fridge and popped the top. "I'm just being honest, Mom. Besides, Aunt Trudy thinks she and I are kindred spirits or something."

"She only wants you to know she relates to your situation. She's trying to help because she understands."

Jo picked up the ball that Mojo dropped at her feet and chucked it down the hall. "She doesn't relate, and we're not in the same situation. She's single because she's been divorced three times after all her husbands found out she's nuts. That's not me."

"Of course it isn't."

Mojo returned with the ball. Jo heaved it even harder. "I don't want to go to singles dances or get an eHarmony or Match dot com account. She can't get it through her head that I'm not interested in finding another man and that our situations aren't the same. I really don't want to deal with it."

"I understand. I just won't mention it to her."

Her mom's disappointment came through loud and clear. "No, Mom, you don't understand. And thank God for that."

Jo realized she would spend Sunday either dealing with her crazy aunt or feeling guilty for making her mom feel bad. It was a no-win situation. "Listen, I'm sorry. You're right. Aunt Trudy shouldn't be alone. I can suck it up for one afternoon. I'll even try to be nice."

"If you're sure—"

"Just call her, Mom."

When she finally extricated herself from the conversation, she grabbed her dinner from the microwave and flopped onto the sofa. Mojo crawled up next to her and wiggled her head onto her lap. Jo ate with one hand while surfing channels with the other until she found a mindless comedy to help her kill the rest of the night.

The morning sun shining through the blinds woke Jo. She scooted to the center of the bed and nestled into the crook of Mike's arm. He shifted to hold her closer, lightly rubbing her back. She kissed his neck and ran her fingers through the soft hair on his chest. She could feel the smile spread on his face as he turned toward her to meet the next kiss. His wet tongue slid across her cheek to her ear then down to her neck.

Wait.

She jerked her head. The licking continued in her other ear. She tried to hold on to Mike, to get back the relaxed, contented mood, but the moment fled. She opened her eyes. All she had next to her was a slobbering dog wanting attention. A late-night infomercial droned on the TV. She had fallen asleep on the couch.

She wiped the slobber from her face. "Mojo, stop!"

Mojo lowered her head and tail. She stared up at her with big brown eyes, her ears flattened against her head. Jo gave the dog a pat on the head to show that she wasn't really angry.

"Damn it, Mike," Jo muttered as she slumped back on the couch. She looked at the clock and saw that it was only one thirty. She rubbed her cheek where it had lain on Mike's chest in her dream. She swore she could smell him.

She got up and shuffled into her office. Sleep wouldn't come after that, and she didn't want it, anyway. She didn't want to go back to that world where she no longer lived.

Some evidence from Mike's case lay on her desk. The murder board, minus the victim's picture, sat center stage. She hadn't been able to bring herself to hang Mike's picture on that cold whiteboard any more than she could leave his case in the hands of Madison.

Jo had pored over the evidence so many times she could recite most of it word for word. She had to be missing some vital piece of the puzzle. Something continuously nagged at the back of her mind. She sat down to go through everything again. She wouldn't stop until she either broke that missing piece free or ended up six feet under. Either way was okay with her.

CHAPTER 4

JO JUMPED WHEN HER PHONE rang. The muffled ringtone told her the phone was buried somewhere on her desk. She shoved aside an empty coffee cup and an ice cream bowl, dropped three binders onto the floor, and lifted a stack of papers. She finally uncovered the device and caught the call before it went to voice mail.

"Riskin."

"Lieutenant Riskin, this is dispatch."

She rubbed her bleary eyes with the palms of her hands and checked the clock. It was 5:52 a.m. "Go ahead."

"A body's been found at 754 South Lapeer."

"I'm on my way. Dispatch Detective Parker to the scene."

"Yes, ma'am."

Jo started a pot of coffee then went to her room to shower. After getting dressed, she pulled her hair back into a loose bun. No amount of makeup was going to cover the evidence of her sleepless night, but she made a quick attempt anyway.

She felt a pang of guilt when Mojo scampered to the garage door and planted herself in front of it. "Sorry, pal, no time for a run this morning." She opened the slider to the backyard. "You'll have to settle for a quick potty break."

When Jo called her in after only a few minutes, Mojo gave her an insolent look before slumping onto her dog bed. Jo clipped on her credentials, grabbed her bag and coffee, then headed out into the cold, dark morning.

As she pulled out of her driveway, she turned off the radio and let the complete silence quiet her mind for what was ahead.

The middle-class homes of her suburban neighborhood were soon behind her, and the lights of the city shone ahead. The lights of the bridges spanning the Grand River that flowed through downtown looked beautiful in the dark. Restored historic buildings with turn-of-the-century architecture sat alongside new high-rises with twenty stories of glass reflecting the river below. Medical facilities that rivaled any around the world rose out of the highest hill in the city and shone hundreds of lights out into the darkness. In another hour, downtown would be teeming with people of all walks of life going about their business, completely unaware that someone had been murdered.

The section of town Jo was heading for didn't shine with bright lights and beautiful historic buildings. With the highest crime rate in the city, the Slope was all too familiar to her. Poverty and hopelessness permeated the streets. The few businesses were run-down and reeked of despair. Anyone who walked through the impoverished area did so with either the confident strut of those who dominate the back alleys or with their heads down, shoulders hunched, and dark hoodies pulled over their heads.

The police would canvass for witnesses, but in the Slope, no one ever saw anything. In Jo's experience, people with money, expensive homes, and plenty of resources couldn't wait to give any dirt they could think of on their neighbor or their best friend, but in poor neighborhoods—where jobs, money, and even homes were a scarcity—no one knew or saw anything. No one trusted the police.

On South Lapeer Avenue, pockets of people stood in the doorways of buildings with barred windows or leaned against dirty paint-peeled walls. A handful were on the stoop of Our Daily Bread, the only place on the street where they could get a free warm breakfast. Even though the place wouldn't open for over an hour, their stomachs brought them there early so the food wouldn't run out before they got their share.

She headed for the rotating blue and red lights. Closer to the address she'd been given, the excitement in the air was palpable. News crews were already gathered at the crime scene tape, vying for the best position to report the latest tragedy. Reporters stood around, drinking coffee and chatting as if they were at a neighborhood picnic.

Jo parked beside some police cars, gulped down what was left of her coffee, threw her bag over her shoulder, then stepped out into the bedlam. A baby-faced officer stood guard outside of the taped-off area. His uniform stretched over a mountainous frame that belonged on a football field. As Jo approached, he shifted to block her access. When she showed him her credentials, he nodded and moved so she could duck under the tape.

On the other side, she turned back to him. "What's your name, Officer?"

The officer shuffled uncomfortably and looked somewhere slightly above her left shoulder. "Jacobs. Um, Douglas Jacobs, ma'am."

Jo held out her hand and smiled. "Lieutenant Riskin. I hate 'ma'am.'"

"Yes, ma'am. Um... Lieutenant. Sorry." He shifted his bulk and looked anxiously over his shoulder.

"Is this your first murder scene?" she asked.

"Yes, it is. I would like to work in Homicide when there's an opening. I asked to be put on off-duty call for Homicide grunt work to get experience." His Adam's apple bobbed. "It's not like it is in the books."

"No, nothing ever is. It's a good idea to gain some experience before you go all in. It's never easy, but it does get easier. Just stay focused, and you'll be fine."

His eyes flickered to hers. "Yes, ma'am. I mean, yes, Lieutenant. Thank you."

Jo straightened her shoulders. "Where am I headed?"

Jacobs pointed toward two uniformed officers standing beside an ambulance about a hundred yards away. "Right over there."

"Thanks." She nodded at the reporters and ever-growing crowd of onlookers. "Keep those yahoos back."

"Yes, ma'am, Lieutenant."

Well, I guess I'm going to be Ma'am Lieutenant to that one.

Jo scanned the parking lot. The Pharmer's Market had been

in business for a long time and ran a legitimate business, at least as far as she knew. Its downfall in recent years was that it had the misfortune to be located next to United Park. At one time, United Park had been a local church's attempt at a youth center, a place where kids could play basketball or skateboard after school to stay off the streets. It had worked for a while with support from local businesses, until those businesses could no longer afford to fund it. When the money dried up, the project failed. The kids who had once felt safe enough to be kids for a few hours after school were forced to either take to the streets or stay out of the area as the drug dealers and gangs took it over. The park was currently nothing more than an empty square with grass poking through cracked cement. Hopscotch and Four Square lines had faded. Rusted poles without backboards or hoops stood at each end of the remains of a basketball court. It was a sad snapshot of the plight of the neighborhood.

The Pharmer's Market was a dingy gray two-story building. Large patches of chipped, peeling paint left the underlying brown brick exposed. On the other side of the barred windows, signs taped to the glass advertised the business hours and cigarette prices. The neon Open sign to the right of the door was dark.

The parking lot was empty, except for one car and a garbage truck. The car was a late '90s Ford Festiva badly in need of a resting place in a junkyard. Jo assumed it belonged to the tenants of the upstairs apartment but wrote down the make, model, and plate number, anyway. She would have dispatch run the information later. A Ridgeline Refuse garbage truck sat close to the pharmacy dumpster. Jo would bet good money that was where the victim had been found.

As she walked toward the ambulance, she spotted two men in Ridgeline Refuse uniforms standing next to the pair of officers.

The older officer nodded as Jo approached and gestured at the garbagemen. "Lieutenant, these are the ones who discovered the body."

Jo held out her hand. "Lieutenant Riskin."

The older one pulled off his work gloves and shook Jo's

hand. "Charlie Schider." He gestured at his partner. "This here is Matthew Terkoff." Charlie sat heavily on the back bumper of the ambulance. His pale cast and watery, red-rimmed eyes told Jo he had probably lost his breakfast somewhere on or near her crime scene. As much as she hated that thought, she couldn't blame the poor guy.

Jo sat next to him. "I'm sorry your day started like this."

He crossed his arms and rested his chin on his chest. His heavy Carhartt jacket bulked up around his face. "Nineteen years on this job and I never seen nothin' like that."

"How did you find her?"

Charlie shrugged and shook his head. "She was just layin' there in the dumpster. We almost dumped her with the trash. We woulda never known she was there if the dumpster wasn't moved."

Jo eyed the bright-green dumpster. "The dumpster was moved?"

Charlie nodded. "It was pushed off kilter. We couldn't get the front loader lined up."

Jo jotted that in her notebook. "What size dumpster is that?"

"Four cubic yards."

"What would it take to move a dumpster that size?"

The man shrugged. "When they're full, they're heavy as hell. I wasn't getting anywhere trying to move it."

Throughout the conversation, Matthew Terkoff had been pacing in front of the ambulance. He moved with a nervous energy that screamed of illicit excitement. His bright eyes darted from the officers to the crowd gathered around the perimeter then over his shoulder to the crime scene. Jo knew the type. Matthew knew he would get his fifteen minutes of fame, maybe even be interviewed for the news. And when the hype died down, he would tell this story over and over to anyone that would listen for years to come.

Matthew stopped and pushed his long hair back from his face. "We didn't touch her. We could see she was dead. I watch crime shows, and I know you can't touch nothin' or you screw up evidence and shit. So I told Charlie, 'Don't touch her. Just call the police.'"

Jo nodded, mentally thanking the multitude of cable crime

shows that seemed to have made everyone a crime scene expert. "You did the right thing by calling the police and not touching her."

Matt smiled and pointed at Charlie. "Told ya."

Charlie regarded him impassively then turned back to Jo. "So what do we do now?"

She motioned the older officer over. "Do you have their full statements?"

He nodded. "We do."

Jo shook Charlie's hand then Matt's. "Thank you for your time. If we have any more questions, we'll be in contact. You're free to go home."

"What about the truck?" Matthew asked.

"We're going to need that to stay here for a short time." Jo nodded toward the younger officer. "He can get someone to give you a ride back to Ridgeline."

The two garbagemen went over to speak with the younger officer, and Jo checked the nameplate of the other. "What do we have, Officer Kingman?"

Kingman opened his notebook. "Not much from those two. Young female found in the pharmacy's dumpster at approximately five fifteen. As they said, they didn't touch anything after they found her. The dumpster had been turned, and Mr. Terkoff was having a hard time getting the forks to line up, so Mr. Schider got out to direct him. The lid was open, and the body was right on top."

"So she was dumped there after the last trash was brought out for the night."

Kingman nodded. "It appears so."

Jo pointed at the wooden stairs that led to a separate entrance on the second story of the Pharmer's Market. "Talk to whoever lives up there. See if that Festiva belongs to him. If it isn't the pharmacy owner, we'll want to talk to him also. Find out what time the pharmacy closed, if he saw anything, what time the last trash was brought out. You know the drill." She stood and looked at the crowd still gathered around the yellow tape. "People are weird, aren't they, Kingman?"

"Excuse me, Lieutenant?"

She waved her hand at the crowd. "Look at them standing around, trying to get a look. They all know there's a dead body here. Why do they want to see it?"

Kingman shrugged. "Morbid curiosity, I guess. They all wonder what death is like. You know, what it feels like. Or they're waiting for the family to come screaming in."

Jo cocked her head and glared at the crowd. "So they can get excited over someone else's pain?"

Kingman shook his head. "I don't think it's excitement for most of them. I think they want to watch from the sidelines and be thankful that it isn't them or someone they love. They can only imagine what it's like, so their curiosity draws them in."

"Well, take it from someone who knows. Your imagination can't begin to prepare you for the life-sucking reality of it." She slid her hands into her back pockets and rocked back on her heels. "When we remove the body, the crowd is going to start dispersing. Get some officers to start taking statements now before they all leave. Then start them on a two-block canvass, door to door. I'm going to need you here."

Kingman pulled off his hat and scratched his bald pate. "I'm going to have to pull a few people in."

"Do it." Jo marched toward the dumpster, where the techs were starting to move in. About ten feet away, she had to step around a splatter of vomit. *Called that one.*

Mallory Wiseman, the assistant medical examiner, was standing on a step stool so she could lean over the edge of the dumpster and snap pictures of the contents. Jo had seen her pull that stool out of her trunk at several crime scenes to hoist up her five-foot-one frame. Although Jo had Mallory by eight inches, they were a pretty even match. Mallory's small frame belied a strength that Jo was made aware of when they had been partnered in a sparring match during a team-building exercise. Before the match, Jo had chuckled at the thought of such a small adversary, but Mallory had put her in her place with quick moves and endless endurance. Jo would never again underestimate an opponent.

"You're quick, Wiseman," Jo said.

Mallory straightened and looked down at her. Her smile didn't quite reach her dark eyes. "I was up for an early-morning run. Had plans for the day and wanted to get an early start. Never made it out the door for my run, but—lucky me—I got to be one of the first ones here."

"Yeah, aren't we the lucky ones."

Mallory nodded at the dumpster. One of its dual-hinged lids was open. "Luckier than her."

Jo took latex gloves from her bag, snapped them on, and stepped onto Mallory's stool. The body of a teenage girl lay on top of a week's worth of trash. She was on her side with her right arm and leg beneath her and the left limbs sprawled as if she had stretched out to find a comfortable position in her bed of garbage. Her long dark hair was saturated with blood. Jo reached in to pull the hair away from the face. Dark smears of mascara pooled around hazel eyes that stared emptily behind long lashes. The mouth was agape. Shimmery cotton-candy lipstick was smeared macabrely across her pale cheek. Jo concentrated on breathing through her mouth so the overwhelming stench of rotting food and blood didn't trigger her gag reflex. Blood, black and crusty, soaked the shoulders of the girl's white shirt, while streaks ran down both the front and back.

Jo stepped down from the stool. "How much time do you need before we can move the body?"

Mallory adjusted her camera lens. "I need a few more shots, then we can get her out of there."

Jo motioned in the direction of the crime scene techs, who were waiting to begin their process. "I'll get a game plan together with the techs. Give me the nod when you're done." She spotted Lynae walking across the parking lot and changed direction to meet her partner.

"Not what I had in mind for this morning," Lynae said. She stopped and stared at Jo. "God. You look like shit."

Jo raised her eyebrows and cocked her head. "Hey, thanks. I can always count on you."

"Sorry. But seriously, are you all right?"

Jo shrugged. "Didn't get much sleep."

"You should think about a little concealer for those bags that have taken up residence under your eyes."

"I'll take that under advisement." Jo pointed at the dumpster. "Now, if you're done assessing my looks, can we talk about why we're here?"

"What do we have?"

"Victim found in that dumpster. Can't really tell much about her yet, but I can tell you it's a kid too young to be ruining our day."

"A kid? Damn it." Lynae shook her head. "What the hell is going on in this city?"

"I wish I knew."

Seeing Mallory step off the stool, Jo nodded toward the scene. "Looks like Mallory's done. We're up." She strode toward the dumpster.

Lynae pulled on gloves as she walked beside Jo. "Fantastic."

Jo pointed at the vomit splatter. "One of the guys who found her upchucked his breakfast, but he had the decency to do it away from the scene."

Lynae stepped gingerly around the mess. "Nice of him to be so considerate."

When they reached the big trash container, Lynae stepped onto the stool and leaned over the side. She pulled the neck of her shirt over her face to block some of the smell, something Jo refused to do out of principle. "Blunt force to the head and neck, multiple." Lynae reached down and shifted the corpse. "No other wounds obvious on the rest of her body. Of course, I can't see much without getting her out of there."

Jo nodded. "Agreed. We need to get her out of there."

Lynae tilted her head. "I can tell you that she's wearing an expensive shirt."

Jo peered over the edge of the dumpster. "How do you know her shirt's expensive?"

Lynae pointed at the logo. "Abercrombie. Ridiculously overpriced but popular."

"I never shop there. It's for teenagers. How do you recognize it? You're almost as old as me."

Lynae looked down at Jo. "You know my nieces. They're almost teenagers, and they love that place. My sister can't afford it, but once in a while she indulges them. Or I do. Besides, it's the place with all the hot models. Who doesn't stop and take a look?"

Jo snorted. "Me. They're teenagers. I feel like a pervert if I even glance at the pictures when I walk by."

Lynae chuckled. "You're such a prude."

"Whatever."

Lynae looked around the area. "This isn't someplace I would expect to find someone wearing expensive clothes."

"It's not all that unusual. Sometimes it's about priorities. I see people living in homes without heat, plastic for windows, no food in the refrigerator, but they're wearing two-hundred-dollar shoes."

Lynae shook her head. "Don't get me wrong. I like my shoes, but I don't get it."

"And hopefully you never will." Jo pulled off her gloves and motioned to Mallory as Lynae stepped off the stool. "Let's get her out of there."

Mallory hovered over the crime scene techs as they laid a body bag on a stretcher in front of the dumpster. "Be careful with her! This is enough of a mess without us losing any trace."

A look passed between the techs. Mallory was cool and collected until it came to moving a body, then she mysteriously turned into a tyrant. She lived for trace evidence and was convinced she was the only one who could properly transport a body without destroying some vital clue.

"What can you tell us?" Jo walked a few steps from the body to get Mallory away so the techs could do their job unhindered.

Mallory followed, but she kept an eye on the scene. "Obvious trauma to the skull. We won't know if that's cause of death until we do an autopsy, of course, but at least half of the blows were severe enough to cause brain hemorrhaging."

"Time of death?"

Staring at the scene, Mallory scowled at some infraction the techs made. "According to body temp and rigor, I would say she's been dead around twelve hours."

Jo glanced at her watch. "So somewhere between six and seven last night."

"Right." Mallory raised her voice. "And that may be all I know if we lose all our trace."

Lynae positioned herself between Mallory and the crime scene. "There should be a lot of blood with wounds like that. Her shirt is soaked, but there's no blood around her or on the garbage she's lying on."

Mallory pulled off her gloves and slipped them into a plastic bag from her field kit. She held the bag out to Jo and Lynae, who snapped theirs off and tossed them in. "She died and bled out somewhere else. She was at that place long enough for the blood to dry before she was dumped here. You're going to find a whole lot of blood somewhere."

Jo watched as the body bag was zipped and strapped to the stretcher. "I'm counting on it. I doubt that we'll find much to go on here, but we'll have to check the dumpster to see if anything came with her."

Lynae crossed her arms and tracked the techs as they moved the body to the ambulance. "There's some serious overkill here. She most likely knew her killer. A crime of passion, anger."

Jo winked at her partner. "That usually means unplanned and careless too."

"Speaking of careless..." Mallory pushed past Lynae and stormed over to the stretcher. "Guys, come on! You think you could zip that bag up all the way? Hey, why don't we just roll her around on the ground for a while and see what we can pick up?"

CHAPTER 5

ONCE THE AMBULANCE LEFT, Jo walked back to the dumpster. "All right, Kingman, we need to go through this garbage. Open every bag. You find anything that you question, bag and tag it. We'll sort it out back at the station."

Kingman eyed the dumpster. "I could use a little help with that, Lieutenant. Everyone I brought in is canvassing the neighborhood."

"There's a young officer holding back the gawkers. His name's Douglas Jacobs. He's looking for some experience in homicide. Why don't you grab him?"

Kingman scanned the crowd. "I don't know Jacobs."

Jo pointed toward the front of the pharmacy. "He's out front. He's huge. You can't miss him."

Kingman's face lit up. "Oh, I know who you're talking about. The Gerber-baby face on top of Mount Everest."

Jo chuckled. "You got it. He seems eager. Keep an eye on him, though. He's completely green."

She began a search of the grounds around the crime scene. The area was unusually clean, considering the location and proximity to a dumpster.

After a few minutes, Kingman returned with Jacobs on his heels. The younger officer's eyes darted around, his head swiveling from side to side. He looked like a bobblehead on steroids.

Kingman opened a field kit, pulled out two pairs of latex gloves, and handed one set to Jacobs. "We have to go through everything in this dumpster, bag by bag. We'll pull out any that are tied and examine the contents outside of the dumpster. But for the loose stuff, we're going to have to get in and sort through it. I hope you don't like your shoes too much."

Jacobs looked down at his enormous shoes. "No, sir. These are standard-issue uniform shoes."

Jo grinned. She'd picked the right rookie. Kingman was going to eat up being called "sir," especially by someone the size of a small truck.

Jo helped the two officers throw out as many bags as they could reach from the outside. When the remaining bags were out of their reach, the officers climbed into the dumpster. She pulled a flashlight out of her bag then got down on her knees to search under the dumpster. The smells of damp asphalt and rust filled her nostrils. Bags thudded on the pavement as the men tossed them out.

"I think I found something!" Jacobs yelled.

Jo bounced to her feet and flipped off her flashlight.

Still standing in the dumpster, Jacobs was holding something over his head like a trophy. "It's a purse. I think it's a nice one." He turned it over in his meaty hands to display the front.

Jo high-stepped over and around garbage bags, pizza boxes, wrappers, and half-eaten food. She recognized the logo on the bag as one of a designer way outside her pay grade. "Let's see if it's hers."

Jacobs hoisted himself out of the dumpster. He reached into the Michael Kors purse, pulled out a lanyard, and held it up. The victim's hazel eyes, sparkling and full of life, stared back out from the Hillview High School ID.

Jo nodded. "That's her."

Kingman pulled himself over the edge of the dumpster and dropped down beside Jo. "There's nothing else in there."

Jo handed him the lanyard. "All right, let's get this bagged."

Kingman grabbed his field kit from beside the dumpster, pulled out an evidence bag, and dropped the lanyard into it. He squatted down to mark the bag.

Jo turned back to Jacobs. "What else is in the bag?"

Jacobs pulled out a wallet that matched the purse. Checking the compartments, he said, "No money. Just a receipt for a taxi."

Jo craned her neck to see the receipt. "Is that from yesterday?"

Jacobs nodded. "Yes, ma'am. Blue Frontier Cab Number Thirty-One. The time stamp says three twenty-five."

"Good job, Jacobs. Get that bagged up and put with evidence."

Red crept up his neck as he worked to suppress a grin. "Yes, ma'am, Lieutenant."

"Make sure he gets that done right, Kingman." For Jacobs's benefit, she put on a stern expression and pointed at the purse. "Do exactly what he tells you. Nothing more, nothing less. Don't guess, don't assume, and don't question. Procedure and chain of evidence is everything. Nothing screws us worse than mishandled evidence."

Jacobs nodded, his wide-eyed gaze never leaving her face. She waved him on, and he turned around, holding the purse out in front of him with both hands as if it were a live grenade. Kingman pulled an evidence bag from his kit and held it open. As Jacobs slipped the purse into the bag, he looked as though the weight of the world had been taken off his shoulders.

"Now we need to tag each piece and get it to the crime scene techs." Kingman gestured at his field kit. "Get a tag out of there, and I'll show you what to do."

Jo nudged some trash out of her way, flipped her flashlight back on, and resumed her inspection of the area under the dumpster. The light caught a glint of something on the side of the container. She moved closer and spotted a silver scrape about eighteen inches from the ground.

She called Mallory over and pointed out the mark. "Can you get me a picture of this scrape?"

Mallory drew the camera up from the strap around her neck, squatted down, and took a couple of close-ups from different angles. She pulled out a measuring tape and handed it to Jo. "I need to get relative location."

Jo slid the tape out, dropped one end to the ground, then held the other end next to the scrape.

Mallory snapped a few more shots. "What are you thinking?"

"Charlie, one of the garbagemen who found the body, said these dumpsters are heavy as hell when they're full. This one was moved, pushed off at an angle, possibly when it was full. Most likely a car did it."

Mallory cocked her head and studied the dumpster. "A solid bump from a car hitting in that spot would push it to that angle."

Jo nodded. "It sure would."

"And you think our killer is the one who hit it. Isn't that a bit of a stretch?"

Jo shrugged. "We'll talk to the pharmacy owner and whoever took the trash out last night. Maybe it's been at that angle all week or they already know who hit it. Right now, I'm just speculating and collecting anything that might be evidence."

Mallory crossed her arms. "The only reason you would ever get close enough to a dumpster that you could hit it with your car is if you're dumping something heavy."

Jo nodded. "Or something you know you shouldn't be dumping. You get close, you're in a hurry, and that makes you careless. It's usually something careless that does our killers in."

Mallory opened her field kit. "Let's get a sample of that paint." She scraped the paint from the scratched area onto an evidence slide and bagged it. "If you're all set, I'll head back to the station and get these uploaded."

"I think I'm good. Thanks, Mal."

Jo walked the scene. She tried to envision that young, well-dressed girl being brought to the dark, empty parking lot and dumped unceremoniously in the trash. *What brought you to this part of town? What could you possibly have done to end up here like this?* She was having a hard time seeing it, getting a feel for it. *Were you simply in the wrong place at the wrong time? No, there was too much overkill for a random victim. This was personal.*

On the way back to the station, Jo had picked up doughnuts and coffee. She walked into the conference room for the morning meeting and found her team already sitting around the table.

She held up the doughnut boxes in her left hand. "I brought treats." She set the bag of coffees on the table.

Charles hopped out of his chair. "Bribery will get you everywhere."

Jo crossed her arms. "Now why would I bribe you, Lainard?"

"You're gonna want to put this one away quick, and that will mean some extra hours or juggling cases."

Isaac picked out a cream-filled and snagged a cup of coffee. "No need to bribe us, LT. Whatever it takes."

Charles elbowed Isaac. "Suck-up."

Detective Morgan brushed crumbs from his silver mustache. "I'm with Isaac. Some of us have been around this department for a lot of years and have seen more than anyone should. But you never get numb to a kid in a dumpster."

Jo scanned the room. "The treats aren't bribery. They're proactive thanks. I knew you'd all react this way." She went to the podium at the front of the room, set down her case log, and leaned her elbows on the scarred wood. "Every case we have open is important to someone, so we'll work this like always. But you're right. I want the bastard who did this to know that we won't lie down and let this happen in our town."

A murmur of assent rose around the room.

Jo gave everyone a moment to get it out of their systems then opened her logbook. "Let's get to work." She listened to updates, took notes, shuffled assignments, and gave direction where needed. Several of her detectives were overloaded by their current cases and were dismissed after the briefing. She asked Charles, Isaac, and Lynae to stay back.

Jo slid into the chair next to Isaac. "According to the school ID found in our victim's purse, her name is Megan Tillman. She goes to Hillview High School. Lynae, get an address on her so we can go ruin her parents' lives."

Lynae grimaced. "Can't wait for that."

Jo gave her a half smile. "Yep, everyone's favorite job. The body was taken to County. It's with Mallory Wiseman in the Trace Evidence Lab right now. She'll contact me if and when they find anything that could be useful. I'll give Kent Alderink a call and see if I can entice him to push our girl to the top of his list."

Charles grinned slyly. "I've heard the medical examiner has a preference for dark chocolate and Crown Royal."

"Well, let's hope it doesn't come to that, but I'll keep that tidbit in my back pocket." Jo turned to Isaac. "I took a paint scraping from the dumpster that looks fresh. Get ahold of your contact in the lab and see how quickly we can get information on the car that left it."

Isaac jotted in his notebook. "I'm on it."

Jo checked her notes. "Charles, I'd like you to contact Blue Frontier—"

"One-eight-hundred-Ima-taxi."

"What?"

Charles smirked. "It's written on all their cars. And it's quirky enough that I remember."

"Huh. The shit you learn. Anyway, get ahold of them and see who drives Number Thirty-One. Our victim had a receipt in her purse. We'll at least know where she was going or where she'd been." Jo leaned back in her chair. "Officer Kingman put a neighborhood canvass crew together. I'm not holding my breath that we'll get anything from that. They've talked to the owner of the pharmacy. He didn't see anything when he took out three bags of trash at ten o'clock last night. He didn't look in the dumpster, but our victim didn't have anything on top of her, so she most likely wasn't there when he took the trash out."

"Does he live in the apartment upstairs?" Lynae asked.

Jo shook her head. "No, that's a rental. The guy who lives up there works third shift, leaves at six twenty every evening. He was very precise. That puts him out of the location too early to be a witness." Jo pointed her pen at Isaac. "We will, however, make sure he was at work last night. At this point, we don't know who this girl knew or why she ended up in that dumpster. Everyone is a suspect."

Isaac checked his notes. "I've got TOD at approximately six p.m."

Lynae added, "Blood evidence indicates that she wasn't put in the dumpster until after she bled out."

Jo slapped her logbook shut. "That's all we've got. Get me something more."

The detectives gathered their things and scattered. Jo grabbed a three-by-four-foot poster board from the supply closet then returned to her office. She logged into the department's secured Sharefile account and perused the crime scene photos Mallory had uploaded. She scrolled down to the clean picture Mallory had labeled for the ID.

The ME had wiped the smeared mascara, lipstick, and blood from the girl's face and combed the trash and snarls from the hair. She couldn't hide the beating the face had taken, but the result was as good as it could be.

Jo hit Print and heard her printer whir to life. She found a close-up of Megan's battered face surrounded by trash and added it to the print queue. When the printer finished, she retrieved the two pictures. She dropped the clean one in her bag to show the Tillmans later. She taped the crime scene one in the center of the poster board. She wrote "MEGAN TILLMAN" in bold block letters above the photo then set the board on an easel in the far corner. She hoped to have a lot more information to add soon.

Jo dialed the medical examiner's office. A smooth baritone voice answered. "Kent Alderink."

"Kent, this is Jo Riskin."

"Good morning, Lieutenant. To what do I owe the pleasure?"

Jo smiled. "You're messing with me, aren't you?"

"Now what gives you that idea? Just because I had the body of a teenage girl brought in this morning with your name on the slip doesn't mean I expected to hear from you within an hour or two."

Jo snorted. "You know me too well."

"Well, this is your lucky day, Lieutenant. It so happens that we're caught up to the point that I can start on your case this morning."

"This morning? That's fantastic. Let me know when you have a preliminary report ready, and Lynae and I will come by."

"I'll text you."

Jo raised her eyebrows. "You're texting now, Kent?"

Kent chuckled. "Even techno-dinosaurs like me have to get with the times, eventually."

"Well, I'm impressed. Thanks. I'll see you later." Jo hung up and shook her head. *Kent Alderink texting. What next?*

Lynae stuck her head in the doorway. "Got an address for Daniel and Joyce Tillman."

"What about missing persons?"

Lynae shook her head. "Nobody with that name or matching her description was reported missing."

Jo scowled. "Interesting."

Lynae gestured at the murder board. "You always put the worst-looking crime scene photo on your board."

Jo grabbed her bag and keys. "Cleaned-up pictures don't belong on a murder board. I want my team to remember what the bastard did to that poor girl."

Lynae nodded. "Then let's get moving."

CHAPTER 6

Driving through the Tillmans' neighborhood, Jo felt a pang of envy. She could work hard her entire life, moving up through the ranks at the department, and still never be able to afford to live in that kind of neighborhood. Public service was not the profession to be in if one wanted an affluent lifestyle.

Lynae whistled. "Damn, this is a nice neighborhood. Not going to get here on a detective's salary."

Jo glanced at her friend. "Weird how you read my mind sometimes."

Lynae wiggled her eyebrows. "I'm in your head."

"Trust me, that's not somewhere you want to be."

Lynae gawked at the houses they passed as though she'd never been in that neighborhood. "What do you suppose a house around here goes for?"

Jo shrugged. "No idea. I just know I can't afford it. At least not if I want to have a car, heat, and electricity. Oh yeah, or wear clothes and eat."

"I'd walk around naked and hungry if I could live in one of these houses. I mean, look at them. I'm totally jealous."

Jo parked the Jeep beside the curb in front of the Tillmans'. The modern colonial two-story home and impeccably manicured lawn belonged in a *House Beautiful* magazine. Dark shutters surrounding the five windows on the second story were a picture-perfect accent for the cream-colored brick. Intricate dentil molding adorned the pedimented dormers on the roof. The place looked flawless. But if the people inside knew she was coming, they would give it all away to anyone who could stop her from knocking on their door.

She knew that kind of pain and loss. "I wouldn't be jealous of these people today."

Lynae gazed at the Tillmans' house. "Do you think the parents were involved?"

Jo shook her head. "God, I hope not. But sometimes the homes that look the most perfect on the outside hold the nastiest secrets on the inside."

"You should put that on a greeting card."

Jo snorted. "Hallmark's got nothing on me."

Lynae opened the door and had one foot out before she realized Jo hadn't moved. She slid back in and closed the door. "You look a little pale. Are you all right?"

Jo stared at the steering wheel until the lines took on a life of their own. "I'm never all right when I have to do this." She took a deep breath and blew it out in a quick puff then grabbed her bag and opened the door. "Let's get this over with."

They walked up the brick sidewalk to the front entrance of the Tillmans' home.

Jo turned to Lynae. "I'll take the lead on this."

"It's all yours."

Jo rang the doorbell, and a dog immediately began yipping inside. She thought of Mojo and made a mental note to call her neighbor, Myla, and ask her to take the dog to the park. Unless the killer wandered into the police station and confessed within the next hour or so, Jo would be getting home pretty late.

From inside the house, a woman scolded, "Brutus, stop!"

Lynae turned to Jo with a look of amusement. "Brutus?"

A woman opened the door then bent down to nudge back the cockapoo yapping around her feet. She straightened and pushed back a strand of dark hair that had escaped her French twist. Her hazel eyes twinkled. "Sorry about Brutus. He's a handful."

Her daughter looks just like her.

Jo smiled kindly. "Joyce Tillman?"

She nodded, her eyes flicking from Jo to Lynae. "Can I help you?"

Jo held up her badge. "I'm Lieutenant Jo Riskin, and this is my partner, Detective Lynae Parker. We're with the Grand Rapids Police Department. May we come in?"

Mrs. Tillman's hand rose to her neck, and she clutched the simple gold cross that hung in the V of her cashmere sweater. "Yes, come in." She stepped back and let Jo and Lynae into the foyer. "Is something wrong?"

"A body was found this morning in the Slope."

"I'm sorry to hear that, but what does that have to do with us? I don't know anyone who lives in that part of town."

Jo kept her eyes on the woman's face. "Mrs. Tillman, when is the last time you saw your daughter, Megan?"

Joyce knitted her eyebrows. "Megan? I saw her yesterday before school."

Jo cocked her head. "She didn't come home last night?"

"No, she spent the night at her friend's house. What's going on? Is this person you found someone Megan knows?"

Jo jotted that information in her notebook. "Do you know where your daughter is this morning?"

Joyce crossed her arms. "Of course I do. She's at school. Why are you asking me so many questions about Megan?" Her eyes widened. "Wait. You don't think...? No. Megan's at school!"

"Mrs. Tillman, we just need to—"

Joyce's eyes darted from Jo to Lynae. "No. You tell me what's going on right now!"

Jo met the other woman's eyes. "Mrs. Tillman, we believe the body we found this morning is Megan."

Joyce shook her head and backed away. "No... no, there's been a mistake. Megan's at school. Call the school."

"Mrs. Tillman—"

"Call the school! You're wrong. It's not Megan."

"We found Megan's purse with the body, and her school ID was inside."

Joyce's breath came in short gasps. "Then someone stole it!" She pulled her cell phone out of her pocket. "If you won't call the school, I will."

Her hands trembled as she punched in a number. She put the

phone to her ear. "Nancy, this is Joyce Tillman." She listened for a beat, her face scrunching into a deep frown. "What do you mean I forgot to call?" She shoved her hand into her hair. "Megan isn't sick. She's there at school. Right?"

Joyce raised her eyes and looked at Jo. "No. Oh, God, no." She dropped the phone and crumpled to the floor. "No... no. Not my baby. It can't be."

Jo picked up the phone, thanked the person on the other end, then disconnected the call.

Lynae squatted in front of her and put a hand on her shoulder. "Mrs. Tillman, can I get you something? Maybe a glass of water?"

Joyce sobbed into her hands and shook her head. Lynae looked up at Jo, who nodded. Jo was pretty certain the woman wasn't their killer.

Lynae held out her hand. "Here, let me help you to a chair."

Joyce stared vacantly at the proffered hand for a second before taking it. Lynae helped the woman to her feet then wrapped an arm around Joyce's shoulders. The look of stunned anguish on Joyce's face paralyzed Jo. She could actually feel the shock, the disbelief, the stabbing pain of loss. Her ears rang, and her stomach clenched.

"Jo," Lynae said over her shoulder as she struggled to lead the distraught mother into the next room.

Jo snapped back and hustled to help. They entered an enormous living room with one wall dominated by a stone fireplace. They lowered Joyce onto a camelback sofa. She perched on the edge of the cushion, her dilated, glassy eyes staring blankly at the Persian rug under the coffee table.

Jo whispered, "I'm afraid she may be going into shock."

Lynae nodded. "Keep an eye on her. I'll get her a glass of water." She hurried toward the back of the house.

Jo sat next to Joyce and gently laid her hand over the other woman's. They sat in silence until Lynae returned with the water. Joyce took the glass and lifted it to her mouth. Her hand shook violently, and Jo reached out to steady the glass.

After Joyce lowered the glass, Jo took it and set it on the coffee table. "Mrs. Tillman, is there someone we can call to be here with you?"

"My husband." Her head snapped up. She turned to Jo, wide eyed. "Oh God! I have to call Dan." A fresh wave of sobs wracked her body.

When the woman regained some of her composure, Jo said, "I'm sorry, but I'm going to have to ask you some questions. I think it would be best to have your husband here, so we only have to go through it once."

Joyce wiped her nose and dabbed her eyes. "Okay. I'll go call him." She stood and walked out of the room.

Jo got up and walked over to the fireplace. A large picture of Megan and her parents, taken at the base of a majestic old oak tree, hung front and center on the stone chimney. Other frames lined the mantel. The photos showed Megan growing from an adorable toddler, through the awkward middle school years, and into the beautiful young woman Jo had seen beneath the blood. Anger rushed through her at the loss of that young life and the pain the parents would feel for the rest of their lives.

Lynae cleared her throat. "Is there anything worse than this?"

"No, this is it. If you can do this part of the job, you can do anything." Jo rubbed the base of her neck then rolled her shoulders.

"How you holding up?"

"I'm fine. This isn't about me, Nae," Jo snapped. She turned back to the pictures to avoid Lynae's scrutiny. Lynae had only asked because she cared, but Jo didn't want to see that look of concern or pity on her partner's face. She could hear the mumble of Mrs. Tillman's voice from the other room then a fresh wave of sobbing as she told her husband the news.

Jo turned back to Lynae. "God, this sucks."

"All we can do is find the bastard who did this and give them at least that."

"Yeah, that's all we can do," Jo said softly.

Mrs. Tillman returned to the room and slumped in the corner of the sofa. "My husband will be here in a few minutes. He works right at Blodgett." She motioned loosely in the direction of Blodgett Hospital, which was only a few blocks from their home.

Jo sat in a chair, and the three of them sat in silence.

Minutes later, the front door opened, and a baritone voice called, "Joyce?"

As her husband bolted into the room, Joyce stood and stumbled over to him. She clenched his green scrubs and collapsed into his arms. "Oh God, Dan."

They held each other, sharing a pain that only they could. When their tears were spent, they sat together on the sofa. Jo and Lynae chose the matching wingback chairs that faced the couch.

Dan scrubbed his hands over his face and looked between Jo and Lynae, his eyes pleading. "Could there be a mistake? Maybe it isn't Megan. Maybe someone else had her ID. Maybe…" He stopped with a choking sound.

Jo inched forward on the seat. "We've identified your daughter visually based on her school ID. When you're ready, we have a photo for you to make a positive identification. I wish I could tell you that I think there could be some mistake, but I wouldn't be here if I thought there was."

Dan met Jo's eyes. "I want to see the picture now. I need to know for sure."

"Are you sure you're ready for this, Dr. Tillman? There are a few things I think I should tell you first."

Jo broke the news about the beating that the girl's head and face had taken the only way she knew how, quickly and gently. There was no way to tell them that would make it any better. Joyce curled up on the sofa, overcome with a new wave of wracking sobs.

Dan stared at the floor and clenched his jaw. "Show me the picture."

"Dr. Tillman, we did the best we could, but I have to warn you that we couldn't hide—"

Dan jumped up and moved so that he was towering over her. "Just show it to me, dammit!"

Out of the corner of her eye, Jo saw Lynae lay her hand on her sidearm. Keeping her gaze on Dan, she held a hand up to Lynae. "Please sit down," she told Dan quietly.

Dan slumped back onto the sofa. She pulled the picture from the back of her notebook and held it out to him.

He took the photo, angling it away from his wife, and stared at it for a moment. He made a gruff sound in the back of his throat and handed the picture back to Jo. "Who would do this to our little girl?"

Jo leaned toward the couple. "We're going to find that out, but we need your help."

"What happened to her?" Dan murmured.

"Dr. Tillman—"

"What happened to her?" he repeated through clenched teeth.

"It's early. There hasn't been an autopsy yet."

He propped his elbows on his knees and ran his hands through his thick hair. The gray sprinkled around his ears stood out stubbornly from the dark russet. "What *can* you tell us?"

"The only thing we know at this time is that she was severely beaten and she was found in the Slope."

Joyce scowled. "The Slope? Why would she be in that neighborhood?" She looked to her husband for answers.

He gripped her hand and shook his head. Dan took a deep breath and stared at Jo. "Was she...? Was there any sign that she was...?"

"We don't have any reason to believe that she was sexually assaulted," Jo said gently. She turned to Joyce. "You said Megan was supposed to spend the night at a friend's house?"

Joyce nodded. "Ashley. She lives just down the block."

"Can you give me Ashley's contact information?"

Joyce pulled the information up on her phone and handed it to Jo. "She's Megan's best friend." She turned to her husband, fresh tears welling. "Dan, why wouldn't Ashley call us if Megan didn't come to her house?"

Dan shook his head and pulled his wife closer. "I don't know, honey. I don't know."

Jo leaned back in her chair and crossed her legs. "Where were you last night, Dr. Tillman?"

Dan scowled. "Where was I? Why?"

"Please. This is just routine. We have to ask."

"I was here all night. I was on call."

"Can you tell us if Megan was having any problems with anyone at school?" Lynae asked.

Joyce looked desperately between Jo and Lynae. "No, everyone loved Megan. I don't know of anyone who would want to hurt her."

Lynae asked, "Was she acting different?"

Joyce looked thoughtful. "Well, she was a little quiet the last couple of weeks, but when I asked her if she was okay, she said everything was fine." She turned to her husband and buried her face in his shoulder. "I asked her, and she said everything was fine."

Jo directed her question to Dan. "Did she have a boyfriend? Were there any problems there?"

"No, no boyfriend. Megan doesn't have time for boys. She's very determined to do well in school and..." He stopped and covered his face with his hands.

Joyce raised her head. "Megan volunteered at Butterworth Hospital once a week, reading to the kids in the oncology ward. She always loved it so much. She was a good kid, Lieutenant. She was so loving and warm. I don't understand why anyone would hurt her."

Jo leaned forward. "We would like to check Megan's phone records to see who she's been talking to."

Dan furrowed his brow. "Don't you have her phone? She always had it with her."

"No, we didn't find the phone."

"Then someone took it. She never left the house without it."

Jo nodded. "That's very likely. With her number, we can trace her calls and texts. It could be helpful to know who she's been in contact with."

Dan rattled off the number then sat back and pulled his wife close.

Jo stood and walked over to the couch. "I'm so sorry for your loss. We will find whoever did this." She laid her card on the end table. "If you think of anything at all, even if you think it's not important, please call me."

Jo and Lynae left the grieving couple on the sofa and showed themselves out. As they walked back to their car, Jo looked around the neighborhood, imagining the peaceful elegance and the security the residents thought money could buy. She could have sworn she heard the shattering of that illusion coming from the Tillman house.

Jo slid into the driver's seat and called Charles Lainard. She relayed Megan's phone number to him. "Find out the carrier and get in contact with them. I want to know who she was talking to."

CHAPTER 7

JO EASED AWAY FROM THE curb. "We need to talk to Ashley Kane and find out if she saw Megan last night, and if not, why she didn't call her parents."

Lynae settled low in her seat. "It doesn't make sense that she wouldn't call if Megan didn't show up and didn't get ahold of her in some way."

Jo adjusted the thermostat. The temperature had plummeted while they were with the Tillmans. "Unless she wasn't really going to Ashley's house in the first place."

"I did that a time or two in high school."

Jo pulled into the parking lot of Hillview High School and parked her Ford Ranger between a red convertible Mustang GT and a silver Mazda MX-5 Miata. "Mrs. Tillman mentioned that Megan volunteered at the hospital. We'll head there after we talk to Ashley."

Lynae scanned the area. "Are we in the student lot?"

"Yeah, why?"

"Look at these cars. When I was sixteen, I bought a 1990 Buick Skylark for two grand. I thought I was the shit."

Jo shook her head. "I'm not even going to tell you what I drove. When I was in school, even the teachers couldn't afford cars like these."

They made their way into the school and headed toward the office. The hallway walls were lined with posters reminding kids to order their class rings, signs encouraging them to climb mountains and reach new heights, and warnings containing drug and alcohol statistics. Several trophy cases were filled with reminders of winning teams dating back as many years as the school had been open. Hillview apparently knew what it was doing on the football field, as that case overflowed into the next. Jo thought of Mike and his love for the game. Sunday afternoons in the fall had been reserved for football, whether with friends, family, or just the two of them. They would don their Detroit Lions jerseys, cover the coffee table with snacks and beer, and spend the day cheering for their fantasy football players. She tucked the memories away as she opened the door to the main office.

The nameplate on the reception desk said Mrs. Dykstra. Behind it sat a harried-looking middle-aged woman talking on the phone while entering information into a computer. Her wide bangle bracelet clattered with every keystroke. The countertop was lined with baskets tagged with things like Senior All Night Party, Athletic Pink Slips, and Yearbook Orders. Next to those were the various forms and permission slips.

Mrs. Dykstra pointed at the sign-in sheet on the counter as she continued her phone conversation. From the half that Jo could hear, some parent was in need of reassurance that Junior's teacher would be in contact. Mrs. Dykstra scribbled a note while brusquely informing the parent that the teacher would contact her as soon as possible but not during school hours.

Jo held up her badge. Mrs. Dykstra arched her eyebrows and again pointed at the sign-in sheet. It was a battle Jo wouldn't win, so she signed her name and noted the time in the appropriate boxes. She smiled at the receptionist as she laid the pen down.

Two students sat in chairs along the wall. One was kicked back with his chair up on two legs and leaning against the wall, while the other had an open chemistry book in her lap.

Through a door on the right, three men were having an animated conversation. They wore matching green-and-gold shirts with the school's mascot emblazoned on the chest. They had the broad-shouldered, thick-around-the-middle look of ex-football players who were no longer burning enough calories.

A couple of minutes later, Mrs. Dykstra hung up the phone and asked brusquely, "What can I do for you?"

Jo held up her badge again. "We'd like to talk to the principal."

"What is this regarding?"

Irritation crept in, but Jo kept her voice level. "This is about us wanting to talk to the principal."

The woman held Jo's gaze for a moment then picked up her phone. "I'll ring Ms. Scheidel. She's in her office."

Jo smiled thinly. "Appreciate it."

Within a few minutes, a slim middle-aged woman emerged from a back office, straightening her navy blazer. She smiled as she approached. "I'm Janice Scheidel. What can I do for you?"

Jo glanced at the eager Mrs. Dykstra, who quickly looked away and busied herself on her computer. "We'd like to have a word with you in private, if we may."

"Of course, follow me." Mrs. Scheidel spun around and headed back the way she had come, her short, dark hair bouncing with each efficient step.

The office fit the woman. A small desk, meticulously neat, sat in the corner with two visitor chairs facing it. A bookshelf held educational volumes and one framed picture propped on the end. No space was wasted on knickknacks. Mrs. Scheidel motioned toward the chairs then stepped behind her desk.

Once they were all seated, Jo got down to business. "Mrs. Scheidel, I'm sorry to tell you that the body of one of your students, Megan Tillman, was found this morning."

"The body? Does that mean...? Oh no." She gripped the cowl of her white turtleneck. "What happened?"

"That's what we're trying to determine. I can tell you that she was murdered."

"Dear God." The principal's voice cracked, and she reached for a tissue box on the corner of her desk.

Jo leaned forward. "Did you know Megan?"

"Yes, of course. I know all of the students. Megan was a good student. She was very involved."

"Did she have any problems with anyone?" Lynae asked.

The principal dabbed at her eyes and shook her head. "No, not that I'm aware of. She was well liked by the teachers. As far as I know, by the students as well. I can't imagine who would want to hurt her."

Jo pulled her notebook out of her bag and flipped through the pages. "We've talked with Megan's parents, and they said that Megan's best friend was Ashley Kane. We'd like to talk to her if you could get her out of class."

"I can get Ashley out of class, but I won't let you talk to her without a parent present."

"She isn't a suspect, Ms. Scheidel. We just want to ask her a few questions."

"I won't have you delivering this kind of news to one of my students without a parent."

Jo realized the woman was right. She had been so focused on finding the killer of a teenage girl that she hadn't thought of the feelings of the girl's friend. With some chagrin, she nodded. "Understood."

Mrs. Scheidel stood and walked to the door. "I'll have Alice call her mother." She opened the door and bumped into Mrs. Dykstra, who had found something to do directly outside of the principal's office.

Mrs. Scheidel smirked. "Alice, how convenient that you're right here."

Crimson crept up Alice's neck. "I was just filing—"

"Of course. Please call Ashley Kane's mother and ask her to come to the office right away. When she arrives, get Ashley out of class."

Alice's eyes flicked to Jo then back to the principal. "What should I tell her this is in regards to?"

The principal raised an eyebrow. "I think if you tell her it's important, she'll come."

Alice turned and clumped back to her desk.

Mrs. Scheidel shook her head then told Jo and Lynae, "I'm going to grab a couple of extra chairs. Would you like some coffee?"

Lynae shook her head.

Jo could almost feel the comfort a hot cup of coffee would bring. She wanted it desperately. "No, thank you. But it might be a good idea to have some water on hand for Ashley and her mother."

Mrs. Dykstra pointed at a mini-fridge behind her desk. "I keep that well stocked with bottled water. I'll be just a minute."

After the principal stepped out of the office, Lynae swiveled in her seat to face Jo. "You turned down a cup of coffee?"

Jo blew out a long breath. "You have no idea how bad I want it. But it seems a bit crass to be kicked back with a steaming cup of java when I'm about to tell a teenager her best friend is dead."

Lynae grimaced. "Yeah, good point."

Jo tapped her hands on her bouncing knees. "I absolutely hate this part of the job. Give me a cranked-up junkie or pissed-off psycho to interrogate the hell out of, but don't make me break the news to anyone that someone they love is dead."

Lynae shifted in her seat. "Have you ever had to notify a teenager before?"

"No, and I—" Jo jolted at the sound of a quiet jangle outside the door. She looked over her shoulder and raised her voice. "Can we help you, Mrs. Dykstra?"

The secretary poked her head around the corner of the door. "I just wanted to let you know I got in touch with Mrs. Kane. She only lives a couple of blocks away, so she'll be here shortly."

"Thank you."

"Is there anything else you need?"

Jo gave her a feral smile. "I think the only thing we need is the door closed."

Mrs. Dykstra huffed and turned on her heel, closing the door behind her.

Jo rolled her eyes. "I bet she regrets wearing those damn bracelets."

The door opened, and Jo sighed then jumped to her feet to help as Mrs. Scheidel attempted to navigate through the door while carrying two chairs. "I'm sorry about the closed door. I wasn't thinking."

The principal set the chairs down then closed the door. "I think we all know why that was necessary. She means well, but it will be best if we leave that closed."

CHAPTER 8

Mrs. Dykstra walked into the office, followed by a petite woman with an oversized purse hanging on her shoulder. The principal smiled. "Thank you, Alice."

The receptionist hesitated, staring at Jo as if trying to read her thoughts, then said, "I'll call Ashley down." She turned and scurried out.

Mrs. Scheidel stood and walked around her desk. "Thank you for getting here so quickly, Julie." She discreetly reached around the woman and closed the door.

Julie Kane eyeballed Jo and Lynae. She tucked a dark mass of wavy hair behind her ear. "Alice said it was important?"

Jo held out her hand. "Mrs. Kane, I'm Lieutenant Jo Riskin with the Grand Rapids Police Department." She motioned to Lynae. "This is my partner, Detective Lynae Parker."

Julie's eyes grew wide. "Detectives? What's going on?"

Jo held up a hand. "Your daughter is okay and not in any trouble."

Julie blew out a short, quick breath. "Okay."

Jo smiled. "I'm sorry, I should have led with that."

Julie laid her hand on her heart. "You may need to give me a minute to get my heart back."

Mrs. Scheidel reached into her mini-fridge, took out a bottle of water, and handed it to the other woman.

Julie smiled gratefully. "Thanks, Janice. It's amazing how quickly your body reacts at the thought of your child in danger." She took a sip and replaced the top then turned to Jo. "All right, if my daughter is okay and not in any trouble, why am I being called to the school to talk to detectives?"

"We have some difficult news to tell your daughter and some questions to ask her. We thought it would be best if you were here with her."

"What do you have to tell her?"

"It's about her friend, Megan Tillman."

"Megan? Is she okay?"

"I'd rather wait—"

A curt knock interrupted them. Before the principal could say anything, the door opened, and the receptionist ushered in a young girl.

Mrs. Scheidel put her hand on the doorknob. "Thank you, Alice. Please hold my calls." She closed the door in the nosy receptionist's face.

The girl clutched her algebra book to her chest and scanned the room. "Mom?"

Julie jumped from her chair and put her arm around the girl's shoulder. "Hi, hon."

"Mom, what are you doing here? What's going on?"

Julie gestured toward Jo and Lynae. "These are detectives, and they need to talk to you. They asked me to be here with you."

Ashley glanced at Jo and Lynae then turned back to her mom. "Detectives? Why?"

Jo smiled at the young girl. "My name is Lieutenant Jo. You're not in any trouble, but we do need to talk to you." She gestured at the chairs the principal had brought in. "Why don't both of you have a seat?"

Ashley stared at Jo as she lowered herself into a chair. Her mom sat next to her and laid a hand on her knee.

Jo leaned forward. "Ashley, I have to tell you something very difficult, and there's no easy way to do it. Megan Tillman was killed last night."

The girl sucked in a harsh breath as her eyes filled with tears. Her blond ponytail bounced as she rapidly shook her head. She covered her face with both hands. Her small frame rocked as she sobbed.

"Oh, honey, I'm so sorry." Julie pulled her daughter close and gently rubbed Ashley's shaking shoulders.

When the sobbing slowed to hiccups, Lynae pulled a couple of tissues from the box on the principal's desk and handed them to the pair. "Ashley, Megan's mom said she was supposed to be with you last night. Was she?"

Ashley wiped her nose. "No. She was supposed to be, but she didn't show up."

"Did you try to get ahold of her, find out why she didn't come?"

"I sent her a text and asked her where she was. She texted me back and said she was going home. I was kind of mad because it was short and—oh God." Her eyes widened. "I didn't even reply. I was mad because she didn't tell me what was going on. Her text just said she didn't feel good."

Her mom squeezed her hand. "Don't be hard on yourself, Ashley. You didn't know."

Jo checked her notes. "What time did you text her?"

Ashley rubbed her eyes with the sleeve of her tunic. "She was supposed to be at my house at six. I think I sent her the message maybe about seven. She texted me back about ten or fifteen minutes later. She just said she was going home and would probably see me tomorrow. I was kinda mad, you know?"

Jo nodded. "Could I see the messages? It would help us to know the exact time."

Ashley glanced at the principal then pulled her phone out of her pocket. She punched in a passcode then handed the phone to Jo.

Jo checked the messages and made notes in her notebook. Ashley had been very close on the time frame. Jo handed the phone back to Ashley. "Do you know where Megan was going after school?"

Ashley shrugged. "I don't know. I think she was working at the hospital."

"I know this is hard, Ashley, but can you think of anyone who would want to hurt Megan?"

Ashley shook her head. "No. Everybody liked Megan."

"Did she have a boyfriend?" Lynae asked.

Ashley glanced at her mom. "No, she didn't have a boyfriend."

Lynae tilted her head. "You don't seem sure of that. Is there something you're not telling us? Was there a boy she was hanging out with? Maybe someone her parents wouldn't approve of?"

Ashley stared intently at her hands. "No." She turned to her mom. "Can I go now? I want to go home."

Julie looked at Jo. "Lieutenant?"

Jo nodded. Ashley and her mother stood up, and Julie put a protective arm around her daughter.

Jo handed Julie a card then met Ashley's eyes. "I'm so sorry about your friend, Ashley. If you think of anything at all, please call me."

Ashley nodded and tugged her mother toward the door. The two walked out of the office and past Mrs. Dykstra. The receptionist watched them leave then turned to glower at Jo and Lynae.

Jo stopped at the reception desk. "Thank you for your help. Mrs. Scheidel will be able to fill you in now."

The woman shrugged nonchalantly. "Okay."

As Jo and Lynae walked past the row of windows outside the office, Jo glanced inside. Mrs. Dykstra was scurrying into the principal's office. They strode through the hallway packed with students ambling to their next classes, then past the racket of the cafeteria, where lunch was being served.

When they stepped into the quiet of the outdoors, Lynae said, "Wow, I don't remember high school being that loud."

"That's because you were one of them making all the noise."

Lynae grinned. "I did have a good time."

Jo unlocked the doors of the Ranger. "What's your take on Ashley?"

"She's hiding something. She hesitated and looked at her mom when I asked about a boyfriend."

Jo slid into the driver's seat. "I agree, but I didn't think we would get anywhere by pushing her right then. She was starting to shut down. We'll see what comes out in the autopsy."

Lynae laid a hand on her stomach. "I know food's never high on your priority list, but it's this girl's lunchtime."

Jo glanced at the dashboard clock. "Yeah, I'm actually a little hungry myself. Let's hit Big O's for a sub then head to the hospital. If that's the last place Megan was, maybe we'll get lucky, and someone will know who she left with."

CHAPTER 9

Butterworth Hospital sat atop the tallest hill in Grand Rapids. Between the main hospital, the attached Helen DeVos Children's Hospital, Lemmen Holton Cancer Center, and all adjoining office buildings, university centers, and parking ramps, the place consumed fifteen city blocks.

Jo parked her Ranger in the massive parking garage across the street from the hospital. She got out of the vehicle and scanned the structure. "Remember this: Level Five-Orange, north side."

Lynae tapped her temple. "Steel trap."

Jo rolled her eyes. "We'll see."

They crossed the skywalk to the hospital and stopped at the information desk. Jo spoke with the woman manning the station and learned that the person they needed to talk with was Marge Balister, the head of volunteer services. The receptionist pointed at a waiting area before picking up the phone.

Lynae took a seat and grabbed a magazine from an end table. Jo paced the lobby and checked her watch every few rotations. After fifteen minutes, she huffed, "What do you suppose is more important in this person's job than talking to the police?"

Lynae shrugged. "This place is huge. If she was on the other side of the hospital, it could easily take this long just to get to us."

A woman who appeared to be in her early sixties rushed out of the elevator and made a beeline for the information desk. Her hospital credentials hung on a lanyard around her neck.

Jo nodded toward the woman. "I bet that's her."

Lynae got up and stood next to Jo. After being pointed in their direction, the woman walked briskly toward them on thick-soled brown shoes that were definitely worn for comfort over fashion. When she reached them, she tucked her clipboard under her arm and held out a hand to Lynae then to Jo. "Marge Balister. I'm the head of volunteer services. I'm sorry to keep you waiting."

Jo took the older woman's outstretched hand. "Thank you for meeting with us, Ms. Balister. I know you must be a very busy woman."

Mrs. Balister patted her short gray hair and laughed. "Yes, I am, but it's not every day I meet with detectives. What can I do for you?"

"I'm sorry to have to tell you this, but one of your volunteers was found murdered this morning."

The older woman laid a hand on her chest. "Oh heavens! This is terrible. Who?"

"Megan Tillman. Did you know her?"

Marge looked at Jo indignantly. She pulled her flower-print blouse down more snugly over her green cotton trousers. "Of course I know her. I've been doing this for thirty-three years. It's my job to know all of the volunteers."

"Can you tell us who Megan worked with?"

"She came into the children's oncology center once a week, on Thursdays, to read to the kids. She didn't really work with anyone other than the kids."

Jo frowned. "She worked only on Thursdays?"

Marge nodded. "That's right."

"Did she come in yesterday for some reason? Maybe to fill in for someone else?"

Marge frowned. "I'm sure I didn't see her yesterday, but let me check my sign-in sheets just to be certain." She pulled the clipboard out from under her arm and flipped several pages back. She ran a finger down the paper then shook her head. "She didn't sign in yesterday."

Jo craned her neck to see the sheet. "Is there only one page per day?"

Marge turned the clipboard toward her. "There's one each day for each floor. Megan only worked in oncology, so she signs in on the fourth floor."

Jo nodded. "I see. Thanks."

"I know you have a lot of people who apply to volunteer and are unable to get in. How did someone of Megan's age manage?" Lynae asked.

"Megan was very ambitious and planned to go into medicine. She wanted hospital volunteer time on her college application."

Lynae crossed her arms. "Her and hundreds of others. What made her different?"

Mrs. Balister regarded Lynae for a moment then sighed. "She babysits for Dr. Markham. He made it happen."

Lynae lifted her chin. "Hospital time is coveted for anyone looking at medicine. Did her connection cause problems with anyone here?"

Marge patted her hair nervously. "It was no secret she was here because of that connection, but she was very good with the kids. I never saw or heard anyone have a problem with it."

"And who is Dr. Markham?" Jo asked.

"He's the chief cardiology surgeon at Butterworth."

Jo wrote the information in her notebook. "Did Megan work directly with Dr. Markham?"

Marge shook her head. "No, not directly. He's a very important man here. He doesn't have time to deal with volunteers. He works in the main hospital, and Megan volunteered at the Children's Hospital. Now that you mention it, though, I did see the two of them talking recently."

Jo's radar pinged. "You saw Megan and Dr. Markham together?"

"Yes. She babysat for his kids, so they were friendly. And I believe the Markhams and the Tillmans are friends. I know that Megan's mother knows Mrs. Markham through committee work, but I think it goes beyond that."

"Mrs. Markham and Mrs. Tillman are on a committee here at the hospital?"

"Oh no, not here. For charities that they're involved with. Mrs. Markham is on so many committees I have no idea how she keeps it all straight or when she sleeps. She's an amazing woman, always has everything perfectly under control, never seems frazzled, never a hair out of place. I don't see Mrs. Tillman in the paper quite as often, but she does her share of charity work also."

Even dressed down as she was earlier that day, Joyce Tillman had given the aura of class. Jo could picture her in an overpriced gown, her hair and nails done to perfection, nibbling on expensive hors d'oeuvres and sipping wine at a charity event where everyone would spend their time one-upping each other. It was the kind of event where Jo would be ridiculously out of place.

Mrs. Balister glanced at her watch and then her clipboard. "I have volunteers who will be waiting for me to check them in. I'm afraid that's really all I can tell you, anyway."

Jo and Lynae each shook her hand again and thanked her for her time. They left the hospital and crossed the skywalk to the parking garage.

Lynae cocked her head. "Level Five-Orange, north side."

Jo grinned. "Nailed it." She dug the keys from her front pocket. "How do you know so much about volunteering here?"

"I applied while I was in college. I needed some volunteer hours and thought working with kids here would be a great way to get them. I wasn't able to get in."

Jo climbed in behind the wheel, and Lynae slid into the passenger seat. After Jo started the car, she said, "I wouldn't think that volunteers would be turned away."

Lynae shrugged. "They can only handle so many people. You have to go through a background check and commit to a certain period of time so there's some consistency. And they can't have so many people wandering around in a hospital, going in and out of patients' rooms, that they don't know who belongs and who doesn't."

Jo raised one eyebrow. "And...?"

Lynae rolled her eyes. "Yes, I called and asked why I didn't get in. I was a little peeved that I got turned down."

Jo smirked. "Ruined your reputation for being perfect?"

"No one has ever accused me of being perfect. But I couldn't see any reason they wouldn't want me."

Jo pulled out into the heavy traffic of Michigan Avenue. "Yet a high school sophomore who isn't earning any credit gets in."

"It's all who you know."

Jo's phone signaled a text message. "Will you check that and see if it's Kent?"

Lynae plucked Jo's phone out of the console. "It says, 'I finished the preliminary report. Please come at your earliest opportunity.'"

Jo grinned. "Well, he's texting. I wonder if he'll ever be okay with shortcuts and abbreviations."

Lynae dropped the phone back into the console. "If he ever throws an emoji in, I'm done."

Jo laughed. "I don't think there's any fear of that. Let's go pay him a visit and see if he can give us any clues about who else Megan may have known."

CHAPTER 10

THE SOUND OF THEIR CLICKING heels echoed in the basement of the county health department as Jo and Lynae made their way to the autopsy room.

Lynae rubbed her arms. "This place always reminds me of a crypt."

Jo regarded the beige walls and cement floor in the long corridor of windowless doors. "They should pipe in some music. Or just open a door or two. You know there are people talking behind those doors."

Lynae eyed the closed doors. "I would feel better if I could hear them."

"I wouldn't last a week here. It's just too quiet."

Lynae shook her head. "It's hard to believe Kent has worked in this dungeon for twenty-four years."

Jo shrugged. "He's the go-to medical examiner for tough cases, so he does a lot of consulting. And he guest lectures at Michigan State. So I think he gets out a lot." Kent was a cornerstone—solid and consistent. He was also a word enthusiast who had authored two books on forensics that were used in college classrooms around the country.

"He's got to be getting close to retirement age."

Jo glanced over her shoulder then lowered her voice. "He's looked exactly the same for as long as I can remember. I don't know what goes on down here, but I don't think he actually ages."

Lynae smacked Jo's shoulder. "Quit it."

Jo checked her watch. "Hey, I have to give Myla a call and see if she can take Mojo for a walk. Go ahead without me. I'll be right there."

Lynae glanced at the door marked Autopsy. "Um, no. I'll just wait right here."

Jo snorted and pulled out her phone. "Chicken." After a brief conversation with her neighbor, she hung up and slid her phone back into her pocket. "I don't know what I'm going to do when Myla goes to college next year."

"Maybe you should start grooming a new Myla now so it won't be such a shock to poor Mojo."

"Yeah, I've thought of that. She's just so great I don't even want to think about replacing her."

Jo opened the door and led the way into the autopsy room. Kent looked up from the scale where he was weighing something pink and gelatinous. He used the back of his bloody gloved hand to slide the protective face shield to the top of his head. Jo knew from old pictures that there had once been a wealth of unruly blond hair on that balding head.

Jo smiled. "Hey, Kent, what's the word?"

He gave them a welcoming smile and said in his gentle baritone, "Icarian."

"Oh, wait. I know this one. Give me a minute." Jo snapped her fingers and pointed at Kent. "Trying so hard that you screw things up." She raised her eyebrows, waiting for approval.

Kent chuckled, causing a lifetime of smile and worry lines to crease his face. His blue eyes sparkled. "Not exactly how Webster would put it, but not bad for a neophyte."

"Not bad? I can even put it in a sentence for you." She smirked. "During the department softball tournament this summer, Nae's fielding was flawless, but she suffered an Icarian fall in her batting."

Lynae's head snapped in Jo's direction. "What? Seriously?"

Jo shrugged. "I'm just sayin', Nae." Her partner prided herself on her softball skills, having been the shortstop for Grand Valley State University's team during her four years there. She was fiercely competitive and continued to play on an adult league during the summer months. Regimented time in the gym and a strict running schedule kept her strong, athletic build in nearly the shape it had been during her college peak.

Lynae threw her arms up. "How many times did I pull our team's ass out of the fire during the season, and all I ever hear about is one game! Are you ever going to let that go?"

"Probably not. It's too much fun. But at least you handle it well." Jo winked at Kent, who shook his head and remained silent.

"Bite me," Lynae replied.

Jo cocked an eyebrow. "Careful, Nae. You're talking to a superior officer."

Lynae dropped her eyes to the floor. "Sorry." Then, looking up, she said, "Bite me, *Lieutenant*."

Jo nodded. "That's better." She turned her attention back to Kent. "Now that I've proven my superiority when it comes to the English language, tell me something I don't already know."

He pulled the shield off his head and laid it on his desk. "Cause of death is brain hemorrhaging due to blunt force trauma to the head."

He removed the organ from the scale and placed it on the waiting tray. Under his protective apron, he wore his usual uniform of perfectly pressed flannel trousers, white button-down shirt, and conservative-print tie. His suit jacket was hanging on the lower half of a coat peg on the door, with his signature fedora on the upper half.

He gestured toward the examination table, where the body lay split open by a Y-incision. "Take a look at the wounds."

Lynae sucked in a deep, steadying breath. Even though they spent their days investigating homicides, the reality of seeing a victim's insides was different. Jo was well aware that autopsies were her partner's Achilles heel.

Kent pointed at a long, oval-shaped contusion on the forehead. "Three of the wounds have this unique shape." He indicated several other deep wounds. "A second weapon was used to make these."

Jo leaned over the body to get a closer look. "Two assailants?"

"I can't say from this. But I can say that the oval-shaped wounds were made first and weren't fatal. Based on the pattern, they were not made from an object hitting her head. They were made from her head hitting an object."

Jo frowned. "Come again?"

"Wounds have what I think of as an entrance and exit, just like a bullet wound. The entrance on these wounds is at the bottom, and the skin and tissue is pushed upward. The head was slammed in a downward motion onto the weapon."

"Couldn't it have been something swung in an upward motion?" Lynae asked.

Kent looked approvingly at Lynae over his wire-rimmed glasses that sat halfway down his nose. "Good question. If the weapon was swung in an upward motion, there would be an exit wound. Skin and tissue would have been removed. There's nothing missing. The tissue is pushed into the skull."

Lynae nodded. "So the weapon was stationary, and her head was slammed into it."

Kent pointed at her. "Exactly. The weapon was oval-shaped and approximately six inches in diameter."

Jo pointed at a purple pattern on the edge of the wound. "What's this?"

Kent indicated another similarly shaped wound on the left temple. "There's a variation of that mark here too. Whatever the weapon was, it had a raised pattern. Unfortunately, we have such a small amount of the pattern that matching it will prove very difficult."

Lynae leaned in to peer closely at the wound. "Maybe a logo?"

Kent nodded. "Most likely. I'm going to run it through our databases. If I don't come up with anything, I'll have Mallory do some digging. She's a little more proficient on the computer than I am."

"Isaac could help with that too," Jo said. "But that isn't the thing that killed her?"

"No, the murder weapon was swung in a downward motion." Kent pointed out several deep, rectangular gashes at the base of her skull. "See the difference? These wounds would have caused most of the bleeding. There was much more force behind these."

"That makes sense. You can take a swing with something much

harder than you could push or pull a head down onto an object." Lynae made an overhead swinging motion.

"Any idea on this second weapon?" Jo asked.

Kent shook his head. "Not yet. I'm still doing preliminary work. Right now, I'm looking at a hammer of some sort, but narrowing that down will take some time."

Jo nodded. "What else can you tell me?"

Kent gestured at some long, thick scrapes along the girl's forearm and the side of her face. "These abrasions were filled with particulates from the paint on the dumpster."

"That's not surprising, since she was found inside the dumpster."

Kent shook his head. "They're too deep to be from simply sliding into the dumpster. I would say the body was scraped along the side of it."

Jo cocked her head. "The killer had to push her up the side of the dumpster to get her in?"

"I can't say he *had* to, but it looks like he did."

Jo checked her notes. "The dumpster is about five and a half feet tall, and Megan weighed around a hundred fifteen pounds. That doesn't seem like that much weight for a man to lift that high."

Kent shook his head. "It isn't, really. Unless the guy was hurt or not very tall."

Jo shrugged. "Or not very strong."

"Or if it wasn't a man," Lynae interjected.

Jo frowned. "That's something to chew on. I'll get a tech to go back to the scene and check the dumpster again for trace. Maybe our killer skinned a knuckle." She turned back to Kent. "Tell me you have something else."

Kent rolled the body onto its side. "Take a look at these marks on the left hip."

Jo and Lynae moved around to the other side of the table. Along the left hip were two deeply embedded half-inch circles. Each circle was made by eight evenly spaced dots.

Kent ran his gloved finger over the marks. "I don't know yet what left these, but I can tell you that, after she died, she was lying on whatever made them."

Jo examined the imprint. "I'll want some pictures of that. That's a distinct pattern. Someone will know what that is."

Kent nodded. "Of course. And now for the worst of it. This was a double homicide."

Jo gaped at him. "What do you mean?"

His eyes softened. "This young woman was pregnant."

"*Was* pregnant? As in, she recently delivered?"

"No, as in still pregnant." Kent pulled back the cloth draped over the upper part of the autopsy table. A tiny fetus lay on a white towel.

Jo's body went numb. All sounds around her faded until she could hear only the ringing in her ears and the thundering of her heart. She stared at the tiny lifeless form with its translucent skin and fine lanugo hair. She let out her breath in a rush. "How old?" she asked, trying to keep her voice steady.

Kent responded, "About three and a half inches, one and a half ounces. I would say this little guy was fourteen weeks' gestation."

"A boy," Jo whispered.

Lynae laid her hand on Jo's arm and gave it a gentle squeeze. "Both the Tillmans and Ashley Kane said Megan didn't have a boyfriend."

Jo looked down at the young girl lying exposed on the table. *Quite a secret you were keeping, Megan.* "I think we'll want to talk to them again." She turned to Kent. "Did you get anything from trace?"

"You'll have to see Mallory. I don't have her report yet."

Kent pulled the sheet back over the tiny form. "I'll have blood work run."

Jo nodded. "Then all we'll need is a suspect to match it to."

CHAPTER 11

Jo and Lynae crossed the hallway to go to Mallory Wiseman's office. Lynae laid her hand on Jo's shoulder. "You okay?"

Jo shoved her hands into her pockets. "The baby just took me by surprise."

"You want me to talk to Mallory? You could go get some fresh air."

Jo shook her head and leaned against the wall. "I lost my baby. I have to deal with that. I can't fall apart and walk away from the job every time something dredges up painful memories."

"I've never seen you walk away from anything, Jo. But this is why you have a partner. There's nothing wrong with letting me handle this while you take a breather."

"Thanks, but I'll be okay."

Lynae leaned on the wall next to Jo. "We have a lot of fun together when we're not breaking bad news or looking at people's insides."

Jo chuckled. "Yeah, we do."

"But you know I'm not here just for the good times. I'm here for the tough stuff too. You think you always have to be strong, but sometimes it's okay to let a friend be strong for you."

Jo closed her eyes and pressed her lips together. She didn't trust herself to talk. Beneath her flippant facade, Lynae had a profound depth. Jo knew that she wasn't the only one keeping something inside. Lynae had a story. Jo just didn't know it yet.

Jo took a deep breath and pushed away from the wall. "We need to see Mallory."

Lynae threw up her hands. "You're the boss."

"And don't you forget it."

Jo knocked on the door and stuck her head in at the same time. Sitting behind her desk, Mallory was talking on the phone. She motioned for them to come in and sit down. Fluorescent lighting gave the small office a yellowish tinge. She had tried to brighten it up with a couple of abstract paintings in bold colors, but Jo thought the effect was more macabre than bright, like balloons and silly string at a funeral.

A minute later, Mallory hung up then tossed her memo pad on her desk. "Nothing quite like making a long-distance notification."

Jo scrunched up her face. "I'll take it over face-to-face any day. But yeah, they all suck."

Mallory leaned back in her chair and sighed. "Feels like a wine-and-comedy kind of night."

"Doesn't every night feel that way in this job?"

"Makes you wonder why we do it, doesn't it? Or why we don't all turn into alcoholics."

"Too many of us are," Lynae said with a humorless chuckle.

"And too many of us are on our way." Mallory pulled the top page from her memo pad, ripped it in half, and dropped the pieces in the trash.

Jo leaned forward and rested her arms on her knees. "You all right, Mal?"

Mallory ran her hand through her hair. "Sorry, I will be. Some days get to me more than others, you know? Like days when I start out doing trace on a fifteen-year-old girl found in a dumpster with her head bashed in. And then follow it up with notifying parents that their twenty-two-year-old who ran away six years ago has finally been found. Dead."

Lynae huffed and shook her head. "Damn, two kids in one day."

Jo shook her head. "Three." She met Mallory's eyes. "Our girl was pregnant."

"Shit, she was young."

Jo leaned back and crossed her legs. "Too young to be pregnant and too young to die."

"There are too many sick fucks in the world. You put one away, and two more crawl out from under some rock." Mallory opened the bottom drawer of her desk, pulled out three candy bars, and tossed one to Jo and one to Lynae.

Lynae started stripping away the wrapping on her bar. "We'll keep putting them away, though. Maybe we'll eventually get ahead of the curve."

"Speaking of putting people away, did you find anything on our girl that will make this quick for us?" Jo asked after swallowing a bite of chocolate.

"Quite a bit, actually. I have two carpet fibers and a hair" —she gestured at two glass vials on her desk—"and I lifted a partial print from the inside of the purse. The wallet, to be exact. And the print definitely wasn't the victim's."

"A print? That's fantastic. Match the print, find the killer." Lynae snapped her fingers. "Case closed."

Mallory snapped her fingers back at Lynae. "*If* we can make a match. And if it belongs to the killer. It could be from someone she knew, a friend or family member, who had handled her wallet for some reason."

Lynae slouched in her chair. "Always the skeptic."

"I've learned to be. I sent the print to the lab to try to get a match with AFIS, but I've seen too many investigations hinge on a set of fingerprints where we never get a hit."

Jo finished her candy bar and licked the melted chocolate from her fingers. "I won't ride my whole investigation on it, but if I've got a solid suspect, I'll find a way to get prints."

Mallory grinned. "I'm sure you will. I'll have to send out the hair and fiber, which will take a while. We don't have that kind of equipment here." Mallory looked around her small lab and shrugged. "It's on my wish list."

"Yeah, it's too bad we don't have a higher crime rate to justify that," Jo said sarcastically.

Mallory snorted. "Be careful what you wish for, right?"

"That hair could easily be a transfer. She was found in a dumpster," Jo pointed out.

"Right, like your dog's hair on your jacket." Mallory pointed at

Jo's shoulder. "Yeah, it's not the smoking gun that the fingerprint has the potential to be, but it could add a nice piece to the puzzle."

Jo looked down and plucked a white dog hair from her jacket. "And we'll take any pieces we can get."

Lynae got up and dropped her wrapper in the trash can beside the desk. "There was no money in her wallet. Whoever left that fingerprint was probably after her money."

Jo nodded. "Not wearing gloves is sloppy. I like sloppy killers. They make our job so much easier."

Mallory tapped one of the vials. "The fibers probably came from the carpet that she was laid on after she died. Blood-pool patterns indicate that she was on her left side for several hours after death."

"Anything significant about the fiber?" Jo asked.

"It's a cut-pile Olefin fiber. Olefin is resistant to moisture and water-based stains, which makes it the primary fiber used in indoor-outdoor carpet. It's also used in vehicles."

Jo drummed her fingers on the chair arm. "With the lack of blood and any other evidence at the scene, we know she wasn't killed there, so it stands to reason she was in a car."

"Unfortunately, I can't say without a sample to match it to that this carpeting came from a particular car or, for that matter, that it definitely came from a car at all. It could even have come from a house, but it's a cheap carpet."

Jo thought about the wealthy homes in her victim's neighborhood. "So it could be a carpet choice, but really only for someone who doesn't have much money to spend on flooring."

"Exactly."

"To me this adds up to a trunk," Lynae said. "That pattern on her side that Kent showed us? Doesn't it stand to reason that whatever she was lying on was something that someone had tossed in the trunk of their car and forgot about? Something that wasn't part of the plan, let's say."

"Sure, we all throw things in our trunks," Jo replied.

Lynae stood and began pacing the small office. "But we don't all just leave things there. Most things go in and out of a trunk on the same day. They aren't left there unless they're a habit. Something that's there all the time or has been there so long you don't think about it. You don't even pick it up as a problem when you're tossing a body in your trunk. Like my bat bag. It's a permanent fixture in my trunk. Never comes out. It's like it's a part of my trunk, and I don't even notice it's there anymore."

"Or my step stool," Mallory added.

Lynae stopped and pointed at Mallory. "Right! Think about it. This is a pretty clean crime scene. We may be able to get DNA from the hair, maybe not, but no guarantee the hair wasn't picked up in the dumpster, anyway. Megan disappeared sometime between two forty-five, which is when she left school, and the estimated time of death, which is around six o'clock. The body wasn't dumped until much later, after the pharmacy closed and they threw their last bag in the garbage. It might have been a crime of passion, but it was well executed and thought out after the fact. Why stash the body on top of something that would leave such a distinct mark unless it's something that you didn't even realize was there?"

Lynae stopped and looked from Jo to Mallory. She shrugged. "It doesn't give us a killer, but I'm getting inside his head."

Jo smiled. "That you are, my friend."

CHAPTER 12

LYNAE HUSTLED TO KEEP UP with Jo's long strides as they walked from the parking area to the station. "We're going to have to tell the Tillmans about the baby, aren't we?"

"I'm afraid so. They probably won't be able to offer any help in the way of who the father was, but they need to be told." She sighed. "We already destroyed their lives. We might as well go all the way and destroy the image they had of their little girl too."

"Can't we send Isaac and Charles?"

"Nice try." Jo glanced at her watch. "It's almost four o'clock. I'm going to check in with Isaac on the paint chip then take a short breather. I'll tell Isaac and Charles to meet us at five o'clock for a briefing, then we'll go to the Tillmans'."

"All right. I'll be ready."

Jo went immediately to Isaac's desk, where he was staring intently at his monitor. "Anything on that paint yet?" she asked him.

Isaac jumped a little then leaned back as far as his chair would allow. He crossed one ankle over the opposite knee and rolled a pencil between his fingers. Even in the short time he had been with her department, Jo had come to expect that posture. "I'm next in line with the lab. I couldn't push it all the way to the top."

She crossed her arms. "Not what I wanted to hear, Isaac. I thought you had an in."

"I do. But I guess not enough of one to bump everyone else."

"Not much of an in then, is it? Let me know when you hear." She arched one eyebrow. "I'll be in my office if you get anything more. Let's touch base in B at five. Let Charles know."

Isaac smirked. "Four o'clock process time, boss?"

Her process time meant allowing her brain to rest so she could think clearly. If it so happened that it was conveniently four o'clock and she could process while watching *Ellen*, then that was no one's business but hers. Jo glared at him in a way that she hoped stopped his heart for a beat. "Is that a problem?"

He dropped the smirk. "Nope."

When she reached her office, she found Lynae sitting in the visitor chair with her head back and her eyes closed. "Comfortable?"

Lynae jumped. "Sorry, I needed a minute. You have a door."

"Been a long day, hasn't it?"

"Yeah, it has, and I have a feeling it's going to be a long night. Do you mind if I stay a bit?"

Jo chuckled and flopped into her chair. "Only if you promise to be quiet. I don't tolerate people talking during *Ellen*."

"I know, and I promise. I've had my head bitten off a time or two about that."

Jo shrugged and turned the television on. "I'm not that bad."

"About *Ellen*, you are."

They used the few minutes before the show began to gather their notes and get some coffee. By the end of the hour, they had regrouped and were ready to meet with the rest of the team.

Lynae stood. "Okay, so maybe you're not completely crazy to watch that show every day."

Jo cocked her head. "I didn't know my sanity was in question."

"Oh, yeah, of course it isn't. I'm just sayin' I feel a little better. You know, ready to go back at it."

Isaac and Charles were already in the conference room. Charles was engrossed in his phone, and Isaac had an open laptop in front of him.

Lynae peeked over Charles's shoulder. "What ya doin'?"

He pulled the phone close to his chest. "Do you mind?"

Lynae slipped into the chair next to him and smiled sweetly. "Not if your wife doesn't."

Charles rolled his eyes and slipped the phone into his jacket pocket.

Jo went to the head of the table. "All right, I know that we don't have anything yet on the paint from Isaac's supposed 'in' at the lab."

Isaac held up a piece of paper. "Not so fast, LT. Just came in." He ran a finger down the page as he read out the information. "Metallic silver paint, number S7842. Found on General Motors vehicles manufactured after 2002."

Jo sat in her chair. "Fantastic. At least now we only have to bring in half the people in Grand Rapids for questioning. GM produces, what, four different brands with about ten different vehicle types?"

Isaac shook his head. "Five different brands if you're going back to 2002. Don't forget the Pontiac."

"Shit. That doesn't give us anything." Jo turned to Charles. "Tell me you got something more from the cell."

Charles leaned back in his chair and tapped his pen on his crossed knee. "The contract is with Verizon. They won't give me the records without a subpoena, which is in the process."

Jo slammed a fist on the table. "Fuckin' red tape. How about Blue Frontier?"

"They were a little more forthcoming." Charles pulled out a notepad and flipped to a marked page. "The victim was in Caleb Isherman's taxi. He dropped her off in the parking lot of the Old Mission Thrift Store on South Division. He said she sat in the car for about fifteen minutes before she got out. Seemed real nervous about something. When she got out, she walked toward Fulton. He didn't stick around to see where she was going."

Jo steepled her fingers under her chin. "Interesting. So we know where she got dropped off, but we don't know where she went from there. Isaac, let's see what we have in that area, say three or four blocks." While Isaac clicked away on his keyboard, Jo continued, "Lynae and I made the notification to Megan Tillman's parents and spoke with her friend Ashley. According to both sources, Megan didn't have a boyfriend. However, she was about fourteen weeks pregnant."

Isaac stopped typing. "I can see where maybe the parents

wouldn't know, but wasn't Ashley supposed to be her best friend? Don't you girls tell your best friends everything?"

Jo raised her eyebrows. "Us girls?"

Isaac swallowed hard. "I meant—"

Jo grinned. "I know what you meant. Yes, us girls do tend to tell our best friends everything. I'll be damn surprised if Ashley didn't know."

Isaac scowled. "You think she's hiding something?"

"Do I think she killed her best friend? No. But she was hiding this, and I'd like to find out what else she knows."

Isaac turned his laptop toward Jo. "There are several clinics in that area offering pregnancy services: free counseling, prenatal care, abortions, everything a pregnant teen would need."

"Give me the address of the one closest to her drop-off point. I'll bet my next paycheck that's where she was heading."

Isaac wrote something in his notebook then tore off the sheet and passed it to Jo. "This is the nearest one. The next clinic is another two miles away, so I'm guessing that's the one it would have to be."

Jo slipped the paper in her pocket. "If there's nothing else, then, Charles and Isaac, you can head out."

"See ya, boss." Charles popped out of his chair and made a beeline for the door.

Isaac closed his laptop and slipped it into his messenger bag. "I'm going to be around for a while tonight if you need anything."

Jo smiled. "Thanks. We're heading out in a few minutes. I'll give you a call if anything comes up."

Lynae massaged her temples. "Heading out means we're going to the Tillmans', doesn't it? Couldn't you just call them?"

"This needs to be done in person."

Lynae sighed. "Yeah, I knew you were going to say that."

"And then I'd like another crack at Ashley Kane before she gets a chance to settle down."

Lynae pulled her hair back and started wrapping it into a bun. "And were you planning on going home at any point tonight?"

"It's still early, and I've got Mojo taken care of. What other reason do I have to go home? If you need to go, I can handle this."

Lynae finished the bun then tucked a loose strand behind her ear. "No, I'm good. You know I have no life."

"We've got all night, then. Let's go solve a crime."

CHAPTER 13

At the Tillmans' house, Jo parked the car then pulled the paper with the clinic address out of her pocket. "While I go do this, why don't you look this place up? Maybe they have evening hours."

Lynae took the paper. "You know I was only kidding about not wanting to do this with you."

"I know, but I've got it." Jo got out of the car and walked to the front door.

Brutus began yipping as soon as Jo rang the bell. A woman of about seventy answered the door. "Can I help you?"

Jo smiled. "I'm here to see Mr. or Mrs. Tillman."

"I'm sorry. They're not here. Is there something I can help you with?"

"Can you tell me where they are?"

The woman frowned. "And who are you?"

Jo pulled out her badge. "I'm Lieutenant Riskin with the Grand Rapids Police Department."

The woman put her glasses on top of her head and looked down her nose at Jo's badge. "Are you the detective who's trying to find out who killed poor little Megan?"

Jo nodded. "Yes, I am. And you are?"

"I'm Sylvia Moore. I live next door. I'm just here to get Brutus for the night."

"Will Mr. and Mrs. Tillman be gone all night?"

Sylvia shook her head. "They'll be back sometime tonight, but I imagine it will be late. They're with Dan's family. I don't think they could stand being in the house today."

"When you see Joyce and Dan, can you please tell them I would like to speak with them as early as possible tomorrow?" Jo passed her a business card.

Sylvia took the card. "I'll see them in the morning when I bring Brutus back. I'll tell them then."

Jo thanked her and walked back to the car. She glanced back and saw Sylvia snapping a leash on the dog. She wondered if Brutus knew Megan was gone forever. If only dogs could talk. He probably knew more about Megan's life than anyone else. She climbed into the car.

Lynae looked up from her phone. "The Tillmans aren't home?"

Jo started the ignition. "No, they're with family."

"That makes sense. Does that mean we're going home?"

"No, we're still going to talk to Ashley. She's been keeping Megan's secret this long. We need to make sure she keeps it for one more night."

Jo drove the one block to Ashley's house and parked in front of the two-story Tudor. "Why don't you take the lead on this? You have more experience with teenagers than I do."

"You're the boss."

They walked up the flower-lined walk to the covered front porch. Julie was standing on the stoop and digging through her purse. Jo cleared her throat.

The woman's head shot up, and she frowned. "Detectives."

Jo smiled. "Hello, Mrs. Kane. Are you on your way out?"

Julie pulled a set of keys from her purse. "I was just going to run to a Redbox and get a movie. I thought it might be a distraction for Ashley. I don't know what else to do."

Jo glanced at Lynae. "Unfortunately, the only thing you can do for her right now is be there for her."

"It's hard to see your child in so much pain."

Lynae nodded. "I'm sure it is. We'd appreciate if you could hold off on leaving. We need to talk to Ashley again."

Julie ran her hand through her hair. "Okay. Come on in." She pushed the door open and led them into a modest foyer that opened into a kitchen and dining area. She pointed toward the table. "Have a seat. I'll get Ashley."

Once the woman had left the room, Jo and Lynae walked past the expansive kitchen, where dark marble countertops glistened against mahogany cabinets. They sat next to each other at the dining room table, and Jo pushed aside a floral centerpiece that obstructed her view of the other side. The dining area opened into a window-lined sitting room with French doors that led to a roomy deck. Every window looked out over a sprawling lawn that ended in a thick copse of trees.

After a few minutes, Julie returned, her arm wrapped protectively around her daughter. The pair sat down with Ashley directly across from Lynae.

"I know it's been a terrible day, hon," Lynae said.

Ashley shrugged and wrapped her arms around her body. Her hoodie sleeves were pulled over her clenched fists.

"We just need a few minutes for you to help us clear something up. When I asked you if Megan had a boyfriend, you hesitated. Is there something you didn't tell us?"

Ashley stared at the table without responding.

Lynae leaned forward. "It's okay, Ashley. We know."

The girl's head jerked up. Her red, swollen eyes met Lynae's. "About the baby?"

Lynae nodded. "Yeah, about the baby."

Julie put a hand over her mouth. "Baby? Was Megan pregnant?" When Ashley nodded, Julie groaned. "Why didn't you tell me? Or tell the detectives?"

Ashley shook her head and swiped a tear from her face with the sleeve of her hoodie.

Her mother laid a hand on her shoulder. "You can't keep important things from the detectives."

Ashley looked desperately at Lynae. "She was my best friend. I told her I wouldn't tell anyone."

"I understand, Ashley," Jo said. She hooked a thumb at Lynae. "Detective Parker is my best friend. If she told me a secret, I would never want to hurt her by telling anyone."

Ashley glared at her mother. "See?"

"But someone killed Megan," Lynae said gently. "Any secret that she might have had doesn't matter to her anymore. If telling her secrets can help us find the person who did this to her, then it's the best thing you can do for your friend."

"She didn't want anyone to know."

Lynae nodded. "And you kept her secret for as long as it mattered to her."

Ashley blew out a long breath. "I guess it doesn't matter anymore. She was so scared of..." She picked at the table runner.

Lynae glanced at Jo. "Who was Megan afraid of?"

Ashley glanced at her mother then leaned forward. "She was going to have an abortion. That's where she was going. She was going to come to my house afterward so if she was sick or something, her parents wouldn't ask questions."

"Do you know where she was going for the abortion?"

The girl shook her head. "I don't remember the name of the place. She didn't really want to do it, you know? But she didn't think she had a choice."

Lynae cocked her head. "Why didn't she think she had a choice?"

Ashley rolled her eyes. "She is... I mean, she *was* fifteen. Her parents would've ki—well, they would've been really mad."

"When we talked with you before, you told us Megan didn't have a boyfriend."

"She doesn't anymore. They broke up pretty much after he found out about the baby."

Julie huffed. "Oh, Ashley, you had to know that the detectives would want to know that."

Ashley slouched in her chair and crossed her arms. "Sorry."

Lynae held up her hand. "We understand, Ashley. And you're telling us now, so that's good. Megan's parents didn't know about her boyfriend. Do you know why?"

"Megan didn't want her parents to know. They wouldn't have liked him."

Lynae frowned. "Why wouldn't they have liked him?"

Ashley picked at her sleeve and shrugged. "He's school of choice. He's supposed to go to one of the city schools."

"Why would that be a problem?"

"You know, he lives in a bad part of town. Megan's parents wouldn't have wanted her to date him or even be in that part of town."

Lynae opened her notebook. "Can you give me his name and address?"

"Hunter Stone. I don't know his address. I went to his house once with Megan. I know the street is all." Ashley gave her mother a sideways glance before telling Lynae the street name.

Lynae jotted down a note. "Is there anything else you can tell me about Hunter?"

Ashley shrugged. "He's kind of a big deal at school."

"Hunter is? Why's that?"

"He's a really good football player. That's a big, stupid deal at our school. I guess that makes it okay that he doesn't really do anything in any of his classes and that he's kind of a jerk."

"You don't like him. Did Megan know that?"

Megan gawked at Lynae. "No. You don't say bad stuff about somebody's boyfriend. I just told her to be careful."

"Why did you think she needed to be careful?"

"I just didn't want her to get hurt. I always thought she liked him a lot more than he liked her. He kind of acted like he was doing her a favor, you know?"

Lynae nodded. "Yeah, I know the type. And when she told him she was pregnant, what happened?"

"He freaked out and said he was going to college and getting out of here and that he wasn't going to be stuck living in a dump his whole life."

"Is that when they broke up?"

Ashley nodded. "Pretty much. He was a jerk to her until she told him she would get an abortion. I told her if that's what she wanted, then okay, but not to do it so she could get back together with him. I didn't want her to regret it someday, and no way he was going to stay with her after he left for college."

"You're a good friend, Ashley."

Ashley slouched even more and wiped away a fresh tear with the back of her hand. "No, I'm not. I should have been with her. I wanted to be, but I had volleyball practice, and she didn't want anything to look suspicious with me missing practice. I never miss. But I should have done it anyway. Maybe she'd be okay if I'd been with her."

Lynae reached across the table and took Ashley's hand. "You can't think that way. There's nothing you could have done to change any of this. This is the fault of whoever did this, not you."

Ashley looked away. "I guess."

"Megan didn't have the abortion, Ashley. We knew about the baby but not about the abortion or about Hunter. This information you gave could really help us."

Tears glistened on Ashley's long lashes as she looked into Lynae's eyes. "It doesn't feel right, you know? Telling her secrets when she trusted me."

"You did the right thing," Jo said. "It's very important that you keep this secret a little bit longer, though. Megan's parents don't know about the baby yet, and we want them to hear it from us first. Can you help us?"

A tear spilled over and ran down Ashley's cheek. "I won't tell anyone. I'm sorry I didn't tell you sooner."

Jo stood. "You told us now. That's what's important."

Ashley laid her head on her mom's shoulder. Julie wrapped her arms around her daughter as the girl started to sob.

Lynae got up, walked around the table, and squeezed Ashley's shoulder. "I'm so sorry, Ashley." She looked at Julie. "We'll show ourselves out."

CHAPTER 14

LYNAE SLID INTO THE PASSENGER seat and propped her feet on the dash. She smiled smugly at Jo. "So I'm your best friend?"

Jo smirked. "I know this is a big moment. Don't let it go to your head."

"Oh, it already has." Lynae pulled her phone out of her pocket. "I'm going to tweet it out. My friends will be so jealous, but I'll be like, 'Bitches, you wish you were me.'"

"Shut up." Jo chuckled.

"Seriously, though, you're my best friend too."

"Well, isn't this a sweet moment. Are we going to read each other's diaries and paint our toenails?"

Lynae slapped Jo's arm. "That's exactly what I had in mind for our sleepover tonight. I'll get the scary movie. You bring the Piggy Polish."

"Deal." Jo started the car. "So back to business. I think this sheds a new light on Megan's situation."

"This Hunter kid breaks up with her right after he finds out about the baby and is pretty freaked out about it. Then she decides not to have the abortion. So you think he knew?"

"It depends on when she decided, but I would think the father of that baby would be the first person Megan would tell. According to Ashley, she left school with the intention of having an abortion. So deciding not to have it had to be a last-minute decision. We'll know more when we get her phone records." Jo looked at her watch. "Give Isaac a call. Get us an address on Mr. Stone. Let's go have a talk with him."

"We've been at this for twelve hours. We could knock off and talk to Hunter in the morning."

"He'll be at school in the morning. I'd rather talk to him at home. Besides, he's a pretty obvious suspect. I don't want to give him any more time than necessary to get his story straight."

"Then we better find out where we're going." Lynae pulled out her phone and called Isaac. After hanging up, she entered the address into the GPS.

Two miles away from the Kanes' house, the neighborhood morphed from exclusive estates to meager shacks. The spacious, manicured lawns were replaced with city lots so small that privacy was a forgotten dream. Jo calculated that she could jump from one roof to the next and make it through the entire neighborhood without much effort. In place of the well-tended, colorful flowerbeds of the Tillmans' neighborhood were overgrown or dead evergreens planted long ago and forgotten. The change was so sudden and extreme that it seemed as though an invisible wall divided the two neighborhoods.

Hunter Stone's home was a small bungalow separated from its neighbor by only a shared driveway. The blue paint was faded and peeling, in some spots showing the weatherworn gray wood beneath. An open one-car garage dominated the miniscule yard. A little girl's well-worn bike, a tool-covered workbench, a set of golf clubs, and stacks of boxes lined the walls.

Jo nodded toward the rusty silver Pontiac GrandAm that sat among the junk. "Nice car."

"Yeah, good ol' GM vehicle. Probably wouldn't be able to tell if any of the scratches or dents in it are new."

Jo stepped out of the car. "Maybe not, but I'd like to get the probable cause to try." They stepped around two heavy plastic lawn chairs and an old ten-speed bike then walked up the steps of the sagging front porch. "I'll take the lead here," Jo said.

Lynae frowned. "What happened to me being better with teenagers?"

"You're better at being nice to them. I'm better at intimidating them."

Lynae knocked on the cracked wooden front door. "No doubt about that."

A young girl of about five or six pulled the door open. Her blond hair was pulled back from her round, freckled face. "Hi!"

Jo leaned over and put her hands on her knees. "Hi, yourself. What's your name?"

"Jana."

"Hi, Jana. We're police officers. Do you have a brother named Hunter?"

"Yep."

"Can you get him for us?"

"Okay." Jana left the door open and ran into the house, yelling for Hunter.

A minute later, she ran back, her stocking feet skidding to a stop on the linoleum floor. "He'll be right here."

Jo smiled. "Thank you, Jana. You're a big help." The little girl beamed. Jo winked at her. "Hey, can you do me another favor?"

Jana nodded seriously. "Uh-huh."

"From now on, if you hear a knock at the door, could you get your big brother or mom or dad before you open it?"

Jana hung her head and shrugged. "Hunter always tells me that too."

"Hunter sounds like a good big brother. You should listen to him."

Jana's blue eyes grew wide. "I don't like to listen to him. He always tells me to stop bugging him. And he won't let me play his Xbox!"

Jo shrugged. "That's what big brothers do. But I'm a police officer, so you can listen to me, right?"

"Yeah, I guess. But he's still a jerk."

A young man sauntered up behind the girl. "Get outta here, runt."

Jana turned around and stuck her tongue out at him. She ran by him and giggled when he swatted her with his beefy hand.

The teenager stepped up to Jo. "I'm Hunter. My sister said you want to talk to me?"

Jo stretched to her full five nine and craned her neck up so she could meet his gaze. He had the same blue eyes as his sister, but his hair was darker. He wore a tight blue Champion T-shirt and gray sweatpants that sagged enough to show that he preferred boxers over briefs. In the pocket of his sweats was the outline of a cell phone. Jo wondered how many messages on that phone were from Megan and when he had received the last one.

An older man rushed into the foyer and inserted himself between Jo and Hunter. "I'm James Stone, Hunter's father. What can we do for you?"

Jo was struck by the resemblance between the two. The only differences were a touch of gray in the father's hair and a softening around his middle. She pulled out her badge and held it up to the older man. "I'm Lieutenant Jo Riskin, Grand Rapids Homicide." Jo motioned toward Lynae. "This is my partner, Detective Lynae Parker. We're here to talk to Hunter about Megan Tillman."

Mr. Stone looked at his son then turned back to Jo. "Why don't you come inside?"

He led them down the hall to a family room with brown shag carpeting and an old green sofa with a matching recliner. Both pieces of furniture faced a flat-screen television that hung on the wall. The pressed-wood coffee table and two end tables were stained with cup rings. Although almost everything looked old and worn, the room was clean and neat.

Mr. Stone turned the recliner to face the sofa and motioned for his son to sit in it. Hunter flopped into the chair and casually leaned back. His father stayed on his feet with his hand on the back of the chair. Jo and Lynae sat on the sofa, which lacked the springs to keep their bodies even.

Jo consciously worked at appearing comfortable. "Hunter, I'm sure you heard that Megan Tillman was found dead this morning."

Hunter nodded. "Yeah, I heard."

"We understand that you were dating Megan."

Hunter shrugged his broad shoulders. "We dated for a while, but we broke up a few weeks ago."

Jo shifted her weight as the sofa tried to pull her toward its center. "What brought on the breakup?"

"You know, just stuff."

"Just stuff, huh? I understand you're quite the football player."

Hunter grinned smugly. "I'm pretty good."

Mr. Stone slapped his son's shoulder. "He's better than pretty good. He's going to play for Michigan State University next year. He's going on a scholarship."

Jo gave them a polite smile. "Good for you."

Lynae scooted forward, obviously struggling with the couch too. "Is that why you chose to go to Hillview, so you could play football with a better team?"

Mr. Stone gave Hunter's shoulder a squeeze. "He never would have gotten recognized going to GR Public. I work at Hillview. It's a good school."

Lynae looked up at the older man. "Are you a teacher, Mr. Stone?"

Mr. Stone shook his head. "Building Services. That's Hillview's way of saying janitor."

Jo stared at the teen. "Hunter, we would like a few more details on why you broke up with Megan. What kind of *stuff* caused the problem?"

Mr. Stone took a step forward. "Why is it important why my son broke up with his girlfriend, Lieutenant?"

Jo raised her eyebrows. "Megan Tillman is dead, Mr. Stone. We're talking to the people who knew her best to understand what might have happened."

"You think Hunter had something to do with that girl getting killed? That's ridiculous."

Jo turned her attention back to the teenager, whose foot had begun to bounce nervously. "We already know a lot about Megan. You need to be honest with us, Hunter."

Hunter huffed. "Fine. She was pregnant, and that's why we broke up. Is that what you want me to say?"

Mr. Stone stared straight ahead. His mouth was set in a straight line, and his jaw clenched.

"That's a start," Jo said.

"She was going to have an abortion." Hunter glanced up at his father then shrugged. "I told her she had to get an abortion, and she said she would."

Jo cocked her head. "You told her she had to have an abortion? Did she have a choice?"

Hunter crossed his arms. "I mean, yeah, I couldn't force her. But she didn't want to have a baby, either."

Mr. Stone glared down at Jo. "That girl wouldn't even tell her parents that she was dating my son! She didn't think they would approve because of where he lives. He wasn't going to give up his future for her."

Jo nodded to acknowledge the man but kept her gaze on Hunter. "So she didn't want her family to know you were dating. Is that right, Hunter? You weren't good enough for her?"

"No, it wasn't like that!"

"Oh? What was it like?"

Mr. Stone spat, "That's exactly what it was like, Hunter. She didn't think we were good enough for her."

Hunter shrank back into his seat and stared over Jo's head.

"Did that make you angry, Hunter?" Lynae's tone was sympathetic and gentle. "First you're not good enough to be dating her, and then she changes her mind and decides to have the baby after you told her to have an abortion."

Hunter gaped at Lynae. "Wait. What?"

Lynae nodded. "Did you try to talk some sense into her and maybe you got carried away?"

"No! I mean... I didn't want her to have the baby, but I didn't even know she changed her mind."

Lynae tilted her head. "You're the father, and she didn't tell you? She didn't call or text you and say, 'I changed my mind, I'm not having the abortion'? She just went ahead and did it without even talking to you about it?"

"Yes! I mean, I didn't know."

Jo leaned forward as much as the sagging couch would

allow. She kept her tone even. "Which is it, Hunter? Yes, or you didn't know?"

"I didn't know," Hunter mumbled.

Jo scowled. "You found out your girlfriend was pregnant, so you broke up with her and told her she had to have an abortion. She was going to do what was undoubtedly the most frightening thing of her life, and you don't even check up on her? You didn't want to find out if she did it or to see if she was okay?"

Hunter ran his hands through his short hair. "I didn't think it was that big of a deal. People have abortions all the time. And I tried to call her, but she didn't answer."

"Having a baby would have really ruined your life, wouldn't it?"

"Yeah, it would have. I mean, if the baby was even mine." He gave them a sly look.

Jo raised her chin. "You're not sure the baby was yours?"

Hunter shrugged. "I don't know. Maybe not."

Jo pulled out her notebook. "Was there someone else at school that you think Megan was dating?"

Hunter shook his head. "Not at school. Nobody there would dare disrespect me like that."

"Then what makes you think it could be someone else's baby?"

"I don't know. There was this doctor she just wouldn't shut up about. Dr. Markham this, Dr. Markham that. It's like she thought he was God or something."

Jo wrote *Dr. Markham?* in her notebook and circled it. "And you think there was something between Megan and Dr. Markham?"

"Sure seemed like it."

"Where were you last night around six o'clock, Hunter?"

"I was home. I came home right after football practice."

Jo jotted that in her notebook. "What time does practice end?"

"Five."

Jo looked up from her notes. "Was anybody here with you?"

"Lieutenant, I think this is enough." Mr. Stone pointed at his son. "Hunter, don't say anything else."

Hunter jumped to his feet. "I didn't kill Megan! Nobody was here with me, but I didn't kill her!"

"Hunter, enough!" Mr. Stone bellowed.

Jo got to her feet. "No one said you did, Hunter. We're just asking a few questions. I only have one more. Is that your car in the garage?"

Mr. Stone held up his hand. "Not another word, Hunter."

Hunter looked from his father to Jo then sat back down in the recliner. He stared at the floor, chewing the quick of his thumbnail.

Mr. Stone inclined his head toward the door. "I think we're done here."

Jo and Lynae walked back into the foyer with Mr. Stone closely behind.

Once there, Jo held out her hand. "Thank you for your time, Mr. Stone."

Mr. Stone looked blandly at the proffered hand then opened the door without a word.

CHAPTER 15

After climbing into the Ranger, Jo slammed the door and stared at the Stones' house. "That kid has a lot to lose."

Lynae nodded. "An eighteen-year-old with a football scholarship? I'd say that's pretty strong incentive to get rid of a baby."

Jo nodded toward the garage. "Golf clubs, tools... without even digging, I can see a gold mine of things in that shed that could have caused the kind of damage that was done to Megan."

Lynae sighed. "We just need a good enough reason for a judge to let us in there."

Jo backed out of the driveway. "Hunter had motive and opportunity."

"We'll have to verify that he was at practice until five o'clock."

"Even if he was, we don't know the exact time of death. He gets done with practice, gets a call from Megan. He picks her up, thinking he'll talk her back into the abortion, but when he can't, he gets angry, maybe panics and goes too far."

Lynae reached into the pocket of the passenger door and pulled out the granola bar and water she had stashed there earlier. "The school is close by, and she was found not too far out of his neighborhood. Kids tend to stick with what they know."

"They do, and right now, he's not only at the top of my list, he's the only one on it. He also has dark hair—a little long for a boy, in my opinion—and a silver car."

"And Hunter's a football player. Athletes have equipment, and that equipment definitely gets left in trunks," Lynae said around a mouthful of granola. "It's the kind of thing people forget about out of habit."

Jo scowled. "But both Hunter and his dad were home, and there was only one car in the driveway. At best, they share the car."

"We'll have to find out Mr. Stone's schedule. Sometimes janitors work odd shifts."

"I'd like to know more about Mr. Stone, anyway."

Lynae raised her eyebrows. "How come?"

"He's got a giant chip on his shoulder. He seemed angrier than Hunter did that Megan wouldn't tell her parents they were dating. It's a pretty big slam when you think someone else doesn't think your kid is good enough. He probably feels like they don't fit in at school. He's the janitor, and all the other parents are doctors and lawyers. I'm sure he goes to the football games to watch Hunter play, but I bet he doesn't hang out with the other parents. He's an outsider."

Lynae frowned. "Is that enough to kill a young girl over, though?"

"That scholarship is Hunter's ticket out. It's his chance to get an education and a better life. Live in a nice house, be a part of that clutch. We all want better for our kids than we have."

"Yeah, we do," Lynae said thoughtfully.

"We both know that people will do crazy things to protect what's theirs. And if Hunter is getting out, in his dad's mind, that may be *his* ticket out, also. If not financially, at least by status. If Stone knew about the baby, he knew that it was a threat to Hunter's future." Jo waved her hand. "It's just an avenue to explore. Obviously, Hunter has the bigger motive, and he's a teenager. Impulse control is not a teenager's strong suit."

Lynae snorted. "Yeah, that's for sure."

"We don't have anything to pull him in on yet, but I'd say he's a strong suspect." Jo glanced at the clock. "It's almost seven thirty. Isaac said he was sticking around for a while. Let's check in with him at the station and see if he has anything for us."

Lynae rolled her eyes. "I don't think he was planning to work all night. The Family Planning Center closed at six, so we'll have to go there in the morning. We'll have the phone records in the morning, also."

"Damn it! So we're at a standstill until tomorrow."

"It's been a long day, Jo. It's time to call it a night."

Jo sighed. "Yeah, you're right." She pulled into the station parking lot.

Lynae hopped out then leaned back in through the open door. "Put it away for the night and get some sleep. You're not sleeping enough. We'll go at it fresh in the morning."

Jo hated the thought of going home to an empty house with only a dog that, try as she might, couldn't quite fill the emptiness. She knew she would spend another night going back over the reports and interviews on Mike's case even though it was all but memorized. Sleep rarely came.

She smiled thinly at Lynae. "Okay, Mom."

CHAPTER 16

JO ARRIVED AT THE STATION at nine fifteen. Another late night at her desk had caused her to sleep through the alarm. She ran up the three flights of stairs, opting out of using the agonizingly slow elevator. *Sweet Jesus, let there be coffee.*

Lynae met her halfway through the bull pen. "Joyce Tillman and a friend are here to see you. I brought them to B."

Jo gritted her teeth. "Shit! How long have they been waiting?"

"Only about five minutes. I told them you had a meeting. I was just going to get them some coffee."

"Perfect. I need a cup desperately." Jo led the way into the break room, where the aroma of coffee blasted her senses. She breathed deeply through her nose. "I feel better just smelling those lovely roasted beans."

"Rough night?"

Jo grabbed a cup from the cupboard. "The usual. You said Mrs. Tillman is here with a friend. Not Mr. Tillman?"

"No, there's a woman with her." Lynae paused in pouring the coffee and gave her a sly look. "Paula Markham."

"Markham? That name just keeps coming up, doesn't it?"

"Yes, it does. I don't know if this woman has anything to do with Dr. Markham, but if not, it's quite the coincidence."

Jo picked up her cup and took a sip. "Interesting. But Mrs. Balister at the hospital did say the Markhams and Tillmans are friends, so we better not jump to anything too quickly."

Lynae shrugged. "Yeah, I know, but I can speculate."

Jo grabbed one of the other cups and nodded at the third. "If you can just help me get the coffee into the room, I'll take it from there. Clear up what you can from your schedule. We'll hit the clinic as soon as I'm done here."

They went into the conference room. Lynae set a cup of coffee in front of Joyce Tillman then nodded toward Jo. "Lieutenant Riskin is available now."

Joyce raised her head and stared blankly at Lynae for a moment before slowly turning her head to Jo. Her face was pale without the help of makeup, and dark rings circled her eyes. Her hair hung limply, so different from the perfect style she had worn the day before. Jo knew the look of a person who had spent the night crying. She had been that person... and still was some nights. She felt a sharp pang of pity for the road that lay ahead of the bereaved mother.

As Lynae left the room, Jo placed a cup of coffee in front of the woman she assumed was Paula Markham then slid into the chair across the table from Joyce. "I'm sorry to have kept you waiting, Mrs. Tillman."

Joyce tilted her head. "My neighbor called me early this morning. She said you wanted to talk to me." She spoke so quietly that Jo had to strain to hear.

"I have some information for you, but it's sensitive." Jo glanced at the other woman.

Paula Markham stared banally at Jo. Her expression gave no clue to the thoughts that might have been going on behind her striking dark eyes. Unlike Joyce Tillman, Paula appeared to have taken the time to perfectly put herself together. Her tailored blouse hugged her frame as only silk could. Her earrings, necklace, and bracelet were a matched set that would probably put Jo back six months' salary. Jo couldn't see her shoes, but she would have bet her right arm that they matched the Gucci purse propped on the table next to the woman's elbow.

Joyce hung her head and picked at the stitching of the purse that lay in her lap. A single tear ran down her cheek. "Dan couldn't come with me. He's not... neither of us is... he can't face it. He stayed with his family. I can't sit home and do nothing." Joyce gestured at the woman next to her. "Paula is my closest friend. She can hear anything you have to say."

Paula gave her friend's hand a squeeze and looked expectantly at Jo.

Jo nodded. "Mrs. Tillman, there's no easy way to say this."

Joyce raised her head. "Lieutenant, my daughter is dead. What could you possibly tell me that could make it worse?"

Like a Band-Aid. "The autopsy revealed that Megan was pregnant."

Paula's face took on an expression of pursed-lip disapproval on the verge of disgust before she quickly exchanged it for a sympathetic-friend look. She patted Joyce's hand, but the gesture seemed feigned.

Joyce whispered, "That's impossible."

"I'm sorry," Jo said. "I know this is hard."

Joyce shook her head. "But she didn't have a boyfriend. I asked her. She would have told me. We were close." Tears rolled down her cheeks.

Jo reached across the table and took the woman's hand. "I'm sure you were close, Mrs. Tillman. But teenagers are masters at hiding things from their parents. She didn't want you to know about her boyfriend."

The pain was palpable in Joyce's eyes. "Why? Why wouldn't she want me to know?"

"Megan didn't think you and your husband would approve. Her boyfriend lives in a rough part of town."

"How would she know someone like that? She would have no reason to go to a bad part of town."

"They went to school together. He was there through school of choice."

Paula Markham sat up a little straighter. "A bad part of town like where you found Megan?"

Fierceness appeared in Joyce's eyes. "Have you arrested this boy?"

"We have not made an arrest, Mrs. Tillman."

"Why not? He obviously had something to do with this. He must be the one!"

"We've talked to him, but we don't have any evidence to make an arrest at this time."

"Didn't he leave anything behind, any evidence?" Paula searched Jo's face eagerly. "Didn't you find anything on her that would help you?"

She wants something to take back to the gossip mill. Best friend, my ass. Jo regarded Paula evenly. "We have some leads that we're following up on, but there's nothing I can discuss at this time."

Paula sniffed. "That's such a terrible area. Someone probably wanted her money and her cell phone. You know how those people are."

Jo cocked her head and gave her a cold stare. "*Those* people?"

"You know what I mean, Detective," she replied, unaffected by Jo's disapproving look.

"What's his name?" Mrs. Tillman asked quietly. "This boy that Megan didn't want me to know about. What's his name?"

"Mrs. Tillman, I don't want you to approach him. We have no reason at this time to believe that he was involved. Nothing good can come from you talking to him."

"I'm not going to talk to him. I don't want anything to do with him. I just want to know his name so I can know one more thing about my daughter. Even if it's something she didn't want me to know."

"Mrs. Tillman—"

"Lieutenant, you know I can find out who this boy is. Please just save me the time and tell me."

Jo nodded. "Ma'am, please let us do our job. It's early, and these things take time."

"How do you plan to do your job if you don't have any evidence?" Paula rebuked.

Jo didn't like the woman. Apparently money and prestige couldn't buy the common decency to know that her words would hurt her friend. "I didn't say we didn't have any evidence, Mrs. Markham. We're following several leads. But processing evidence takes time, and it's only been one day. There is always evidence, and the evidence speaks for the victim. The evidence will speak for Megan."

"Of course it will. I'm sorry. This is all so difficult." Paula put her arm around Joyce's shoulders. "Is there anything I can do to help? Our family has resources. We know the right people. If there's anything we can do to help, we will."

"I appreciate the offer, but money and influence aren't going to matter here. The only thing that will help us is evidence." Jo turned back to Joyce and gripped her hand. "I will do my best to find whoever did this to your daughter. You have my word."

Joyce wiped her eyes with a tissue she had pulled from her purse. "I need to know everything. It's all I have to hold on to."

"Of course. Stay with your family and friends. I'll call you with any new information."

Joyce nodded and stood. Paula followed suit, throwing her purse over her shoulder. She touched Joyce's elbow and led her to the door.

Jo glanced at Paula's feet as she followed them out of the room. *Yep, the shoes match the purse.* After the women got into the elevator, Jo headed back through the bull pen.

Once again, Lynae met her halfway. "You have a visitor waiting in your office." Lynae's eyes glinted with a mischievousness that made Jo certain she wouldn't be happy about whoever was waiting for her.

Jo needed a couple of minutes to mull over her conversation with Joyce and Paula. "Who is it, and why do you have that stupid grin on your face?"

"It's Jack Riley. He's hot, and he's here to see *you*."

Jo scowled. "The prosecutor? What's he doing here?"

"I don't know, I didn't interrogate him. He just said he wanted to see you and would wait until you got back."

"I told him to let me know when the verdict came back on the Schneider trial. I thought he would just call, not actually come here."

Lynae smirked. "I guess he wanted to see you personally."

Jo glared at her. "Don't you have something to do?"

Lynae turned toward her desk. "Yes, very important police business that does not involve your personal life."

Jo stopped outside her office and took a deep breath. She plastered a smile on her face and opened the door. Jack stood and smiled broadly as she walked into the room. His blond hair had its usual semi-messy look, as if he had just stepped out of the wind… or bed.

Jo did her best to ignore the familiar flutter in the pit of her stomach. "Mr. Riley. What brings you here?"

"It's Jack. I just stopped by to tell you that the verdict came back on Schneider. First degree, life without possibility."

"That's fantastic. I have to say I would have been surprised if it had come out any other way. We had that case pretty well sewn up."

Jack nodded. "It was airtight. Your team did a great job. But it's always good to hear the words. You never know what a jury will do."

"That's true. I've seen some real surprises over the years."

Jack shoved his hands in his pockets and rocked back on his heels.

Jo searched for something else to say. "We're on a new case. Should be bringing another bad guy in for you soon." *Bad guy? Really, Jo?*

"I heard about the young girl in the Slope. So tragic."

"Murder always is, but it's harder when they're so young."

Jack pulled out one hand and swung a key chain around his forefinger. A glint of gold from a wedding ring shone in the light. "Well, I should go. I just wanted to let you know." He opened the door then stopped and turned back to Jo. "I was wondering… would you like to have dinner with me some night? Or catch a movie?"

Jo raised her hand and adjusted her wedding ring. "No, I don't think so."

"Oh, I thought—"

"Well, you thought wrong." Jo nodded at his left hand. "Why don't you take your wife out to dinner instead?"

Jack looked down at his wedding ring as if seeing it for the first time. "Oh... I—"

Jo wanted to end the awkwardness and get him out of her office. "Thanks for stopping by to let me know about the trial. I'm glad it's over."

"No problem." After giving her a short nod, he left her office.

CHAPTER 17

LYNAE SLIPPED INTO JO'S OFFICE and shut the door before Jack had even cleared the bull pen. "Well?"

"Well, what?" Jo banged her notebook onto her desk, got up, and walked over to the file cabinet.

"What did he want?"

"To tell me we got a guilty verdict on Schneider. No big surprise there, but nice to have it over, anyway."

Lynae crossed her arms. "That's it? He came here to tell you that instead of calling, or even e-mailing?"

"Yep." Jo opened the top two drawers, peeked inside each, then slammed them. She couldn't remember what she was looking for.

"Did that file cabinet piss you off, or is there something more you want to tell me?"

Jo dropped into her chair and began rummaging through the desk drawers. "Neither."

"Come on."

Jo leaned back in her chair, knowing Lynae wasn't going to leave her alone until she spilled. "He asked me out to dinner."

Lynae grinned. "Seriously?"

"No, I'm making it up."

Lynae ignored the sarcasm. "When are you going?"

"I'm not." Jo stared blindly at the paperwork on her desk.

"Why not?"

Jo shot her an exasperated look.

"Jo, why not? What can it hurt to go out for dinner or drinks?"

"He's not my type."

Lynae threw her hands up. "How is that even possible? He's *everyone's* type."

"I put my amazing detective skills to work and noticed that he's wearing a wedding ring. I wouldn't go out with a married man."

Lynae sat on the corner of Jo's desk. "Riley has been a widower for a little over a year. Sometimes good detective work takes research."

"Oh, shit." Jo dropped her elbows on her desk and rubbed her forehead.

"What's wrong? I thought you didn't want to go out with him."

Jo looked miserably up at Lynae. "I told him to take his wife out to dinner."

"You did not!" Lynae looked horrified.

"I did. I didn't know. Why didn't you tell me?"

Lynae shrugged. "You never really seemed interested in him. I didn't know he was going to show up here."

Jo sighed. "What's his story?"

"His wife died of cancer. All I know is she was pregnant and refused treatment because of the baby. By the time the baby was born, it was too late, and she went pretty quickly. It was their second kid. I think his oldest is about four now, and the baby must be about a year and a half or so."

Jo flopped back in her chair. "Oh God, that sucks. How do you know all this? He's only been in Grand Rapids for a few months."

"I make it a priority to know as much as I can about hot guys just in case it's ever important. Which in this case it clearly is."

Jo groaned. "Shit, now I feel like an ass. I thought he was just another good-looking guy who thought he could step out on his wife and get away with it."

"Now you're gonna have to make nice, especially if you're ever going to want anything from him. And considering his position, I'm guessing you will."

"It's not that. It's just wrong to leave it like that, all awkward. I have to apologize. He has to know that I didn't know."

"I'm sure he's figured that out." Lynae walked over to the door. "Now if you'll excuse me, I have shit to do."

Jo rolled her eyes. "I'm right behind you. I don't really have anything to do in here. We're still going to the clinic, right?"

"Yeah, I just need to get my stuff."

After Lynae left, Jo straightened her desktop a little while thinking about the discussion with Joyce and Pushy Paula. She couldn't decide if Paula had actually acted suspicious or if she just didn't like the woman on a personal level. Hoping they might learn something more at the clinic, she grabbed her things, along with the folder containing the photo of Megan.

As soon as Jo stepped out of her office, Charles intercepted her. "I've got the phone records from our victim's cell." He handed her a sheaf of papers. "The top three numbers are Ashley Kane, Hunter Stone, and her mom. In that order."

"Not surprising from what we know."

Charles pointed at the first number. "Last text sent was at seven twenty-eight to Ashley Kane."

"That jibes with what Ashley told us," Lynae said. "But according to Kent, Megan would have been dead well over an hour by the time that message was sent."

Charles let out a low whistle. "Cold bastard sent a text from her phone after he killed her."

"Smart bastard," Jo said. "If Megan had simply not shown up, Ashley would have gotten worried. She might even have said something to her mom and started the ball rolling toward finding Megan a whole lot earlier than this guy wanted."

Lynae walked over to join them. "And the guy was lucky. He could have just as easily sent a message to Megan's mom saying, 'Don't worry, I'm going here or there.' Her mom wasn't expecting Megan to come home, so that would have made her suspicious."

"Ashley's text worked out perfectly for him, didn't it?" Jo pictured the distraught teenager. "I think I'll keep that little bit of information from Ashley. She has enough guilt over this." She flipped to the second page. "Anything interesting before that?"

Charles put a finger on a highlighted number. "Several incoming texts from young Mr. Stone. Seems he was very intent on getting in contact with her. Also two phone calls from him. The last two outgoing texts before the one to Ashley are at four twenty-nine and four thirty-two. Hunter Stone and a Steven Markham."

Jo stared at the report. "Dr. Markham?"

Lynae raised one eyebrow. "Wonder why Megan was texting Dr. Markham at a time like that."

"His name has come up too many times. I think we need to have a talk with the doctor and see why he's texting with our victim. You with me?"

Lynae hitched her purse strap onto her shoulder. "Wouldn't miss it for the world."

CHAPTER 18

Jo and Lynae were led into Dr. Steve Markham's corner office on the seventh floor of Butterworth Hospital by Rita, a friendly middle-aged nurse. Rita kept up a constant chatter about how long the doctor would take to meet with them and why she had to wait in the office with them. Even with their police credentials, they were not allowed to wait unattended in the doctor's office, where he might have patient files. Jo understood that rule and agreed with it, but she certainly wouldn't have been offended if the nurse had chosen to wait with them in silence.

As Rita prattled on, Jo scanned Dr. Markham's office. As the attending physician of the cardiac unit in one of the country's highest-ranked hospitals, he was almost required to have an office that reeked of prestige and pomp, and his certainly fit the bill. The large cherrywood desk had a glass piece fitted perfectly to the entire top. Open on the desk was a Franklin planner with handwritten notes and appointments. She tried to read it upside down, but the scribbled shorthand made it impossible. Jo found it interesting that he kept a paper calendar and decided he must have a bit of an old-fashioned side.

A gold pen stood in a holder engraved with "State of Michigan Medical Society." The pedestal was angled perfectly for someone who didn't plan to use the pen but wanted visitors to be able to read the engraving. Manila folders with color-coded tabs were neatly stacked to the right of the computer monitor, which displayed a screen saver of two kids playing on a beach while a baby watched from a toddler seat. The kids were laughing and dirty, and the camera had caught the perfect moment when one threw sand in the air.

The wall of windows overlooked the city and let in the blindingly bright sun that made it easy to forget that it was fifty-two degrees outside. Two framed pictures had been placed on the windowsill on either side of a thriving blue orchid and immaculately trimmed miniature bonsai tree.

How does a doctor of Markham's standing have time to worry about trimming a stupid little tree?

The wall across from the desk hosted a matching cherrywood bookshelf. Jo left Lynae holding up the conversation with Rita and wandered over to take a closer look. Among books with titles like *Advances in Cardiac and Aortic Surgery* and *Atrial Fibrillation after Cardiac Surgery,* the shelves held more family pictures, including a wedding photo with the happy couple posed on the steps of the Grand Rapids Cathedral of St. Luke.

Paula had been even more beautiful in her youth, with shining black hair that fell just below her shoulder blades and was held back on the sides by the band of white roses that completed her veil. Her bright smile and stature gave her the look of someone who had just won something they had fought hard for, the expression Olympians wore when they stood on the winner's podium. The good doctor would definitely have been considered a prize. His thick dark hair reached his collar and was slightly messy, the kind of hair that a woman would immediately imagine running her fingers through. His piercing blue eyes and mischievous, lopsided grin dared everyone to join him in whatever fun thing he would do next. Jo had no doubt that he left many broken hearts in his path. *I wonder if one of those hearts had belonged to Megan.* The thought left a bitter taste in her mouth.

Other pictures showed the doctor and his wife at black-tie events and with another couple holding a golf trophy at what had probably been a charity tournament. In every photo, they looked happy, relaxed, and wealthy. Yet somehow, the joy didn't look real. Each image looked staged, the perfect couple doing perfect things.

As the years progressed in the pictures, Dr. Markham's

hairstyle became more businesslike and his posture more staid. His smiles lost their daring.

The family pictures taken on various vacations and holidays always displayed the children in spontaneous and fun poses, but everyone looked perfect in every photo—perfect smiles, perfect hair, perfect clothes. The infant from the screen saver was in only one other photo. Before Jo could contemplate the meaning of that, Dr. Markham strode into the office.

"I'm sorry to keep you waiting, Officers." He spoke in a quiet, commanding baritone. He turned to Rita. "Thanks for sticking around, Rita. I can take it from here."

Rita exchanged smiles with Jo and Lynae then made her exit. The doctor walked around and sat behind his desk.

"You have a beautiful family, Dr. Markham," Jo said as she took the seat Rita had vacated.

He smiled. "My kids have their mother's good looks."

"Have you been married long?"

"Right after medical school. Paula wanted to get married sooner, but I didn't want to try to fit a wedding in during the final semester of school. Paula and I went to Stanford together. She was on the golf team, and so was my fiancée at the time." He chuckled. "They're why I learned to golf, although I'll never be as good at it as Paula."

"I met your wife this morning when she came into the station with Joyce Tillman."

He closed his eyes and shook his head. "It's so tragic about Megan. I can't get over it. Dan and Joyce are very close friends of ours. I can't imagine what they're going through. Paula has been with Joyce almost constantly since we found out. But Dan... he isn't talking, even to me."

"Megan babysat for your kids, right?" Lynae asked.

He nodded. "Yes, after school two afternoons a week while Paula did volunteer work. Also sometimes on the weekend if I wasn't on call and we could manage to get away for a night out."

"And you helped her get a volunteer job at the hospital?" Lynae asked.

He folded his hands on his desk. "Megan wanted to be a doctor and thought volunteering at the hospital would look good on a college application. I agreed and used what pull I have to make it happen."

Lynae smiled. "That was nice of you."

"As I said, Dan is a good friend of mine. I wanted to help her in any way I could."

"Was she good at her job here?" Jo asked. "Did she have any problems with anyone that you're aware of?"

"I don't really know. I never heard any complaints, but I'm a surgeon. I'm not involved with the volunteers. You would have to talk to Marge Balister."

"We did, and she said the same." Jo cocked her head. "I thought you might have more insight since Megan was more than just a volunteer to you."

He shrugged. "We had a few conversations about the job, and she said she liked it. But nothing came up that would lead to this. I can't imagine what Megan could have been involved in that would."

Jo leaned forward. "Can you tell me why Megan contacted you shortly before her death?"

His eyebrows knitted as he frowned. "What do you mean?"

Jo returned his blank look. "I mean, why did Megan Tillman contact you an hour before she died?"

"I haven't talked to Megan this week, and I don't remember her calling." He pulled his phone from his pocket and began scrolling. "I don't see a missed call from her."

Jo retrieved the phone log from her bag and laid the report on his desk. "She sent you a text at four thirty-two p.m. the day she died."

Something flickered across his face as he stared down at the printout. She couldn't tell if it was recognition or fear. Then it was gone, replaced by his normal calm facade.

He raised his eyes back up to Jo's. "I don't understand. I never got a text from her."

Jo jabbed a finger at the number on the printout. "Isn't that your cell phone number, Doctor?"

"Yes, it is, but I never saw a message from her that day." He looked back down at his phone and began flicking his thumb across the screen again. "I can show you my messages."

"Messages can be deleted, Doctor. But phone records can't."

"I don't know what to tell you. I did not receive a message from Megan the day she died."

Jo frowned. "Have there been other text messages that you haven't received that you're aware of? Is something wrong with your phone service?"

He shook his head. "Not that I know of."

Jo took the printout from his desk. "But you're saying this one from Megan didn't come through."

"I'm saying I never saw a message from Megan that day."

"That day? But you did receive these texts from her on the other days?"

He sat back in his chair. "Yes, I did receive other texts from her."

"Are you in the habit of texting with teenage girls, Doctor?"

He huffed. "No, I'm not, Lieutenant. But that is how teenagers communicate, and the situation with Megan was… different."

"How was it different?"

Dr. Markham took off his glasses and rubbed his eyes with one hand. "Megan came to me as a doctor. She needed to talk to an adult that she could trust."

"As a doctor? So she needed medical advice?"

He sighed. "She came to me because she was pregnant and didn't know what to do. She wanted advice."

Jo nodded. "Yes, we're aware of the pregnancy. And what did you tell her?"

"I thought an abortion would be the best thing for her and encouraged her to have one. She was hesitant. It went against her beliefs, and she was very frightened."

"Did you discuss this with her parents?"

Dr. Markham jerked as though Jo had slapped him. "Of course not. There's doctor-patient confidentiality, Lieutenant."

Jo glanced around the office. "Do you have anything on record here that you were acting as her physician?"

"No, it wasn't in an official capacity. There wasn't any reason for that."

"Yet, you still concerned yourself with doctor-patient confidentiality enough not to talk to your good friend, Dan?"

Dr. Markham massaged his left shoulder then leaned forward, resting his elbows on the desk. "That's how I thought of it and treated it. I didn't want to betray her trust by talking to her parents without her consent. I had encouraged her to have the abortion because she had such a bright future. She was a very smart, ambitious young woman. I didn't want an unexpected pregnancy to stop her from fulfilling her dreams. I told her she wouldn't be able to achieve everything she wanted in life if she had a baby to care for."

Jo rubbed her forehead. She could feel a headache starting behind her eyes. "Teenage girls usually talk to their friends, or if they're smart, they talk to their parents. I'm finding it hard to understand why she would go to you with this problem unless you were especially close to start with, or you had some other interest in whether or not she had the baby."

Dr. Markham glared at Jo. "I don't know what you're trying to say, Lieutenant, but I assure you my relationship with Megan was completely aboveboard."

"Okay, then tell me why Megan confided in you about the baby."

"Megan was our babysitter, and I always walked her home in the evenings. I didn't like the idea of her being out alone if it was late. One night when I walked her home, she seemed very upset, so I asked her if something was wrong. She blurted it all out like she just couldn't keep it in anymore. She asked me what she should do. After that, I looked into options for her, and we talked about them. That's it."

"Did you suggest one of the clinics in the area?"

He nodded. "I have some connections at the Family Planning Center. I suggested she go there and talk to a counselor."

"And did she talk to a counselor?"

"Yes, she said she did and that she had decided that she should have the abortion so she could have a life."

Jo opened her notebook. "Did she say who she talked to?"

"No, and I didn't ask. I was just relieved that she had decided to have the abortion."

"I bet you were."

"I was relieved *for her*, Lieutenant." He rubbed his shoulder again. "She had sent me a few messages recently and was doubting her decision. I understood, to an extent, but I encouraged her to talk to the counselor again, and I hoped that she would make the right decision."

"Why didn't you encourage her to talk to her parents? Maybe even go with her to help ease the conversation, since you're such good friends?"

He opened his hands, palms up. "I tried. She didn't want them to know, and as I said, I wasn't comfortable having that discussion with Dan behind her back."

"What do you know about her boyfriend?" Lynae asked.

"I don't know him, but I knew he wasn't going to be any help, and it sounded like his father had a problem with the two of them dating. It wasn't a good situation."

Lynae tilted her head. "She told you that?"

"Only in passing. I was just helping her with her situation. We didn't talk about much else. Do you think the baby or the abortion had something to do with her death?"

"We're exploring all avenues right now," Lynae said, "but that would be a motivator, don't you think?"

Dr. Markham nodded slowly and leaned back in his chair. "To some people it would be."

Jo studied him silently until he shifted uncomfortably, removed his glasses, and began to clean them on his jacket. "Your wife didn't appear to know anything about the baby."

His hand froze. "You told her?"

Jo wondered if she'd hit a nerve. "I told Mrs. Tillman. Your wife was there with her," Jo replied. "Why didn't you tell her?"

"There was no reason for her to know," he replied as he put his glasses back on.

Jo thought about Mike and the long conversations they would have about anything and everything, delving deep into cases, family dynamics, and even topics that sometimes had no real significance in their lives. If Markham's relationship with Megan had truly been innocent, if it was just a case of a young girl needing an adult to talk to, she couldn't imagine him keeping it from his wife. "And was there a reason for your wife not to know?"

Dr. Markham leaned forward. "Paula is a wonderful woman. She's intelligent, generous with her time and money, a loving mother and wife. Her one weakness, however, is discretion. I'm afraid my wife doesn't keep a secret very well, and I didn't want this to get back to the Tillmans. I didn't want to betray Megan's trust."

Jo decided she would have to chew on that for a while. "Can you account for your whereabouts on Tuesday evening?"

He gaped at her. "Am I really a suspect here, Lieutenant?"

"Your number came up on the phone of a murdered teenager at a time very close to her death. Unless you can give a solid alibi, we can't cross you off our list."

He pushed his hands through his dark hair. "Tuesday is my paperwork night. Paula and I have dinner out, and then I come back to the office and work late to catch up on my paperwork."

"What time did you have dinner?"

"Paula had some errands to run, so it was a little later than usual. I met her at Leo's at seven thirty."

Jo scribbled the time and place in her notebook. "So you were here in the hospital until you met your wife at seven thirty? Can anyone verify that?"

He sighed and shook his head. "I don't know. I spend the time in my office by myself. That's the point. Most days I'm coming and going at all hours around here, but I have the same routine every Tuesday. Ask anyone."

Jo looked up from her notes and stared coldly at the doctor. "I don't care about every Tuesday, just this one."

He stared blankly at his desktop, then his head jerked up. "I said good night to Julie at the desk when I left. I remember because she made a comment about date night."

"Is Julie working now?"

"No, she's off today. She'll be in tomorrow at noon."

Jo nodded and made a note to talk to Julie. "Would date night be one of the nights that Megan would normally babysit for you?"

Dr. Markham shook his head. "No, Paula's mother picks the kids up from school on Tuesdays and keeps them overnight."

"Quite a handful for Grandma," Jo commented, nodding at the computer screen.

He gave Jo a crooked grin. "That picture is a bit old. They're not quite as much work anymore. But Grandma enjoys every minute of it."

Jo smiled. "I bet she does. And you said your wife was running late?"

"Yes. She said she spent a little more time than usual with the kids. She reads with underprivileged kids in an afterschool program. It put her whole schedule off." He smiled tenderly. "Must have been a special kid because she doesn't usually deviate. She's a bit of a stickler about her schedule."

"So you got the call from your wife, but you didn't get the text from Megan?" Jo asked.

"Paula called my work number. I forgot—" A brief look of confusion crossed his face.

Jo leaned forward. "Forgot what?"

He cleared his throat. "I forgot that Paula had called my work number. I probably left my phone lying somewhere."

"I would think a doctor would have to have the phone obsession that most of the rest of us have, checking messages constantly," Lynae said.

"I have a pager. If there's an emergency, that's how they contact me. And I was here, so my phone wasn't that important."

"What kind of car do you drive, Doctor?" Jo asked.

"I drive a Lexus, why?"

"And the color?"

"Black." Dr. Markham glanced at his watch and stood. "If we're done here, I have patients to see." He raised his hand to his shoulder then dropped it.

"Did you hurt your shoulder?" Jo asked.

He looked down at his arm as if it had moved of its own free will. "Tendonitis. My doctor blames it on tennis." He gave Jo that crooked grin again. "I don't blame anything on tennis."

Jo thought of the scrapes on the side of Megan's lifeless body. Whoever put her in that dumpster had a reason for struggling to lift her. Maybe that reason was tendonitis. She filed the thought away for later and stood with Lynae. "Thank you for your time, Doctor. Please contact us if you think of anything that may help."

"Of course, but I believe I've told you everything I know."

Jo took one more look around his office. She thought about her own little cramped space with ugly beige walls and cheap pressed-wood bookshelves. She decided she wouldn't want to trade. His office left a bad taste in her mouth. And it didn't have a television.

CHAPTER 19

LYNAE JABBED AT THE ELEVATOR button. "Well, he had an answer for everything."

Jo tapped her foot impatiently as they waited for the door to open. "In my experience, an adult and a teenager having a secret that involves a baby is never a good thing. And when the adult doesn't talk to his wife about it, it's even worse."

The doors opened, and Lynae stepped inside first. "He's a highly intelligent man. He has to know about phone records. Why would he risk everything by texting a teenager he's involved with?"

Jo leaned her head back against the elevator wall. The lack of sleep had suddenly slammed her body like a brick wall. "No one ever thinks they're going to get caught. Plus, if criminals weren't stupid, our job would be a lot tougher."

Lynae rocked on the balls of her feet and drummed her fingers on the wall behind her, the wound-up yin to Jo's tired yang. "Aren't we really stretching it to think that Megan was sleeping with two men? It doesn't fit. Her parents didn't even think she had *one* boyfriend."

"Teenagers can be great at deceiving their parents. Didn't you say earlier that when you were in high school, you would tell your parents that you were going to a friend's house when you were really with a boy?"

Lynae crossed her arms. "Only once or twice."

Jo smirked. "Okay, your story. What about the doctor's bad shoulder? That would be a good reason to have to push a small body like Megan's up the side of that dumpster."

Lynae shrugged. "Yeah, that's a strike against him. On the

other hand, the paint chip that you pulled from the dumpster was silver. The doctor drives a black car."

"It was only my speculation that the paint came from the killer's car. It could have been there for a long time, for all we know."

"You seemed pretty sure before."

The elevator doors opened, and Jo pushed away from the wall and walked into the hospital lobby. "I know. I'm trying to make it fit."

"We have to fit the suspect to the evidence, not the evidence to the suspect."

Jo stopped in her tracks and stared at her partner. "God, that sounds like something Mike would say."

Lynae pointed at her. "It's something *you* said to *me* when we worked our first case together. Remember, I was trying to jump on the first person I thought was guilty? I wanted to solve that case fast and make a name for myself."

"Damn, I give great advice. And it probably was something that Mike told me once upon a time." Jo opened the hospital door and stepped into the cool October air. "Of course, you're right, and I know it. I can't force the evidence to fit him or ignore evidence that might prove his innocence. I have to work with the evidence first and find the person that fits it."

"Then let's start from scratch. Your gut says that he knows something he's not telling us."

"Yeah, that's where we start. It's an odd situation with a young girl confiding in a man old enough to be her father, but that's not a crime. Maybe he's just a very good listener or comfortable to be around. Who knows?"

Lynae shrugged. "But he has a strange tie to a dead teenager."

Jo grinned. "So I'm gonna pick him apart piece by piece."

"If his timeline checks out, it would have been pretty tough for him to pull this off. There would have been blood splatter, so he would have needed a change of clothes, maybe even a shower."

Jo pulled out her keys and unlocked the Ranger. "Which he could have had at the hospital. He would know where to take a shower, and no one would question why he was there."

"The car would have been a mess," Lynae countered before getting into the passenger side.

Jo slid into the driver's seat and started the engine. "It's possible he left the cleanup for later, but it would be very tight, and there's always a risk in leaving a mess in a car. And then there's a wife at home to deal with later. He knew she wouldn't be home because she had called to tell him."

Lynae buckled her seat belt. "He hesitated over that, did you notice? He thought twice about his wife calling, leaving it wide open that the house was empty. And that he had told us that."

"I noticed that look, but that was his alibi. We had to know why his routine changed. There's something he's not telling us, though. I can feel it. We just have to figure out what that something is."

"And we will. Personally, I'm sticking with the boyfriend," Lynae said.

"He's young and impulsive. If something was going on with Megan and Dr. Markham, and Hunter found out, that might even be motive."

"He thinks he's all that, and now he's been dissed by this girl," Lynae added.

Jo raised an eyebrow. "Dissed?"

"Disrespected, you know..."

"I know what it means. I've just never heard anyone over the age of about seventeen say it. And I think it's been about five years since I've heard any seventeen-year-olds use it."

Lynae huffed. "Oh, so now you're Miss Language Police."

"*Mrs.* Language Police. And yes, I'm adding that to my résumé."

"I'm sure that will help land you a captain's spot."

"Then I'll leave it off."

Lynae grabbed the sissy bar as Jo stomped on the accelerator to enter traffic. "You don't want a cushy desk job, bossing people around, not having to deal with this shit we're doing right now?"

"Are you kidding?" Jo grinned. "I live for this shit."

CHAPTER 20

JO PARKED IN THE LOT behind the Family Planning Center and grabbed her bag from the backseat. They were three blocks from where the Yellow Cab driver had dropped Megan off, and since the good doctor had suggested it to the teenager, they were pretty certain it was the right place.

As they walked up the long sidewalk to the front entrance, Lynae eyeballed the protestors. "I wonder if any of them talked to Megan."

"It would be worth asking." Jo pulled Megan's picture from her bag.

Lynae plucked the picture from her hand. "I've got this. I'll meet you inside."

As Lynae hustled over to the line of protestors, Jo slipped into the cool, tiled entrance of the clinic.

A young woman looked up from behind a glass window and smiled as Jo approached. Her smile faded when Jo held up her badge. "What can I do for you, Officer?"

Jo gave her a friendly smile. "Lieutenant Riskin with the GRPD. I'd like to talk to someone about a young girl we believe had an appointment here on Monday."

The woman frowned. "I'm sorry, but we can't release the names of our patients. There are confidentiality rules."

Jo pulled out Megan's autopsy picture. "I don't think she would care about confidentiality if it helps us find whoever did this to her."

The receptionist's face turned a shade of gray-green. "I'll get the doctor."

Jo nodded. "Thank you."

Lynae pushed open the heavy glass entrance doors and made a beeline for Jo. "No luck out there. They all come out as a group once a week, and today's their day."

"Maybe other groups come out on other days. There always seem to be protestors at these places. If it comes down to it, we can track down who's here on Mondays."

A woman wearing an exam coat and stethoscope came through the doors from the back with the receptionist. She smiled thinly and held out her hand. "I'm Dr. Theresa Lipscomb."

Jo shook the woman's hand and introduced herself and Lynae. "Thank you for seeing us. We'd like to talk to you about a girl we believe was here on Monday."

Dr. Lipscomb glanced around the waiting room, where four women were studiously ignoring them. "Why don't we talk in my office?" She turned and walked back through the door she had just entered. Jo and Lynae hustled to follow her.

She led them into a small office overrun with files. "I apologize for the mess. We don't have the funding to be completely computerized yet, so I'm stuck with paper. I haven't found much time for filing recently." She motioned to the visitor chairs across from her desk. "Please have a seat."

Jo and Lynae settled into the hard plastic chairs.

Jo handed the doctor the autopsy picture of Megan. "Do you recognize this girl?"

Dr. Lipscomb stared at the picture for close to a minute, shaking her head. Jo thought the doctor was going to say she didn't recognize Megan, but the woman said, "Yes, I recognize her. She was here this week." When she handed the picture back, her hand shook.

Jo took the photo and slid it back into her bag. "And you met with her?"

"I talked to her briefly then left her to get changed. When I came back, she was gone." Her shining eyes were dangerously close to spilling over with tears. "She looks like she was beaten in that picture. What happened to her?"

"She was murdered."

Dr. Lipscomb closed her eyes and let out a long breath. "God."

"Was anyone here with her?" Lynae asked.

"No. I asked her if she had someone and told her we prefer it, but she didn't have anyone. She insisted that she had someone who was going to pick her up when she called."

Lynae raised her eyebrows. "And did someone pick her up?"

The doctor held out her hands. "I don't know. As I said, she was gone when I came back to the room. I went to the waiting area to see if she was still here. Sometimes young girls change their minds and then come back, or they sit in the waiting room, trying to make up their minds. If I see them there, I'll talk to them, usually suggest they wait and come back when and if they're sure. But she wasn't there. The receptionist said the girl just walked right out the door without stopping."

"Did anyone else talk to her while she was here?" Jo asked.

"Karen. She's a nurse and the counselor here. She had spoken to the girl prior to the day of the procedure to tell her what would happen and what her options were. We have mandatory counseling here."

"Is Karen here today?" Jo asked.

"Yes, she is. I can get her for you when we're finished."

Jo nodded toward the window. "I see you have protestors outside. Is that pretty standard too?"

The doctor didn't look at the window. "We have someone out there almost every day."

"Do they ever give you a hard time, harass employees or patients as they're coming in?"

"No, I think the days of abortion clinic bombings and murdered doctors are over. They don't really bother anyone. They just gather out there and walk with their signs. Some of them are from local churches, and they're very peaceful, even friendly in their way. Sometimes they talk to the women who are coming in."

Jo cocked her head. "Does that cause a problem?"

"Not usually. We have the rare occasion when someone gets aggressive, but usually there aren't any problems. If they stop someone from having an abortion, that doesn't bother me. It's a tough decision, and if someone walks away from it, then that's what's right for them."

"Did any of the protestors talk to Megan?"

She shook her head. "Not that I heard. I don't know what happens outside unless someone tells me."

"Thanks for your time, Doctor." Jo passed her a card. "I would appreciate it if you could get Karen for us. Can we talk to her in here?"

Dr. Lipscomb stood up. "Sure. I'll get her for you."

After the doctor left the room, Lynae said, "Not much help there."

"Maybe we'll have some luck with the counselor."

Dr. Lipscomb brought Karen into the office and introduced her. Before closing the door, the doctor said, "I'll have to leave you and get back to my patients. I've got your card. I'll call if I remember or hear anything helpful."

The counselor settled into the doctor's chair, giving the springs a much harder workout than the petite doctor had.

Jo handed her Megan's picture. "This girl was found murdered yesterday. I understand you counseled her previously and saw her on Tuesday."

Karen spent a moment staring at the picture then brought a hand to her chest. "Yes, I talked with her… Megan. I felt so bad that she was all alone. She was so young and frightened… and confused. She put on a tough front, but I wasn't really surprised when she disappeared."

"Does that happen often? Girls disappearing out of the rooms?"

"No, not really. Many of them come in here and are not questioning their decision. I still do the counseling, but their minds are made up. Occasionally, we have someone like Megan who isn't so sure she's doing the right thing, and sometimes they walk." Karen looked down at the picture again then handed it back to Jo. "I actually pushed her a little not to have the abortion. Did that have something to do with her murder?"

Jo slid the photo back into her bag. "We don't know. We're just following every lead. Did she talk to you about her relationship with the baby's father, her parents, or anyone that she might have been worried about or afraid of?"

Karen looked thoughtful. "She was worried about her parents, but she was equally worried about her belief that abortion is wrong. She was very torn. I encouraged her to talk to her parents, but she said she couldn't, that they would kill her if they knew."

Lynae sat up straight. "She actually said that her parents would kill her?"

Karen shook her head. "She's fifteen, Detective. Kids use that terminology. I don't think she thought her parents would actually kill her. She was a good kid from a good home who made a mistake. I think she just meant that she would break their hearts or that their perfect world would be marred. You don't think her parents had anything to do with this, do you?"

"Right now, we can't rule out anything," Lynae replied.

"That's really all I have. I talked with her, gave her the pamphlets to look over, and helped her fill out some paperwork. That's it. I was surprised when she actually showed up for her appointment, and not surprised when she walked."

"You're friends with Dr. Steve Markham." Jo stated it as a fact.

Karen smiled. "With Paula, his wife, actually. I've gotten to know Steve over the years, but I've known Paula forever." She cocked her head slightly. "I'm curious how you know that?"

Jo waved it off. "I just saw you in a picture in Dr. Markham's office. You were with the Markhams and another person holding a golf trophy."

"Oh, that!" Karen laughed heartily. "We were in a charity golf tournament together one year. I was the handicap. Paula actually took me out shopping for the right outfit to wear that day. If I was going to be on her team, I had to look the part. I don't usually do charity events unless I'm behind a desk, passing out name tags, so I guess I needed a little coaching."

"I hear ya!" Lynae chuckled. "I wouldn't know how to fit in at something like that."

Karen's eyes softened. "Paula took to it like she was born into it. She never missed a beat. Personally, I wouldn't want to try to be perfect like that all the time. But I guess that comes with the territory of being married to someone like Steve."

Lynae narrowed her eyes. "Someone like Steve?"

"Oh, you know, someone in his position, with his social standing. His tax bracket. He's a very nice man and quite fun to be around, but there are so many obligations. Paula's always been very ambitious, knew what she wanted, but she also knew how to cut loose and have fun. I don't see that anymore. It all looks so glamorous, but I think there's too much pressure to be perfect."

"I imagine there is." Lynae glanced at Jo.

Jo took the hint and picked up the questioning. "Did you recognize Megan when she came in for her first appointment with you?"

Karen nodded. "I did, but she didn't seem to recognize me, so I never said anything to her. I thought it would make her uncomfortable."

"Did you tell anyone that she had been here? Or that she left without having the abortion?"

Karen stared at Jo for a moment. "That would be a breach of confidentiality."

"To your knowledge, has Dr. Markham ever recommended this facility to anyone needing your services?"

Karen shook her head. "Not that I'm aware of. But Paula has, so it makes sense that this would be the place that Steve would think of."

"Mrs. Markham has brought girls here in the past?"

"Paula works with a lot of underprivileged kids, and they're the most likely teens to need our help. There have been a few times when she's taken one under her wing and helped her through this process."

"She sounds like quite the woman," Jo replied.

Karen nodded and smiled with genuine affection. "She is indeed. She's the ideal wife for a man like Steve."

"How did you say you met her?"

"We've been friends since grade school. We lost touch for a

while when she went to Stanford. I couldn't afford a school like that, so I stayed in the area. We reconnected when she came back to Grand Rapids."

"It's tough to be the one without the money," Lynae said.

Karen waved her hand in front of her face. "Oh, Paula's family didn't have money. In fact, she grew up very poor. On the wrong side of the tracks, if you will."

Jo cocked her head. "Wasn't she on the golf team at Stanford? Golf isn't exactly a poor man's sport. And to get good enough to play for Stanford, she must have had lessons."

Karen nodded. "She did have lessons. Paula's father mowed the grass at Egypt Valley Golf Course, and Paula would tag along when she was little and there was no one home to watch her. Apparently, she had one old club that her father had found lying on the course, and she would hit ball after ball with it. The pro there took an interest in her and offered lessons in exchange for her father doing yard work."

"She wouldn't have made it to college and ultimately the life she has without those lessons," Lynae replied.

"It was her ticket out. And Paula wanted out. When Paula wants something, she goes all in, so she was a very good protégé for the pro to take on. He helped her, and she made him look good."

Lynae whistled softly. "That's quite the ticket."

Karen held up her hands. "Don't get me wrong, Paula was a good student and did very well academically. Stanford doesn't keep bad students, no matter how good they are athletically. She was an English major. I thought she would be a language arts teacher." She stopped and frowned. "I'm sorry, but what does this have to do with that poor girl's murder?"

Jo shrugged. "I'm sure nothing. I just saw the picture and recognized you."

Karen folded her hands on the desk. "I wish I could be of more help."

Jo stood and handed her a card. "You've been a great deal of help. Thank you. If you think of anything else, please give me a call."

Karen looked at the card then dropped it into the front pocket of her pink scrubs. "Of course."

Lynae shook her hand then hustled out the door behind Jo.

CHAPTER 21

Lynae buttoned her coat as they walked back through the parking lot. "I can see the storm brewing in your head. What are you thinking?"

Jo glanced back at the brick building. "She was here, ready to have the abortion. Markham recommended the place, so he would have known where she was. She sends him a text after she decides not to go through with it. If he's not involved, then why would she do that?"

"She also contacted Hunter," Lynae countered. "I would find it hard to believe that he didn't know where she was going to have this done. I know they weren't technically together, but I would think he would know that much."

"Yeah, maybe."

They got into the Ranger and buckled up. Jo glanced back at the clinic as she exited the lot. Megan had made a tough choice in that building, and she had paid for it with her life. Jo was certain of that.

"Maybe it had nothing to do with the baby, " Lynae said. "She had no money in her wallet. Maybe this was a simple robbery. Or it could have been one of the protesters who didn't know she had changed her mind and wanted to scare people away from the clinic."

Jo shook her head. "Neither really fits. A simple robbery doesn't end in murder with fiber trace from the trunk of a car. You rob them and move on. Even if the robber was crazy enough to kill, he wouldn't transport the body. And the few rogue protesters who've gone off the deep end and killed someone have wanted people to know what they've done and why. Otherwise they're not making a point. The way she was beaten tells me this is personal. There was too much anger for anything else."

Jo's phone rang. She glanced at the screen but didn't recognize the number. "Riskin."

"Lieutenant Riskin, this is Detective Mick Conner from the Ottawa County Sherriff's Department."

Jo glanced at Lynae and shrugged. "What can I do for you, Detective?"

"I've got a detainee here, brought in on possession with intent. Third time for this guy. He's looking at Class A-II felony. Gonna do some serious time." The detective's voice was deep and slow, bringing horses and miles of white fence to Jo's mind.

"Sounds like a great guy."

"Suddenly he wants to talk to you."

Jo scowled. "Oh yeah? Who is he?"

"Name's Treyton Brocht. Goes by Treybro."

Jo went through her mental Rolodex and came up empty. "That's original, but it doesn't mean anything to me. He asked for me by name?"

"Yep. Said he has some information that you'll want to hear."

"Probably looking for a deal on something I've got open. Did he say what?"

Detective Conner hesitated then said, "He just said it's on a case that's real personal to you."

All of the blood in Jo's body froze then rushed en masse to her heart, making the pounding almost unbearable.

"Lieutenant?"

Jo loosened her white-knuckled grip on the phone. "Do you think he's legit? I don't want to waste my time."

"I don't know, Lieutenant. He said he'll only talk to you."

Jo glanced at the clock and calculated the trip. "I can be there in about forty-five minutes."

"He's not going anywhere, and neither am I," Detective Conner drawled.

Jo hung up then pried her fingers loose from the steering wheel before telling Lynae, "Drug dealer at Ottawa County wants to talk to me. Says it's about something that's real personal to me."

Lynae laid her hand on Jo's arm. "I'm going with you."

Jo shook her head. "Not necessary. Most likely this guy just heard my name and wants to blow some smoke to try to get a deal. That's all it ever is."

"Then we'll find that out together. I'll stay behind the glass, but I'm going along. No use arguing, it will only waste time. Isaac and Charles can take care of anything we've got going here."

Jo shrugged. "Okay. I guess I could probably use the company."

"Yeah, you can tell yourself you have a choice if it makes you feel better."

"At least make yourself useful and get ahold of Isaac. I want him to dig up anything he can find on Steve Markham. Maybe there's something in the doc's past that wants to jump out and help us."

While Lynae made the call, Jo thought about the man sitting in the Ottawa County Jail. She refused to get her hopes up. Every time she had followed a new lead, she'd let herself hope that it could finally be the piece she needed to break the case wide open. And every time, that hope had been crushed. She was sure her heart could take being broken only so many times before it would shatter beyond repair.

But she knew there was someone somewhere who knew what had happened that night, and come hell or high water, she would find that person. She would worry about her heart later.

CHAPTER 22

Jo and Lynae waited at the security desk until Detective Conner came out and walked them through the nearly empty bull pen and into the observation room of Interrogation Room 3. The detective was exactly what Jo had anticipated from their short conversation. He was in the latter part of his fifties with salt-and-pepper hair, heavy on the salt. He was fit for a man his age but definitely softening around the edges. He stood a couple of inches taller than Jo and wore blue jeans and a sport coat over a crewneck T-shirt.

Jo stared through the one-way glass at the man who, despite herself, she dared to hope had some piece of legitimate information for her. Treyton Brocht slouched in one of the hard plastic chairs that seemed to exist in every station across the US, his legs splayed out in front of him. He wore the practiced, bored look of the chronically arrested. His Crown Holder jeans were cinched ten inches below his waist, and the bottoms pooled around his unlaced DC shoes. His dreadlocked hair reached the shoulders of his black hoodie, which was unzipped over a Wiz Khalifa Rolling Papers T-shirt. That was pretty much standard attire for a man of his profession.

The beige-walled room held nothing but a single table and four chairs, intentionally empty and plain for its calming effect on people. After twelve years on the job, Jo had her doubts about the legitimacy of that tactic.

"Did he tell you anything?" Jo asked Mick.

"No. We have him nuts to the wall on the charge. 'Scuse my language."

Jo chuckled. "No need."

"Anyway, he suddenly clams up and says he's not saying anything until he talks to you. I'm guessing he just wants to make a deal, give you some bullshit. But just to be safe, I didn't want you to miss anything that would help an important case."

"I appreciate the call." Jo reached for the doorknob.

"Are you sure you don't want me to go in with you?" Lynae asked.

"No, I got this," Jo said as she stepped out. She closed the door and stood in the hallway, gathering her courage and tamping down her hopes. When she felt she was as ready as she would ever be, she entered the interrogation room.

As she walked in, Treyton raised his head. "Took you long enough." His tone was filled with defiance.

So this is the way he wants to play. Jo shrugged and lowered herself slowly into the chair across from him. "I've got more important things to do than come running every time some low-level bagman wants to talk to me."

Treyton slumped even lower in his seat and crossed his arms. "I ain't no low-level bagman."

"You're sitting in here looking at fifteen in state, aren't you?"

Treyton shrugged and looked away, his only sign of agitation a compulsively bouncing foot.

Jo leaned forward and laid her palms flat on the table. "Listen, don't waste my time. What do you want with me?"

"I didn't do nothing, and I ain't goin' down for this bullshit. I want a deal."

Jo smirked. "What am I going to give you a deal for? From what I hear, they got you solid on this."

"I got information you're gonna want."

"Information on what? I've got a lot of cases, Treybro." Jo said his name slowly, her voice dripping with contempt. She wanted him to know she didn't give a damn about his street cred.

"I got information on a cop got killed. Shot."

Jo concentrated on keeping her breathing steady. "I'm not working anything involving a police officer."

"Word is you been asking around on it, anyway." Treyton shrugged and looked away. "It ain't your case, tell me who to talk to. I know you cops all stick together. Somebody'll want what I got."

"Okay, you give me something I can use, and we'll talk about a deal."

"What can you do for me?"

Jo raised her hands. "I don't even know what you have, and this isn't my jurisdiction. I have to check out your so-called information. But I'll tell you this. If you're giving me straight-up information and it checks out, I'll go to bat for you on your charges."

"Go to bat for me? What the fuck does that mean?"

"Right now, you got nothing to lose. You tell me what you have, and don't bullshit me, and I'll do everything I can."

"How do I know I can trust you? I give you what I got, and you could give me nothin'. Ain't gonna be nothin' I can do 'bout it then."

"I can't do anything unless you give me something. You know that. I gave you my word. That's all I can do right now."

"Your word. Right." He stared at Jo.

She stared back, unblinking. She fought against her own body to keep a calm exterior while everything inside her wanted to grab the little shit and shake him until whatever he knew fell out.

After what felt like an eternity of a silent battle of wills, he finally licked his lips nervously and said, "All right, look. Talk to Tonya Mereck. She got sick a' gettin' knocked around by her old man, so she come my way. I know how to treat a woman, know what I'm sayin'?" He looked Jo up and down suggestively.

"Yeah, I'm sure you're every woman's dream man," Jo deadpanned. "So what does this have to do with this case?"

"This guy told her he killed a cop, even gave her the gun to hide for him. She put it together and said it was the guy you're lookin' for."

Jo waited a beat then slammed back into her chair. "That's it? That's what you called me all the way out here for? How do I even know she's talking about the same cop?"

"How many cops get shot in Grand Rapids?"

He had her on that. But she was thankful that number was low for several reasons.

"Why didn't she go to the police?"

Treyton rolled his eyes and snorted. "Why would she? What the police ever do for her? Never gonna happen 'less she needs somethin' or she's pissed enough at him."

"So she was pissed enough at him to tell you, and you kept it to yourself until you needed something."

Treyton leaned back and kicked his legs out in front of him. "That's the way it works."

"Where can I find this Tonya?"

"I don't know. I ain't seen her in a while. I don't know where she's stayin' now. Heard she might be back with him."

Jo raised her eyebrows. "I thought you knew how to treat a woman?"

"I do. That chick just don't know what's good for her." Treyton sat up again and put his hands on the table.

"Do you know how to spell her name?"

"Yeah. She had it printed on everything she owned, like she thought everybody was gonna steal her stuff." He spelled it for her. His leg bounced nervously. "But that's good shit, right? Now you're gonna do me a solid, right?"

"I will, as soon as I know you're not just blowin' smoke. I talk to Tonya and she gives me something that I can use, I'll do what I can for you." Jo stood on shaky legs and headed for the door.

"You tell her she ever wants a real man again, she knows where to find me," he said to her back as she walked out of the interrogation room.

When she walked into the small observation room, Lynae said, "He's a real charmer."

Jo shook her head and looked back through the glass. Treyton was once again slouched in his chair. She turned to Mick. "Do you know that Tonya Mereck he mentioned?"

He frowned. "I'm thinking the name is familiar, but I'm not sure. We can check the system."

"No problem. We can do that ourselves. I just wondered if you knew anything about her." She stuck out her hand. "Thanks for the call, Detective."

Detective Conner shook her hand. "It's Mick, and I hope this leads to something that makes it worth your trip."

Jo smiled into his kind green eyes. "I'll keep you in the loop if it does."

"I would appreciate it. Not sure there's much you're going to be able to do for him on his charges. Three-time drug losers don't really get breaks."

"If this breaks this case open, I'll put in the word like I said I would, but in the meantime, I'm not losing any sleep over it." But Jo knew she would lose plenty of sleep over Treyton Brocht and his casual reference to "the cop that got killed." And she could already feel the burning hope in the pit of her stomach that maybe the lead would turn out to be real.

CHAPTER 23

Before starting the car, Jo dialed Isaac's cell. It seemed to take forever for him to answer.

"This is Breuker."

"Isaac, you still at the station?"

"Of course. I have no life."

"I need you to find an address for me. Tonya Mereck." She spelled the last name for him. "Whatever else you're doing can wait."

"I'm on it. What's up?"

Jo could hear the clicking of his keyboard and knew that he had already started the search. "Just a lead I'm following. Need it right away."

"Got it right now." He reeled off a Grand Rapids address.

She jotted the information in her notebook. "That was fast. Do a cross reference and see if anyone else is listed at that same address."

"The apartment is rented to a Drevin Clayburn."

"Okay, run a background check on both of them. I want to know if there's anything outstanding that we can bring either of them in on. I don't care how minor. I'll hold." Her mind was racing. After all the hours of digging through reports and following dead-end leads, something as simple as a drug dealer trying to cut a deal could give her the lead she needed.

After a few minutes, Isaac came back on the line with the discouraging news that there were no outstanding warrants for either Tonya Mereck or Drevin Clayburn.

"Drevin has a record as long as my arm, but there's nothing on Tonya," he added.

"What kind of charges on his record?" Jo asked.

"A dozen or so minor possessions, then he stepped up to possession with intent and possession of a stolen vehicle. Topped that off with one domestic."

Drugs and stolen vehicles. Sounds promising. "Get me a list of any known associates. Anybody I can squeeze. Who filed the domestic?"

"Tonya Mereck."

"Perfect. Thanks, Isaac." Jo felt the adrenaline pulsing through her body as she hung up. She tore out the page with the address on it and passed it to Lynae. "I've got a good feeling about this, Nae."

Lynae grabbed the paper and entered the address into the GPS. "Let's go talk to Tonya Mereck and see what she has to say before we get too excited."

Jo started the car. "What happened to the eternal optimist?"

Lynae turned as far sideways in her seat as her seat belt would allow. "I don't want you to pin your hopes on a small-time drug dealer. I've seen you go through too many highs and lows on this case. I don't want to see you hurt again."

Jo shifted the car into gear and pulled out onto the street. "Hope's the only thing that gets me out of bed in the morning."

CHAPTER 24

Jo parked in front of the Lafayette Park apartment complex. The five-story brick building was within walking distance of downtown, and it overlooked a small park.

Lynae looked around. "Not bad."

"Yeah, not what I expected. I wonder if Mr. Clayburn has an actual job on record."

"I doubt it. There's plenty of money in drugs."

They got out of the car and headed for the door. There was a better chance of a response if they made it to the apartment, so they followed someone inside instead of using the intercom. They exited the elevator on the second floor and easily found the correct place a few feet down the hall. Lynae stood to one side, hand on her holster, while Jo knocked.

A woman pulled the door open as much as the chain would allow, cautiously peering out, her brown eyes too large for her thin, pale face. A fresh bruise, deep red at its center and fading only slightly on its edges, swelled below her left eye, probably no more than a day old.

Jo held up her badge. "Tonya Mereck?"

"Yes. What do you want?" The woman glanced over her shoulder. "I didn't call the police."

"We'd like to talk to you about Treyton Brocht. May we come in?"

Tonya again looked over her shoulder. When she turned back to them, her expression had changed from cautious to frightened. "No, you can't come in."

"Tonya—"

"Hold on." She closed the door to release the chain then stepped out into the hallway, shutting the door behind her. She instantly lost the deer-in-the-headlights look. "My boyfriend's sleeping. I don't want to wake him up. Now what is this about?"

"Do you know Treyton Brocht?"

"Yes, I know him."

"Have you recently had a relationship with him?"

Tonya's dull brown hair hung limply around her bony shoulders, and she pushed it behind her ears. The effect made her look like a waif. "We went out for a while. I wouldn't call it recent. What is this about? Is Trey in some kind of trouble again?"

"He is, but that's not really why we're here. He contacted us last night and told us that you have information about the murder of a police officer two years ago."

Tonya frowned and shook her head. "I don't know what you're talking about."

"According to Mr. Brocht, you told him that a person involved in the murder of a police officer confided in you regarding the circumstances." Jo knew she was rushing and that she should finesse the girl, but she wanted answers, and she didn't want to wait.

"Trey is making that up. I don't know anything about a cop getting shot."

"You have no information regarding that shooting?"

"No, I don't know anything."

"Can you tell me why Mr. Brocht would contact me and specifically tell me that you have this information if you don't?"

"I don't know. You'll have to ask him. If he's in trouble, he'll say anything to get out of it. He's real good at lying," she said, crossing her arms and gripping her biceps with hands so thin Jo wondered how the bones didn't snap under the pressure. With the motion, her sleeve fell back, and Jo noticed bruising around her wrists. "I don't know anything, and I gotta get back inside."

"That's a nasty black eye. You get that running into a door?" Jo asked, looking deliberately at the door to her apartment.

Tonya raised her chin but avoided looking Jo in the eye. "Is a black eye against the law, Officer?" She glanced again at the door.

She's trying to be defiant, but she's meek and afraid. Not a very convincing combination. "Nope, not against the law to have one but real often against the law to give one. You think your boyfriend would be able to tell us how that happened?" Jo turned toward the door. She desperately wanted to get inside the apartment to get a look at Drevin Clayburn.

Tonya quickly stepped in front of the door, the first move she had made that showed an actual backbone. "You got no reason to go in my place. I told you I don't know what Trey's talking about, and you got no reason to worry about my eye. I think you should leave."

She's more afraid of the man behind that door than she is of us.

"Tonya, if you're afraid of him, we can help," Lynae said softly, laying a hand on the tiny woman's shoulder.

Tonya shrugged off the hand. "Why would I be afraid of someone?"

Lynae looked pointedly at her bruised face. "The black eye you can brush off to most people, but this"—she reached out and pulled Tonya's sleeve up around her wrist—"this kind of bruising only comes from a grip." Lynae wrapped her hand around her own wrist to demonstrate her point.

Tonya pushed her sleeve back down over her wrist and crossed her arms. "Are we done here?"

"You filed domestic abuse charges against Drevin Clayburn fourteen months ago," Jo said.

"That was a misunderstanding."

"A misunderstanding? How is domestic abuse a misunderstanding?" Jo let her irritation show more than she meant to. She had to get herself under control. The last thing an abused woman would respond to was hostility.

Lynae stepped forward and angled her body so that she essentially stood between the two. "Tonya, I know how hard it is, but you don't have to live like this. I can help you."

The woman snorted. "You know how hard it is? What do you know about it?"

"I can help you," Lynae repeated.

"I don't need help. You, in your perfect little worlds, coming in here asking me questions, telling me you can help me. Acting like you know what my life is like."

"Tonya—"

Tonya held up her hand. "I don't have to talk to you. I don't know anything about Trey's problems. He's just making that up to cut a deal on whatever stupid thing he's done now. And don't act like you understand my life. You don't understand shit."

Lynae blew out a hard breath. "Yes, I do understand. I know that you feel trapped, like you can't function without him. Some days, it's like you don't even think you could breathe without him. You wouldn't know how to because you've lost your sense of yourself, your confidence, your worth. You're only what he tells you you are, and he tells you you're nothing without him."

Lynae motioned to the apartment door but never took her eyes off Tonya. "You're dependent on him because he made sure of that. This is *his* apartment. The only roof over your head, and it belongs to *him*. Maybe you don't work because he said you didn't need to, that he would take care of you."

Tonya looked over her shoulder, glaring at the door as though the apartment itself were responsible for her pain.

Lynae leaned forward and softened her voice. "You don't have friends anymore or talk to your family because, according to him, they're trying to turn you away from him. When you do talk to them, they try to tell you to leave him and that he's bad for you. But that only proves his point. 'See? They're trying to get between us. They don't really love you, and if you love me, you won't talk to them anymore.' He tells you that no one else would ever love you like he does. And because he's stripped you of your self-worth, your confidence, you believe him. You really believe that no one else will love you and that he's the best that you deserve."

Tonya stared at Lynae, tears glistening in her doe-brown eyes. She looked away, hugging herself tighter and biting her bottom lip.

Lynae took a deep breath and swallowed hard. Her voice quivered. "His moods dictate your life. When he's happy, when things are going good for him, he's the nicest guy in the world. He loves you and treats you like a queen. He buys you nice things, takes you out at night. But then his mood changes in a heartbeat, and you have no idea why, what happened. You rack your brain trying to figure out what you did wrong, what you could have done different. The apartment isn't clean enough, your clothes aren't right, why is that guy looking at you like that. You're a slut, you're stupid, it's no wonder no one else loves you, why you have no friends and your family never calls.

"And then he hits you."

Tonya closed her eyes and turned her head away, her lips tightly pressed together.

Lynae pressed on. "The first time, you're so shocked that you can't think. You want to deny that it happened. You're embarrassed. You don't want anyone to know, so you hide it. He's a nice guy, right? He didn't mean it. He tells you that afterward. He didn't mean it. You just pushed him over the edge, but it won't ever happen again. You believe him because you want to. And you tell yourself that if it happens again, you're going to leave and never look back. And for a while he's so nice, over-the-top nice. And just when you're comfortable, it happens again. You think you know what you did wrong, and if you don't do it again, he won't have any reason to hit you. You can change; you can be what he wants you to be. You just have to remember not to do that one thing again. But it's never one thing. The next time, it's something else. And every time you think it won't happen again, that this time his promise is true and things will be different."

Lynae put both hands on Tonya's shoulders. "It's never different, though, is it? Tonya, it's never going to be unless you make it different. You, and only you, have the power to change it. But I can help you."

Jo noticed that her partner's hands were shaking a little. The two women stared at each other for a minute, a deep understanding seeming to pass between them. Lynae had always been good at playing the good guy in the questioning of suspects, but that bit she had just done went beyond her acting skills. Jo was learning something new about her partner, something she felt she should have already known about her friend.

A noise from inside the apartment made Tonya jolt and turn toward it. "I have to go. I don't know why Trey said what he did, but I can't help you. I'm sorry, but I just can't." She opened the door and walked back into what was no doubt her hell.

Back in the car, Jo stared out the windshield for several minutes before starting the engine and pulling away from the curb.

Lynae blurted, "She's lying."

"I know."

"She's afraid of him and what will happen if he's questioned but not arrested, or arrested and not convicted."

"I know." Jo drove in silence for a few minutes, the only sound coming from the windshield wipers rhythmically pushing away the light drizzle that had begun to fall. She hoped Lynae would just tell her, but apparently that wasn't going to happen. "Are you going to tell me what the hell that was all about?"

"I thought I could get her to open up."

"That's not what I'm talking about, Nae."

"It's not important."

Jo eyeballed her partner. "I think it is."

Lynae sighed and gazed out the window. "It seems like a lifetime ago."

"Tell me," Jo said softly.

"I was in college, away from home and living on my own for the first time. He was so amazing at first. The nicest guy you've ever met. Everyone loved him, and he treated me like I was the most important person in the world. I really thought that he was it, he was the man I was going to spend the rest of my life with."

Lynae leaned her head on the window. She was quiet for so long, Jo thought she might not finish. "What happened, Nae?"

"Without me even realizing it, he became my whole world. I

got so wrapped up in him, so dependent, that when he turned on me the first time, I don't think I really believed it was happening."

Jo clenched her jaw. "You forgave him."

Lynae sighed. "He was so sorry, so contrite, that I convinced myself that it wasn't as bad as I had thought and that it would never happen again. After I let him get away with it once and stayed with him, it became a pattern. I didn't know how to get out."

Jo slammed her hand on the steering wheel. "Jesus, Nae, you're smarter than that!"

Lynae jumped at the outburst. "It's not about being smart, Jo. It's not only people who are stupid, or ugly, or poor, or whatever people want to believe it is. It can happen to anyone, and it does happen all the time to normal people like you and me."

"Why didn't you just leave? Kick his ass to the curb and walk away?"

Lynae shook her head. "It sounds so easy. But when you're in the middle of it, it's different. You think it will change, that you can somehow make it right, make yourself right, so that perfect person you were dating will come back to stay. He convinces you that he's acting the way he is because of *you*, that *you* are the problem. And you think if you can just be good, do everything right, he'll love you and..." She hung her head. "It's so hard to explain. I guess the best analogy is that it's like suddenly finding yourself in a cult you didn't know you had joined."

Jo glanced at her friend. "How did you finally get out?"

"I was in the Criminal Justice Program at Grand Valley, and we started working with the police department. One of the officers, Nancy Reisler, took me aside one day and talked to me. She had spotted the signs, and she wanted to help me. I denied it at first, told her she didn't know what she was talking about, all the same things we just heard from Tonya." Tears ran unchecked down Lynae's cheeks. "It took me a while, but the day I had to go to class with a broken wrist and abdominal bruising so severe I had been spitting up blood, I decided to put my trust in her."

Fighting back her own tears, Jo grabbed her friend's hand. "My God, he broke your bones? Did you have him arrested?"

Lynae pulled a Kleenex from her bag, wiped her eyes, and blew her nose. "No. I didn't want anyone to know. I was trying to be a cop. I thought if anyone knew, they would never hire me. How could anyone think I could be a detective, be strong enough to deal with the demands of this job, be smart enough to solve cases, if I wasn't even strong and smart enough to get out of an abusive relationship?"

"You just said it has nothing to do with how smart someone is."

Lynae pointed at Jo. "What was your first reaction? Would you have hired me if you knew?"

"That's not a fair question."

Lynae threw her hands up. "Why not? The first thing you jumped to was that I should have been smarter than that. It's the common misconception. Women who stay in abusive relationships are seen as weak, unintelligent, pushovers. I would have thought the same thing if I hadn't lived it. So it's not something I want to put on my résumé."

"But you finally got out with the help of this officer?"

Lynae smiled. "Nancy. It was hard, and there were times I almost went back to him, but she was always there. She always managed to talk me down. He would show up at my place and try to talk his way in the door. I know now that if I had let him in, even just to talk as he kept claiming he wanted, he would have been back in my life. So whenever he came over, I would call Nancy, and she would be right there in uniform. Eventually, he found a new girlfriend and left me alone."

"I'd like to meet Nancy."

"You'd like her. She most likely saved my life. I still see her quite often."

Jo thought of cases she had worked in which the bruising had eventually turned to murder. The boyfriends or husbands would rant their self-perceived justification for killing the "bitch," "slut," or whatever their name of choice was. She had seen too many bodies, young and old, broken by someone who claimed to love them, someone they thought could change, or who they thought was the best they could get. She knew that Lynae was right. Jo's perception had never been that the women deserved it, but she might have been guilty of mentally holding them a little responsible because they didn't have the will or self-confidence to walk away. She would never have put the strong, intelligent, beautiful Lynae Parker in that group.

Jo squeezed her partner's hand. "I'm sorry, Nae. That must have been hell."

"It was, but I'm a stronger person for it." She chuckled. "Not that I would recommend it as a strength-building exercise."

"Is that why you don't date?"

Lynae shrugged. "I don't trust my own judgment. Adam seemed like such a great guy. Perfect, really. Anytime I meet a guy that seems great, my mind goes to Adam. I'm afraid I won't see it coming again."

Mike's face popped into Jo's mind. "Not every guy that seems great is going to turn out to be shit. Some of them actually turn out to be exactly what they seem."

"I know. I just don't trust myself to figure it out."

Jo scowled. "You wouldn't let that happen again."

Lynae shook her head. "No, absolutely not. The problem now is that I run for the hills immediately so I don't have to find out that I was wrong again. We've both seen the pattern with other women. We all tend to have a type of guy that we're attracted to, and too many times we put ourselves right back in the same spot. I'm not going to let that happen."

"Well, you have me now. I'd kick his ass."

Lynae snorted. "No doubt about that. I just wish I could have convinced Tonya to talk to me about it."

Jo sighed. "I still don't have anything I can arrest this Drevin guy on, and I don't even know if he's my guy. My gut says we're onto something, but judges don't sign arrest warrants based on my gut."

"They should. Your gut's usually right. But I'm not giving up on Tonya. Those bruises were fresh. She had him arrested once, so she has the moxie. We just have to get her to do it again."

Jo pulled into the station parking lot. "We can't do any more now, so let's call it a night."

Lynae looked at her skeptically. "You're going to go home and put it away for the night?"

"I'm going home. I never said what I'm going to do when I get there."

CHAPTER 25

JO SPENT A SLEEPLESS NIGHT going over Mike's case file, looking for anything that would link Drevin Clayburn to the drug bust. She found nothing. Eventually, she decided she wouldn't be able to concentrate until she cleared her head. She took Mojo for an early-morning walk, but she still felt restless as she got ready for work. She poured coffee into a travel mug then dialed Lynae's work number.

Her partner's husky voice came on the line. "Homicide. Detective Parker."

"You're in early this morning. I expected to get your voicemail."

"Trying to suck up to the boss after spilling my guts last night."

Jo pinned her phone between her ear and shoulder and rummaged through her bag. "We're friends first, Nae. I'm glad you told me. That's not something you should keep from a friend. It's too bad you decided to suck up by coming in early on a morning I'm going to be late, though."

"Jo Riskin late two days in a row? Now there's something to write home about. Did something new come up?"

Satisfied that she had everything she needed for the day, Jo clipped her badge on her waistband then flung her bag over her shoulder. "No, I just decided it will help if I talk this all over with Mike. I'm going to go there for a little while this morning, talk it all through, and see if anything hits me."

"Jo—"

"It doesn't hurt anything, Nae. It helps me clear my head."

"Talk it through with me. You want my help on Mike's case, but you haven't given me all the details yet. We can meet at MadCap, have some coffee, and go through the whole case. We're waiting on reports for Tillman, anyway."

Jo gave Mojo one last pat then slipped out the door to the garage. "We'll do that, I promise. But this morning, I want to talk it over with Mike. I won't be too long. We should have the phone records by the time I get in. In the meantime, update the murder board with Hunter Stone's information and the paint. And run DMV records. We already know Stone will show up, but we'll see if we hit anyone else of interest."

"I'm on it."

Jo drove straight out of the city and headed toward the small rural town where she had grown up. Traveling down the familiar country road past golden hay fields with giant rolled bales, apple orchards dotted with red and yellow, acres of corn dead on the stalks, and pastures filled with grazing cows and horses, she began to relax. She slowed as she came up behind a John Deere combine using the road to move between fields and taking up more than its half. She pretended not to notice when the driver waved her around. She was in no hurry, and puttering behind the behemoth piece of machinery gave her more time to enjoy the peaceful scenery. She swung into the Happy Apple fruit stand and spent more time than she should have picking out the perfect pumpkin.

At the cemetery, she pulled into the parking lot and parked toward the back. Tall evergreen shrubs stood sentry along the perimeter of the lot, like guards protecting the residents.

When Jo was a kid, she had enjoyed walking through the cemetery with her mom, who stopped at any tombstone that bore her family name or that of one of her friends. The history of her small farming community had always fascinated Jo. The commonality of so many names within the cemetery told a great deal about the people who lived there. Generations of farming families, mostly from Germany, had settled in the area to start a new life. Armock, Umlor, Dietrich, Rasch, and Klein were all names that could still be found in the community, their ancestors carrying on the family farms for generations.

Strolling through the vast cemetery, Jo passed headstones that dated back almost two hundred years, some names and dates barely readable as the stone had weathered and smoothed out over time. Marble family monuments dominated the plots, while small inlaid markers named the individuals buried within. Only one tombstone bore the name Riskin. The flowers around the stone were fresh, and the inlaid badge was always polished. Jo made sure of that. She stood in front of the dark-gray marker and read the inscription for the thousandth time: Michael David Riskin.

She set the pumpkin on the stone in front of his name. Fall had been Mike's favorite time of the year, and every year they had spent what Jo had considered a ridiculous amount of time walking through pumpkin patches, looking for exactly the right shape and size for him to carve. He acted like a little kid, hopping over rows to run to a potentially perfect gourd only to slump in disappointment when he found the flaw that kept it from becoming his. And when he did find that perfect choice, that one pumpkin that was meant to be his, he would beam with anticipation, his green eyes dancing with excitement, as he described exactly how he would use its unique characteristics to carve the perfect jack-o'-lantern. Jo, on the other hand, would grab the first pumpkin that wasn't rotting, knowing that her pathetic carving skills would destroy any unique characteristics that it held, anyway. She would roll her eyes and sigh loudly every time Mike rejected yet another pumpkin, but she secretly loved the yearly ritual.

Her eyes were drawn to the second inscription on the stone, "Michael David Riskin, Jr." She pulled the toy John Deere tractor out of her pocket and laid it in front of her baby's name. Her son had never had a chance to be born. She had never had the chance to be the mom that she so desperately wanted to be. He would have been over a year and a half old if the trauma and stress from Mike's murder hadn't caused her to miscarry. Whoever the son of a bitch was that she was hunting, he had killed not only her husband, but also her son. Her anger and hatred for that unknown person simmered inside her, playing over and over in the back of her mind like a Benedictine chant. At one time she had been afraid it might consume her, but she was getting it under control. She would never find the perp and bring him to justice if she went over that deep end. She had to keep it together for Mike… and for little Mike. She had to find the killer and make him pay for what he had done to her family.

She sat down on the grass in front of the tombstone and started talking. During their years together, she and Mike had talked and debated through every topic either of them had an interest in, and sometimes ones they didn't. Her husband had helped her through some of her early cases, giving her guidance from the couple of years' experience that he had on her. And she liked to think that she had helped him through some of his. He had shown her how to see things from the logical, black-and-white side, while she had shown him how to see the human being behind every crime. Although they worked in different divisions and precincts, they had been a great team.

She told him about the bombshell Lynae had dropped the night before and lamented the upcoming dinner with Aunt Trudy. When she ran out of the easy topics, she picked at the grass silently for a few minutes.

The dampness from the early-morning dew suddenly felt cold on the backs of her legs. "I have a new lead."

You've had a lot of those over the years. What makes this one different? His voice was still so clear in her head.

"I don't know, but I really have a good feeling about this one."

Did she give you anything you can use?

"No. According to my source, her boyfriend pulled the trigger."

Bring him in.

Jo pulled out a handful of grass and flung it to the side. "I don't have anything to bring him in on. No outstandings, no probable cause for a search warrant, nothing. I have the secondhand story of a drug dealer looking for a deal."

That's not enough. You couldn't get her to talk?

"She's afraid of him. And she should be."

Why are you so sure this one is legit?

Jo shrugged. "Just a gut feeling."

You have to go with your gut. It's usually right. Keep an eye on him. He'll make a mistake, and when he does, you'll be there to make sure he pays for it. You'll find a way, Jo. I have faith in you.

Jo gazed at the dark stone. "What if I don't, Mike? What if I never find the person who did this to us? I don't know if I can live with that."

You have to live with it, Jo. You have to find a way to be okay. You know I only want you to be happy.

"I know. I'm just not sure I can be."

She leaned her head back and stared up at the bright-blue sky. A dog barked in the distance. A car that needed a new muffler rumbled by. Life just kept going on. The sun kept coming up in the morning, the seasons continued to change, and everything moved forward. Except her.

She looked out over the open hay field adjacent to the cemetery and thought about how desperately Mike had wanted to buy that field and turn it into a driving range. She wiped a tear from her cheek. *Stupid golf.*

Golf! Jo sat up straight. "Holy shit, that's it."

She hopped to her feet and planted a quick kiss from her hand to the tombstone. "Thanks, babe."

Jo jogged back to her car. She dialed Lynae as she slipped into the driver's seat.

Her partner picked up on the first ring. "Parker."

"Cleats."

"Okay…"

Jo pulled out onto the quiet country road, no longer interested in the scenery. "That's something you would leave in the trunk of your car and forget about. You said as much about your softball bag. Cleats would be the same thing, right?"

"Exactly the same. Are you thinking of Hunter Stone's football cleats?"

"That's one possibility. The other is golf cleats."

"Golfers wear cleats?" Lynae asked.

"What kind of athlete are you?"

"The kind that plays softball. I only tried golf once, and it was way too slow for me. Besides, my softball swing gave me a bit of a slice."

Jo passed a slow-moving vehicle. "A golf club would give you a bit of a slice to the head too. That hammer-type wound could be the end of an iron."

"Didn't the good doctor mention being a golfer?"

"Yeah. Not as good as his wife, but still a golfer. I also saw golf clubs in Hunter's garage."

"Time to have another chat with both of them."

"Agreed. I'm stopping by the morgue to run this by Kent on my way in. We'll go from there."

CHAPTER 26

JO MARCHED INTO THE MORGUE. "Morning, Kent. What's the word?"

Kent looked up from his desk, his bright eyes twinkling over the glasses that sat low on his nose. "Vituperate."

Jo raised her hands. "I don't even have to think about it. I know that I don't know that one."

"It means to use harsh or abusive language."

Jo nodded. "I'll remember that since I'd like to vituperate all over whoever did this to Megan Tillman."

Kent removed his glasses and wiped a hand over his face. "Indeed, so would I."

"That pattern on her hip, I think it may be from a cleat."

"You would be correct. More specifically, FootJoy golf cleats."

Jo was a little disappointed that she hadn't brought anything new to the table. "You were way ahead of me."

Kent winked. "It's my job, kid." He pulled a photo out of a file and laid it on the desk. The picture showed the hip wound next to a measuring tape with each section marked for size. He turned to his computer and pulled up a 3-D image of the wound with the distance between each mark measured and labeled. He then opened a graphic of a FootJoy cleat and overlaid it on the wound picture. "It took a while, but through the process of elimination, I found an exact match."

"Does this tell you the shoe size?"

Kent shook his head. "I'm afraid not. The cleats are the same size on all adult shoes."

"Did your process get us a golf club as the murder weapon?"

Kent pointed at Jo. "Right again. More precisely, an iron, possibly a seven or a nine."

Jo crossed her arms. "You're kidding me. You actually know which club?"

"Golf clubs each have their own angle, 'loft' in golf terms. Anyway, I was able to measure those angles here and here." Kent pointed at two isolated wounds in the pictures.

"Any defensive wounds?"

"None."

Jo cocked her head. "So she probably knew her assailant, went with him willingly, and was then taken by surprise."

Kent nodded. "Most of the damage is to the top and back of her head and shoulders."

Jo shook her head. "He hit her from behind. Coward." For some reason, that extra insult irked her. "Can you determine the assailant's height based on the impact?"

Kent shook his head. "I'm afraid not. Scrapes on the victim's knees and palms indicate she was on her hands and knees at some point. That would give any adult a good amount of height over her."

"Have you determined the first weapon?"

"That one has been more difficult." He sorted through the other pictures in the file then handed one to Jo. "There was a large contusion on the back of her head. When I shaved the hair, I found bruising in this pattern. The shape and size indicates a gearshift—"

"Wait. You mean like the gearshift in a car?"

"Yes. Or truck. But the raised pattern is throwing me off. I've searched for a gearshift with that pattern, but it doesn't exist in the manufacturer database."

Jo held the photo up to the light and peered at it. "It looks like the *S* in the Michigan State logo. It could be custom made."

Kent nodded. "It does, but there's something in the center that doesn't fit. That's where the pattern breaks down."

"Megan's boyfriend is bound for MSU next year, but he's going on scholarship. I can't see him having the money to have a custom gearshift made. Plus, he shares a car with his dad. Could it be something else?"

"It's always possible. It could be any kind of decorative item of some sort stuck in the ground or something. But the shape of the outline really does make me think it's a gearshift."

"With the MSU connection and the cleat pattern, I think it's enough to bring Hunter back in for questioning. Maybe I can shake the answer out of him. And there's a place in town, ShapeShifters, that makes custom gearshifts." Jo had given one with a detective shield to Mike the Christmas before he was killed. It was in a box somewhere in her home office. It was one of the things that she would never get rid of but couldn't bring herself to look at.

"I checked them out online. Nothing matches."

She handed the photo back to Kent. "Yeah, but if you're willing to shell out the extra money, they'll make whatever you want. I'll get in contact with them and see if they've made any with that logo."

Kent slid the pictures back into the folder. "I'm afraid we have no match on the hair. The DNA was compared to all criminal databases, state and federal."

"I'm not surprised. I don't think we're dealing with someone who's been in the system. This is personal, and I doubt anyone that close to Megan would be in the system."

Kent smiled sadly. "But someone close to Megan *deserves* to be in the system."

Jo nodded. "We'll find him and put him there."

CHAPTER 27

Jo stepped off the elevator and made a beeline for the break room. Her mug was empty, and that was unacceptable. Once she had her coffee in hand, she headed for her office.

A man was sitting in a chair beside Lynae's desk. When he saw Jo, he jumped to his feet. "Good morning, Lieutenant. I'm Officer Doug Jacobs."

Jo smiled at the young officer. "I remember you from the Tillman crime scene. What can I do for you?"

"I just wondered if there was any progress on the case."

"We're interviewing friends and family. We don't have a lot to go on yet, but I'm hopeful that today will bring us something." Jo leaned against Lynae's desk and crossed her arms. "Why do you ask?"

Doug turned his city-issued hat over and over in his hands. "I've been thinking about it, and I thought maybe I could help. You know, do some grunt work or something."

"I appreciate the offer, but I don't have any room on my payroll right now."

"No, ma'am. I would work on my own time. I'm off shift right now."

Jo liked his ambition and wished she could help him, but she didn't have time for an inexperienced cop vying for a detective slot. She paused to consider how to let him down without dampening his enthusiasm. "I'll have to think about it and talk to my captain."

"Thank you, ma'am… um, Lieutenant."

Jo leaned toward Lynae. "Kent gave me a solid lead. We need to go visit ShapeShifters."

Lynae grabbed her coat from the back of her chair. "Never heard of it."

"Custom-made gearshifts and steering wheels," Doug said.

Jo cocked her head. "You know of it?"

"I'm kind of a car guy. And my buddy works there."

What the hell? "Why don't you ride along, then? It can't hurt to have a familiar face with us."

Doug's face split into a grin. "Yes, ma'am."

"You gotta quit that *ma'am* thing, though." Jo grabbed her ringing phone from her pocket. "Riskin."

"Lieutenant, someone is here to see you," Aneace from the main reception desk drawled in her smooth, made-for-radio voice.

"What is this, visitor day?"

"I sent out a memo. You probably ignored it."

Jo chuckled. "Who is it?"

"A woman with a young boy. They asked to talk to you specifically."

"Send them up." Jo turned to Officer Jacobs. "Shouldn't be long. Stick around if you want to go with."

"Yes, ma—" He stopped when Jo pointed her finger at him.

Lynae tried to stifle a laugh and snorted. "We'll wait here for you, *Lieutenant.*"

Jo met the visitors at the elevator. The boy looked to be about ten years old. His clothes looked old, probably bought secondhand or maybe handed down from an older sibling, but clean. His hair was cut close to his head. The only concession she could see to the streets was the LeBron hat worn cocked slightly sideways on his head. He had brown hair, chubby cheeks, and large brown eyes.

Mom had the same worn but neat look with the addition of the tired eyes of someone who worked too hard and worried too much. Jo guessed she was probably ten years younger than she looked.

Jo held out her hand to the woman. "I'm Lieutenant Riskin. What can I do for you?"

"Angela Heard. This is my son, Jeron. He has something to give to you."

Jo smiled at the boy. "What do you have for me?"

He glanced at his mother, who gave him a stern look. He pulled a plastic bag out of his pocket, gave his mother one last defeated look, then handed it to Jo. Inside the bag was a white iPhone 6 encased in a purple LifeProof case.

He hung his head, seeming suddenly very interested in his shoes. "I think it was that girl's phone. The one that got killed and put in the trash."

Making sure not to snatch it as quickly as she wanted to, Jo took the phone from his outstretched hand. "What makes you think that?"

"I looked at the pictures on it. A bunch of 'em are selfies of the girl. I saw her picture on TV." A pained look came over his face. "It's a sweet phone."

Jo raised an eyebrow. "I bet you could have sold it on the street for a pretty decent amount."

"That's what I was gonna do." Jeron shot a glance at his mom. She didn't reply, but her eyes spoke volumes. "Phone like that'll get you a couple hundred. It's like new. That case would get you twenty."

I bet that's what the person who ditched it was counting on. Jo smiled. "But you brought it here instead."

His mother laid a hand on his shoulder. "I'm trying to raise him to do the right thing."

Jo looked into the woman's weary brown eyes and smiled. "Looks like you're doing a good job."

"It's not easy living where we do."

Jo bent down to get eye level with Jeron. "You did the right thing bringing it in here. This could help us find the person who killed her. Her name was Megan, and she was only fifteen years old." She wanted him to know that she was someone other than "that girl," that she had a name, parents, friends, and dreams of a future, just as he did.

Jeron nodded eagerly and pointed at the phone. "I put it in a bag in case there's something on it like fingerprints or somethin'." He appeared to be warming to the idea of helping the police.

Jo mentally crossed her fingers that he hadn't destroyed any evidence before he got the phone in the bag. "That's a very smart thing to do. How did you know you should do that?"

He shrugged shyly. "You came to my school last year. You told us how to be safe and to trust the police. And that we should tell someone we trust if we know something."

Jo held up her hand for a fist bump. "And you listened very well." Looking around the bull pen, she caught Charles's eye and motioned him over. "Our junior detective here brought us a phone that could very well be Megan Tillman's. Let's get it dusted and swabbed. Maybe we'll get lucky and get a fingerprint. Then let's see what those texts had to say."

Charles took the phone and hustled away. He looked as excited as Jo felt.

Turning back, she noticed Jeron eyeing her detective shield hanging on her belt. "You did a good thing, Jeron. Maybe someday you'll be wearing one of these."

He gave another nervous glance at his mother then said, "It came out of a car. I saw it."

Jo's pulse quickened. "You saw a car and this phone coming out of it? When did this happen?"

"Really late Monday night."

Angela's head snapped to her son. "What were you doing outside late at night? You know better. It's not safe."

Jeron looked up at his mother with big, innocent eyes. "I was sitting on the porch roof. That's safe, right?"

Angela let out a long, slow breath. "Safer than being on the street, I guess."

"Why don't you tell me exactly what you saw?" Jo said.

"I was sitting on the roof, and I saw a car, a really sweet car, come out from the alley by Pharmer's. And I saw something come flying out the window right onto the sidewalk by the park. I could see it was shiny." After giving his mother a sideways look, he added, "I thought it was a gun."

"So you went and got it?" Angela's voice rose a full octave. "In the park?"

Jeron hung his head and mumbled, "Sorry, Mom. I just ran and grabbed it and came right back to the house."

Jo asked, "Do you know what kind of car it was, Jeron?"

"I don't know. It was dark. I just saw the back. The taillights were sweet."

Taillights could distinguish a car. This kid is golden. "I would really like it if you could sit with one of my officers. You can describe the taillights to him. Maybe you can help him figure out what kind of car you saw." Jo motioned at Isaac to get his attention, and he stood and walked toward them.

Angela looked up at the large old-fashioned clock that hung in the bull pen. "I have to get to work, and Jeron has to go to school. My boss wouldn't care if my son was saving the whole world from aliens, he'll still fire me if I'm late."

"Would it be okay if we take him to school after he talks to my officer?" Jo asked. "He couldn't be in a safer place, and I'll make sure he gets to his classroom."

Jeron's dark eyes widened in panic. "I can't go to school with no cop!"

Jo chuckled. "I'm not wearing a uniform. No one has to know."

"You came to my school. 'Sides, a uniform don't matter. I would know you were a cop just how you look."

Huh, who knew? "Well, how about Officer Breuker?" She waved at Isaac standing beside her. "He could maybe pass as an uncle, right?"

Jeron looked Isaac up and down then shrugged. "Yeah, I guess. He still kinda looks like a cop, but not as much as you."

Isaac smirked. "Gee, thanks, kid."

Angela gave Jo the details on the school location and classroom while Isaac led Jeron back to his desk. "I'm going to have to hold you up for just a few minutes. We'll need to go down to the booking office to take your fingerprints. If there's a problem with your boss, I'll talk to him."

Angela frowned. "Why do you need my fingerprints?"

"We're going to dust the phone for prints. If we find yours

or Jeron's, we need to eliminate them from our list. We'll have to print him as well."

Angela looked across the room at her son with a worried expression.

Jo laid a hand on the woman's shoulder. "Don't worry. Isaac will stay with him, and he'll make a game out of the fingerprinting."

Angela smiled. "Thank you. I don't want him to be afraid to come to the police."

Jo nodded. "Neither do we."

CHAPTER 28

After waiting with Angela through the fingerprinting process, Jo went back to Lynae's desk. "Hey, we've got a couple of major breaks on Megan Tillman. We got her phone and maybe even a make on the car."

Lynae asked, "How? The kid?"

Jo nodded. "Yeah. He's with Isaac now. Let's go see Charles. He's got the phone. It should be dusted by now."

Doug stood up, but Jo motioned for him to sit again. She almost laughed at the deflated-little-boy expression that came over his face. "Sorry, Doug. We're still going, but we need to check on something first. Just stay here another few minutes."

They walked over to where Charles was working on his computer. Engrossed in the screen, he didn't look up until Jo planted her hands on his desk and said, "Tell me that phone has something."

Charles jumped a little then grinned. "It was covered in partials, but we did manage to pull one complete. The lab is putting a rush on running it."

"Good work. People handle each other's phones all the time, but if a print from the phone matches the one we pulled from the wallet, then we have something."

"Now if any of the suspects had their fingerprints on file, this could be useful."

Jo snapped her fingers. "There was a time period when parents were having their kids fingerprinted in case they went missing. I think Missing Persons keeps those on file. Hunter would be in the right age bracket to have had that done."

Charles jotted down a note. "I'll check with them."

Jo pointed at the cell. "What about the texts?"

Charles picked up the phone and thumbed to the texts. "The texts weren't erased. There's one to Hunter at four twenty-nine that says, 'Can you pick me up? We need to talk.' Of course, it's in texting shorthand."

"Funny, he failed to mention that she asked him to pick her up. Add that to the MSU mark, and I think it's time to bring Hunter in and ask a few more questions. But this time, I want him in *my* house, not his." Jo turned to Lynae, who had walked over to join them. "Give Mr. Stone a quick call and tell him we'll be bringing his son in for questioning this afternoon."

When Lynae stepped away, Charles set the phone down and leaned back in his chair. "I don't know about Hunter. I talked to his coach, and he said Hunter was on the practice field until just after five o'clock. No phones allowed, even in the locker room. Kent has time of death between five thirty and six o'clock. Hunter would've been pretty hard pressed to pick her up and kill her in that time frame."

Jo nodded. "That is pushing the limits, but it's always possible that the TOD is off a little."

Charles gave Jo a knowing look. "You gonna tell Kent that?"

She chuckled. "I can't see any reason we need to tell Kent. What he doesn't know won't hurt him."

Lynae returned, sliding her phone into her pocket. "James Stone is not a happy camper right now."

Jo shrugged. "Can't be helped. I hope the kid didn't do it, but there's a lot pointing his direction."

Charles held his hand up. "Hold on. The next text, at four thirty-two, is even more interesting. 'I can't do it. I'm a… I'm a…'"

Doug cleared his throat. "I'm going to."

Charles looked back at the officer sitting alone by Lynae's desk. "Is that so hard to spell out? Why don't you come look over my shoulder to help me decipher these?"

Doug jumped to his feet and stepped behind Charles's chair. Charles winked at Jo.

Doug cleared his throat and squinted at the phone screen. "Anyway, it says, 'Karen's right. I can't do it. I'm having the baby. I'll give your money back probably tomorrow. Gotta tell my parents. Will you help?'"

Jo slammed her hand on the desk. "Son of a bitch. Hunter *did* know!"

Charles raised an eyebrow at Jo and smirked. "That message didn't go to Hunter Stone. It went to Dr. Steve Markham."

Jo's eyes widened. "I'll be damned. The prestigious Dr. Markham was paying for Megan Tillman's abortion?"

Charles nodded. "*And* he knew that she had changed her mind and was planning to tell her parents."

Lynae whistled. "Smoking gun."

"Who's this Karen she mentions? Do we need to check her out?" Charles asked.

Jo shook her head. "No, she's the nurse that did Megan's counseling at the clinic. We talked to her already. She's a friend of Paula Markham's."

Charles frowned. "If Dr. Markham was the baby's father, it's interesting that he would send her to the clinic where his wife's friend works."

"Megan went there alone. Unless she chose to tell them, there's no way anyone at the clinic would know who the father was." Jo pointed at the phone. "What else does that tell us?"

Charles turned his attention back to the phone. "There's no reply from that number. There are three incoming from Hunter Stone. The first one at five twenty-six says, 'I'm going to get there as fast as I can.' Another at six twelve says, 'At the clinic. It's closed. Where are you?' Then at six twenty-five, the last one says, 'Come on, Meg, where are you?' Phone records show that he tried to call her six times after that."

"He sounds desperate," Lynae said.

Jo nodded. "He does sound desperate, but that's easy to do in a text. There's no acting involved. Don't forget that the perp sent a message from Megan's phone after she was dead. He was thinking very clearly. This could just be more of the same."

"The next text is incoming at seven thirteen from Ashley Kane, 'Where are you?' Megan's reply was at seven forty-two. 'I'm not feeling well, so I decided to go home. I'll see you at school tomorrow.'"

"Huh." Doug frowned.

Jo looked up at him. "Huh, what?"

He shoved his hands in his pockets. "Oh, um, I'm sure it's nothing, Lieutenant."

Jo leaned on the corner of Charles's desk and crossed her arms. "Relax, Officer. I don't bite. What's on your mind?"

Doug pointed at the phone. "Well, ma'am... Lieutenant, I do a lot of texting, and it's just that that's a lot of whole words and punctuation. It looks like somebody's mom sent it or something."

"Let me take a look." Jo held out her hand, and Charles dropped the phone into it. She read the message then scrolled through the texts before it. "Good catch, Doug. That text doesn't fit the pattern of Megan's previous texts, or any of the others for that matter. It does look like somebody's mom sent it. Or dad." She passed the phone back to Charles.

Lynae smiled. "That might be a point in Hunter's favor."

Jo nodded. "And a strike against Dr. Markham."

At the sound of the elevator, Jo glanced at the doors and quickly hopped off the desk. Marcus Quinn strode into the bull pen. The station captain's black suit was a striking contrast to his silver hair. Jo respected him for his sharp mind and keen eye for minute detail. He had been off the streets for over twenty years but had never lost his edge.

Jo straightened to look up at the imposing six-foot-four figure of her boss. "Captain Quinn."

He smiled and nodded. "Lieutenant. Just the person I want to talk to."

"What can I do for you, Captain?"

"What kind of progress have you made on the Tillman case?"

"You have good timing, sir. We just caught a break and got our hands on the victim's cell phone. The killer dumped it in the Slope, and the boy who found it brought it in this morning."

Captain Quinn crossed his arms. "Considering the general feeling toward the police in that area, I'm sure the perp never thought it would find its way here."

Jo grinned. "I'm sure he didn't. The messages on the phone shed some new light on the case. We'll be bringing in two suspects today for interrogation."

"Who are your suspects?"

"The victim's boyfriend, Hunter Stone. Text messages indicate that she sent him a message shortly before her death and asked him for a ride. We have reason to believe she was transported in the trunk of a car. Also, two weapons were used, and one of them appears to have the logo for MSU on it. Hunter has been offered a football scholarship to MSU."

The captain nodded. "He sounds like a solid suspect."

"Yes, sir. We've just learned, however, that he was at football practice until after five o'clock, and Kent has TOD between five thirty and six. That would make the timing very tight but possible."

"Who else are you looking at?"

"A Dr. Markham was one of the last people our victim sent a text to. According to her message, he was paying for her abortion. He's a surgeon at Butterworth. At this point, he's my primary suspect."

Captain Quinn scowled. "Dr. Steve Markham?"

"Yes, sir. Lynae and I spoke with him yesterday, and he indicated that he was helping Megan in a doctor-patient type relationship. He failed to tell us that he was paying for the abortion. I find that very unusual."

"Yes, it is, but not unusual enough that you should bring him to the station."

Jo looked up into her boss's shrewd green eyes. "Sir?"

"Steve Markham is an important figure in the medical community, as well as with all the charitable organizations that he contributes to. His family has been well known in this area for several generations both politically and charitably. I believe there's even a wing at the hospital that bears their name. This is not a family that we want to insult or embarrass. I don't want you to step on any toes."

Jo grabbed the phone from Charles and handed it to the captain. "With all due respect, sir, we're investigating the brutal murder of a fifteen-year-old girl who was thrown in a pharmacy dumpster like yesterday's trash. That teenage girl was sending text messages to this suspect, an adult male, shortly before her murder. She was pregnant, and he was paying for her abortion. At this point, I'm not really worried about Dr. Markham's toes."

Captain Quinn flicked his finger across the screen, scrolling through the texts. He sighed and passed the phone back to Jo. "Tread lightly until you have something more, Lieutenant. Don't haul him in here. Get me something more than a few text messages, and when you do, go to his home and speak with him. No accusations, just questions. If you have reason to believe there's more to it, and can back that up with some evidence, then we'll bring him in."

"Am I to give the same courtesy to the young man from the poor neighborhood, sir?"

He shook his head. "Sometimes we have to play the game, Lieutenant. It won't compromise the case to go to Markham's home."

Jo gritted her teeth and looked her captain square in the eye. "Yes, sir. Anything else?"

"I'm going to need you to talk to the press."

Jo winced. "Sir, you know how I feel about the press."

"Yes, I do, but it doesn't change your job, and that's part of it."

Jo looked over her shoulder at the bull pen. "I think Isaac Breuker would be a good face for the press. He's got the look, he's charismatic, and—"

Captain Quinn laid a hand on her shoulder. "This has to be you. You're the lieutenant in charge of this case. This is a young girl from an affluent family. The press wants a piece of this, and you know how to handle them."

Jo gave him an eyebrow-raised half smile. "I'll deal with them if they catch up with me."

"There's a reporter outside right now."

"Fantastic." Jo rubbed the back of her neck, where the tension was already building.

The captain held up his hand. "There's no reason to mention Dr. Markham at this time."

"Of course not, sir. There's no reason to mention any suspect at this point."

"Keep me informed on your progress." He turned and marched to the elevator.

Jo watched him until the doors closed. She shook her head and decided to shake the conversation off as well. He was her boss, and she would have to play the political game whether she liked it or not. She grabbed her coat and nodded to Lynae and Doug. "Ready?" Without waiting for a response, she headed for the stairwell.

Lynae matched Jo's pace down the stairs while Doug kept one step behind. Lynae glanced at Jo. "Sure pays to have money, doesn't it?"

Jo rolled her eyes. "It sure does. One guy is born with a silver spoon in his mouth. He gets into the best college, gets the most beautiful girl, and lands the best job. He might not be any smarter than the poor kid down the street, but he has the advantage. Then he finds himself in trouble, and his family's name and money walk him out of that as well."

"It can't walk him out of it if he's guilty. If he did this, he'll pay for it."

"He won't pay for it as much as Hunter would if it's him."

They reached the lobby, and Jo spotted a young woman pacing outside the door. Jo moaned. "God, why do I have to deal with the press?" She took a deep breath and opened the door.

The young woman scurried over, and Jo wondered how she managed to move so fast in that tight pencil skirt. "Lieutenant, Terri Cross with the *Sentinel*. I'd like to ask you a few questions about Megan Tillman."

Jo crossed her arms. "Go ahead."

The reporter held up a recorder and raised her eyebrows. At Jo's shrug, Terri turned the recorder on and held it between them. "What can you tell me about her death?"

"Megan Tillman was murdered."

Terri stared at Jo, obviously waiting for more. When Jo didn't accommodate her, she asked, "Do you have any suspects?"

"At this time, we're following all leads and expect to bring in some persons of interest before the end of the day."

"And who are those *persons of interest*?"

Jo cocked her head. "Really?"

Terri raised her eyebrows. "The people have a right to know."

Jo shook her head. "At this point, the people do *not* have a right to know because we are only following leads. I won't speculate until we have an actual suspect."

The reporter grimaced. "Do you know how she was killed?"

"Megan was killed by blunt force to the head. We did not recover the murder weapon."

"Anything else you can tell me about this case?"

Jo scowled. "I can tell you that I'll find whoever did this. And when I do, they'll never see the outside of a prison again. You can print that. Now if you'll excuse me, I have a job to do." Jo turned and walked away with Lynae and Doug beside her.

The reporter called out, "Has there been any progress on the murder of your husband?"

Jo whipped around.

Lynae gripped her arm and turned to the reporter. "Why don't we stick to the Megan Tillman case?"

The reporter looked at Jo then took a step back. With a nod, she slid her recorder into her jacket pocket.

Lynae nudged Jo toward the parking lot. "C'mon, Jo. It's just what they do. They chase police cars and ambulances around town, hoping to fall into a good story. They'd sell their own mothers to get a good story."

Jo clenched her fists. "They don't care about the victims or how much their stories hurt the ones they left behind. The more brutal the murder, the better the story. And God knows our freedom gives us the right to read every gory detail over and over. Ratings are all that matter, and grief sells."

Jo stomped to her vehicle and opened the door. She flopped into the driver's seat and sat staring blindly at the steering wheel, trying to calm her anger. She hated reporters with a passion. She knew it was part of her job to talk to them, and she did it when she absolutely had to, but it burned in her gut like hot coals.

After Mike's murder, she had pored over the articles written about him, practically memorizing every line, including the stories with their innuendos that he had somehow been involved with the drug deal that had ultimately led to his death. She had been pouring salt on her own wounds, but she couldn't stop herself. She needed the pain, needed to suffer. She seethed over the misleading information and the conveniently quoted "anonymous sources," but she read on. One night, she could no longer control her anger or the searing pain over Mike's memory being tainted by those who didn't know better. After reading the latest front-page story, she snapped and upended her table, scattering all the articles that she had collected and smashing the glasses and dishes that had accumulated there. Anything that didn't break in the initial onslaught did when she continued her rampage, throwing anything she could get her hands on. Spotting poor Mojo cowering in a corner made her finally stop.

She collected all of the articles, shoved them into her wastebasket, and lit them on fire. She stood, her hands clenched in fists that wanted to fight, tears running down her face, and watched the small fire consume the scapegoat of her anger. While she was lost in her misery, the fire grew. Stunned, she gaped at the flames. The sides of the wastebasket bowed outward, and in seconds, the flames were licking the ceiling. Fight-or-flight kicked in. She scrambled to get to the sink and get the fire extinguisher she kept beneath it. When the fire was extinguished, she looked around at the damage she had inflicted and knew she was on a path that would destroy her. That was the first night she had driven to the cemetery to talk to Mike. It was also the night she decided she would never again read a newspaper article about his murder.

When Jo brought her attention back to the present, her hands and jaw were tightly clenched. Lynae was sitting in the passenger seat, staring at her with a worried expression. In the backseat,

Doug studiously kept his face turned to the passenger window, but his bouncing knee gave away his nervousness.

Over two years later, and the anger can still get the better of me. Jo forced herself to relax her hands. "Let's get to ShapeShifters."

CHAPTER 29

THEY WALKED INTO A STOREFRONT office with a clean reception area complete with live plants, comfortable chairs, and a big-screen television. Behind the desk were two glass windows displaying clean offices with computers attached to the largest monitors Jo had ever seen. The force had provided her with a whopping nineteen-inch screen.

"This is ShapeShifters?" Lynae ogled the reception area like a tourist. "I expected a body shop. You know, with the smell of oil and men covered in grease. Where are the filthy jeans and striped shirts with names over the pockets?"

Doug grinned. "The shop's in the back. This is where they meet with customers and help them pick out their customizations."

The receptionist looked up at them. "Dougie! How are you?"

Doug's eyes flicked to Jo. He shuffled his feet and shoved his hands in his pockets. "I'm good, Tracy. How 'bout you?"

"Much better now that you're here." Her heavily bangled wrists clanged on the desk as she leaned forward and revealed more cleavage.

Crimson crept up Doug's neck. "Um... well..."

Jo found the scene entertaining, but she had come to kind of like the kid, so she stepped in. "We'd like to talk to Dan. He's expecting us."

Tracy turned to Jo and gave her a smile a few watts lower than the one she had favored Doug with. "Sure, hon. I'll go get him." She got up and walked through a door on the back wall.

Lynae snorted. "Dougie?"

Jo held up her hand. "Let's give him a break, Nae." She was determined never to call him Dougie. Unless he deserved it.

Doug gave her a grateful look.

Tracy returned with a man who more accurately fit the role Lynae had expected. She winked at Doug then settled back behind her desk.

"Hi, I'm Dan." He shook Jo's and Lynae's hands. "Doug tells me you want to talk about a gearshift we made?"

Jo pulled the pictures of the imprint on Megan's skull from her bag. "Well, we don't know that for sure yet. But we suspect these marks were left by a gearshift, and you're the only game in town that customizes them."

Dan raised an eyebrow. "There are some other places online that make them. We just happen to be the best."

Jo smiled. "No doubt."

Dan studied the picture for several seconds. "This looks like the Michigan State *S*. We do a ton of those. I can get you a list of people who've ordered them."

"What about this?" Jo asked, pointing at the center then running her finger along the faint jagged line.

He pulled the picture closer and squinted at it. "You sure that's part of the shifter?"

"It's possible that's a secondary mark. How about you get me those records on the MSU buyers, and we'll start there."

Dan nodded. "Sure, it will just take a few minutes."

Jo's phone rang. She checked the screen then stepped a few feet away to take the call. "Hey, Isaac. What do you have for me?"

"LT, according to the kid, I think we're looking for a Cadillac. They have pretty distinct taillights. He couldn't remember anything else."

"That's pretty good from a ten-year-old, I'd say. I'm getting a list from ShapeShifters. We'll see if we can make a comparison. Run Dr. Markham through the DMV and see if he happens to own a silver Cadillac. That pretty much rules out Hunter Stone as a suspect. We'll hold off on bringing him in for now."

"I talked to Julie Mertens from the hospital, and she confirms

Dr. Markham left around seven fifteen. She remembers the conversation about date night."

Jo ran a hand through her hair. "Any entrance or exit to his office that she wouldn't see?"

"There's a card-access-only door at the end of the hallway. He could go in and out through there."

"Are there records on who uses that door?"

"No, it's only basic security."

Jo rubbed the back of her neck. "So he has an alibi, but it's got the potential for giant holes in it."

"Exactly."

"All right, I want you to do some digging since we have to play this politically. Find everything you can on Steve Markham's past. I want to know if he's ever been in any kind of trouble before, anything he's gotten away with or bought his way out of. Get me the dirt you're so good at getting."

"Best part of my job." She could hear the grin in his voice. "Also, Charles checked with missing persons, and you were dead-on. Hunter's parents had him fingerprinted several years back. The print from the phone is a match."

Jo paced the small waiting area. "What about the wallet?"

"Different print. Not a match to the kid."

"All right. Considering we believe we're looking for a Cadillac, let's hold off on the kid. We have that print in our back pocket if something more turns up. Concentrate on Markham for now."

"One more thing, LT. That woman you wanted me to check into… Tonya Mereck?"

Jo froze. "What about her?"

"I have a friend who's an EMT. Said she was brought into Emergency last night."

"Oh, shit. What happened to her?"

"Fell down her apartment stairs. Sounds like her injuries are pretty extensive for a fall. Of course, my friend couldn't give me details. He shouldn't even have told me she was there. She's in ICU and hasn't regained consciousness yet."

"Damn it!" Jo yelled.

The conversation going on at Tracy's desk came to a halt. All eyes turned to Jo.

Jo waved a hand, turned her back to them, and lowered her voice. "Did they bring the son of a bitch in?"

Isaac was quiet for a breath. "What son of a bitch?"

"The son-of-a-bitch boyfriend, Drevin Clayburn. The guy she filed the domestic against. Beats her up when he feels like it. Have they brought him in yet?"

"And she's still with him? What is wrong with these women?" The disgust was clear in Isaac's voice.

"Don't be so fucking judgmental," Jo snarled. Her mind had Lynae in that hospital bed, busted and bruised by the man she loved.

"Whoa, sorry, LT. Who is this woman, anyway?"

"Someone I need alive."

"I don't have any more for you. All I know is the neighbor who called it in said she found her at the bottom of the stairs."

Jo pinched the bridge of her nose. "Okay. I need to know the minute she regains consciousness."

"I'll call the hospital and tell them she's a witness you need to talk to."

"That'll work. Thanks, Isaac."

Jo walked back to the others. She shook her head discreetly when Lynae gave her a questioning look.

Lynae glanced back down at the printout in her hand. "You remember doing any work for a Cadillac, Dan?"

"A Caddy? I don't get many of those. We mostly do muscle cars. I don't do all the designs, though. I'll check with my partner. He's out right now. I can give you his number if that helps."

"We'll go through this list and see if anything stands out. I would appreciate it if you would check your records and check with your partner. Call me if anything hits."

Dan nodded. "You got it."

Doug slapped his friend's shoulder on the way out. "Thanks, Dan."

As soon as they had cleared the door, Lynae said, "I want a Grand Valley gearshift."

Doug stole a sideways glance at Lynae. "They do all of the university logos and mascots. I could probably get you a discount."

"Thanks, Dougie!" Lynae gushed.

Despite her mood, Jo couldn't stop her snort as the red crept back up Doug's neck.

In the car, Jo relayed her conversation with Isaac. "Tonya's in bad shape, Nae. If she doesn't make it, I'm back to nothing."

"We'll hope for the best. At least at this point, we have Drevin's name. Shithead like that is bound to get in more trouble. Worst case, we work backward from that."

"Yeah, that's something."

"We'll get the bastard, Jo. I want him for you first, second for Tonya. He belongs in a cage."

"If he's our guy, he belongs six feet under."

Jo could feel Lynae staring at her. "Don't forget you play by the rules, Jo."

Jo gripped the steering wheel. "Sometimes the rules change."

CHAPTER 30

JO STORMED THROUGH THE DOOR of the station and made a beeline to Isaac's desk. Before Isaac could even look up, Jo blurted, "What do you have for me on Markham?"

Isaac pointed at a thick folder. "Plenty. For someone born with a silver spoon in his mouth, this guy's had some bad luck. I printed off the big stuff."

"That's a lot of reading. Break it down for me."

"The Markham family has boatloads of money, and they make sure everyone knows it. They give to plenty of high-profile charities, and they even have a wing at the hospital with their name on it, along with a family picture hanging in the hallway of said wing. They show their faces in the press real often. Granddad was a politician, Dad a doctor. He's got two brothers and a sister, so with him that makes two doctors, a surgeon, and a lawyer."

Jo smirked. "Sounds like the beginning of a joke. Anything shady in the family?"

Isaac shook his head. "No, just the typical accusations slung at a politician. Nothing that stuck."

"It's pretty easy to make things go away when you have that kind of money and pull. What's the bad luck?"

Isaac pulled out a printout of a newspaper article from the folder and passed it to Jo. "This article is from 1993. According to this, Markham's fiancée died when she fell from an apartment balcony. She was at an off-campus party near Stanford University. The fall was ruled an alcohol-related accident."

Jo gazed at the picture of a young Steve Markham, his head bowed, standing by a graveside. The caption read, 'Steven

Markham, grandson of State Representative Henry Markham, mourns the loss of his fiancée, Sheila Fitzgerald.' Jo studied the grainy black-and-white photo and spotted Paula Markham standing in the background. She remembered that Paula had been his fiancée's roommate. But the woman seemed to be staring not at the coffin of her roommate but at Steve Markham. *Had eyes for him back then, didn't you, Paula?*

Jo passed the article back to Isaac. "What else?"

He pulled another small newspaper copy from the folder. "This is an obituary for his son, Joseph H. Markham. He died at four months of SIDS."

Jo blew out a long breath. "That's awful. Sudden infant death syndrome can be hard to disprove. Was there any suspicion related to the death?"

"The boy had Down's syndrome and a host of other medical conditions. The autopsy showed constriction of the airway. Nothing in here to indicate it was questioned at all."

"Did Kent do the autopsy?"

"No, it was handled by someone named Bradley Gaint."

Jo nodded. "He was here before Mallory. There's no reason to suspect anything, but I'll see if Kent can take a look at the results, anyway."

Isaac frowned. "You really think this doctor killed our victim?"

"There's a lot pointing his way. The fact that he was paying for her abortion would normally be enough to get me a search warrant, but it won't be in this case. For some reason, my gut can't be completely convinced that he's guilty. But I feel like, if nothing else, he knows something. That and the fact that we've got jack shit else to go on. Any other bad luck I should know about?"

Isaac handed the folder to Jo. "Besides being linked to Megan Tillman, no."

"Good, quick work on this."

Isaac grinned. "I aim to please, LT."

Jo threw her laptop bag over one shoulder and hefted her shoulder bag onto the other. It was time to call it a night, and even though she had her bag full of work, she really didn't want to spend the night alone. She caught Lynae at the elevator. "Hey, how about dinner?"

Lynae scrunched her face apologetically. "I kinda have plans to meet somebody for dinner tonight. I can cancel, though. No problem."

Jo waved her hand as they stepped into the elevator. "No, you're not going to cancel. Are you actually going on a date?" Jo thought of their conversation from the other night and knew she would have to tread lightly.

Lynae put her hands on her hips. "I told you, I don't date. This is just dinner. If it turns into something for tonight, then it does. But that will be it."

"Seriously? So you'd go home with him for the night, but you won't go on a date with him?"

"I don't date. It's that simple."

Jo eyed her friend. "It's not simple, and we both know it."

Lynae threw her hands up. "See? This is why some things are better left unsaid. You know what? Screw it. Let's go to a movie."

Jo decided to drop the subject. She hated the thought of her friend wasting herself on one-night stands, but Lynae was a big girl and had to make her own decisions. "Go on your 'not date,' Nae. You never know when you're going to meet the guy that will make it worth the risk. Just think about it before you go home with him."

Lynae smirked. "Oh, believe me, I think about it. What about you, though?"

The elevator doors opened, and Jo stepped out first. "Don't worry about me. I've got stuff to do."

"No, you don't."

Jo grinned and bumped Lynae's hip with her heavy bag. "Bite me."

CHAPTER 31

SITTING ON THE SOFA WITH Mojo's head in her lap, Jo flipped through Markham's file while Detroit Tigers baseball played in the background. Mojo jerked her head up and looked at the back door. A second later, she jumped off the couch and ran to the door, her tail wagging.

Jo set the file down and followed her. "What's got you so excited?"

The doorbell rang, and Mojo went into an excited frenzy. Jo peered through the window and saw Lynae holding a six-pack.

Holding Mojo by the collar, Jo opened the door. "Since when do you knock?"

"Since it's dark out and you have a .38 Special." Lynae held up the beer. "I come bearing gifts."

Jo grinned. "Come on in. I thought you had a 'not date' tonight."

Lynae walked in and headed for the kitchen. "I did, but it turns out he wanted to skip the dinner, drinks, and getting-to-know-you portion of the evening and just head back to his place. I'm not that cheap of a date."

Jo knitted her brow in mock consideration. "Close, but not quite."

Lynae's mouth dropped open then morphed into a half grin. "Fuck you."

"Apparently you're not into that tonight." Jo grabbed a beer and ducked as Lynae tried to smack her.

Lynae opened a beer of her own and put the rest in the refrigerator. She followed Jo into the living room, settled into her favorite recliner, and grabbed the television remote.

Jo made a grab for the remote. "Hey, don't worry, I wasn't watching that game, anyway. It's only the playoffs."

"Boring. Just watch the highlights later."

Jo sighed. "And this coming from a softball player."

Lynae waved a hand. "Totally different game. And it's completely different when you're playing it."

Jo cocked her head. "So what's going on?"

"Nothing, why? I just thought I'd stop in since my night out turned into shit."

Jo glowered at her. "You better not be here because you feel sorry for me not having a life."

"You have a life." Lynae nodded toward Jo's home office. "It's right behind that door."

Jo pulled her legs up underneath her. She patted the seat next to her, giving Mojo the go-ahead to join her. "Seriously, Nae, don't worry about me."

Lynae changed the channel. "Not worried at all. I just came over here to hang out with my friend. But if you keep nagging me, I'm gonna take my beer and leave."

"All right, as long as we understand each other. Do I need to break out my diary and Piggy Polish?"

"I wondered what was taking you so long." Lynae kicked the footrest back on the recliner and spilled beer down the front of her shirt. "Damn it!" She jumped out of the chair and stood staring down at her wet shirt while Jo laughed.

At the sound of the doorbell, Jo gave Lynae a questioning look. "Did you order pizza too?"

Lynae shook her head. "Nope, but it's a good idea. I didn't even get dinner out of my jerk date."

"Make the call while I get rid of whoever's here. And grab a dry shirt from my room." Jo got up and went to the door. She pulled back the curtain to see who was interrupting her suddenly enjoyable evening. "Oh, shit." She knew she couldn't pretend not to be home, so she put on a smile and opened the door. "Aunt Trudy! What are you doing here?"

"Is that any way to greet me? Come here and give me a hug!"

Aunt Trudy grabbed Jo and pulled her into a strong hug. The woman's Estée Lauder perfume was so overwhelming Jo could feel it in the back of her throat.

Aunt Trudy let Jo go and pushed her way into the house. Jo followed her into the kitchen. She understood why the woman had been married three times. She was attractive, especially for a woman her age, and her small frame exuded an energy that women in their thirties would love to have. Unfortunately for the men she married, she was somehow able to keep her crazy hidden until after the weddings.

"What brings you out at this time of the night, Aunt Trudy?"

Aunt Trudy scrutinized the kitchen and shook her head. "So clean in here. Can't even tell you live in it."

"Things stay pretty clean when it's just me and the dog."

She laid a hand on Jo's cheek. "A girl like you shouldn't be alone. You're so pretty."

Jo sighed. "Aunt Trudy, can we not have this conversation?"

"I'm sorry, honey. I just hate to see you alone."

Jo looked down at her faithful furry friend sitting dutifully at her side. "I'm not alone. I have Mojo."

"You know what I mean, Joellen. That's why I'm here." She reached into her purse and pulled out a brochure.

"What's that?" Jo asked in her most uninterested voice. She didn't bother to look at what was in her aunt's hand.

Aunt Trudy clapped her hands like a five-year-old at a birthday party. "A singles cruise! I just got back from the singles dance, and they passed these out. I had to come right here!"

"Aunt Trudy—"

"Marilyn Mickleson—she does my hair—you know she has a son about your age, and—"

"Aunt Trudy, can we just—"

Trudy grabbed Jo's hand. "Anyway, she's been on two of these cruises, and she said they're loads of fun. And crawling with eligible men."

"I bet they are." Jo didn't even attempt to keep the sarcasm out of her voice.

Trudy squeezed Jo's hand. "I'm going to find husband number four. I can feel it."

Jo pulled her hand away. "Good for you. I hope that works out for you. But I don't think—"

"I won't take no for an answer. It would be good for you, Joellen."

Jo leaned against the kitchen counter and crossed her arms. "Don't you think it's up to me to decide what's good for me?"

"I don't think you *know* what's good for you. You need to get out and meet some people. Some men people." Trudy laughed.

Jo gave up on *I don't want to meet a new man*. "I don't think a singles cruise is something I would enjoy." She hoped Aunt Trudy would understand *I won't like it*.

Trudy waved a dismissive hand. "Nonsense." She took off her coat and hung it on the back of a chair.

Oh, God, she's staying.

Trudy pulled out a chair and sat at the table. "Do you have any wine, dear? I could use a glass."

Lynae walked into the room, buttoning the shirt she had borrowed from Jo's closet. "Pizza's ordered."

Trudy gaped at Lynae. "Oh, I didn't realize you had company."

Lynae stopped in her tracks with a deer-in-the-headlights look.

Jo pushed away from the counter. "Aunt Trudy, this is my partner, Lynae Parker."

Beaming, Lynae held out her hand. "Nice to meet you. I've heard a lot about you."

Trudy looked Lynae up and down before taking her hand in a limp shake. "All good, I hope."

Lynae somehow kept a straight face and sincere voice. "Of course."

Jo pulled a bottle from the wine holder and reached for a glass. "Aunt Trudy stopped over to invite me to go with her on a singles cruise."

"Oh... interesting."

Trudy raised a penciled-in eyebrow. "You don't approve?"

Lynae shrugged as she sat across from Trudy. "I just can't see a singles cruise being something Jo would be interested in."

"How does she know if she doesn't give it a try? I'm going, so she'll be with someone she knows. She can meet my friends. They're such a hoot! And it would be good for her to get back in the game, so to speak."

Jo's shoulders tensed as she took out her frustration with the bottle opener. She set a glass in front of her aunt, grabbed two more beers, then sat down next to Lynae.

Trudy took a sip of her drink. "So we need to—"

"Hey, Jo, I was in the middle of telling you about the guy who tried to pick me up at the grocery store. So anyway..." Lynae jumped into an animated story that included cantaloupe, a bag of frozen shrimp, and crashing grocery carts. It was completely made up and an obvious attempt to knock Trudy off course.

Jo was grateful, but she knew her aunt. Nothing would keep that woman from something she wanted.

When Lynae had exhausted her topic, Trudy took advantage of the lull in conversation. "Now, we have to get busy planning our trip. It's only a month away. I know it takes time to arrange to be away from your job." She leaned toward Jo conspiratorially. "Maybe if you meet someone, you won't have to work that horrible job anymore."

"I *like* my horrible job," Jo said through gritted teeth.

The doorbell rang. Lynae stood up, ran her hand across Jo's upper back, then gave her shoulder a squeeze. "I've got it."

Jo smiled up at her and watched her walk to the door. When she turned back to her aunt, the woman was frowning and her wineglass was stopped halfway to her mouth. But then Trudy smiled and took a sip of her wine.

Lynae returned to the kitchen and put the pizza on the table. "Would you like to join us for pizza, Aunt Trudy?"

Trudy shook her head. "No. No, thank you. We had food at the dance."

"Well, there's plenty if you change your mind." Lynae got a couple of plates from the cabinet and handed one to Jo as she sat back down next to her. After grabbing a slice of pizza, Lynae picked the mushrooms off her piece and put them on Jo's, while Jo did the same with her pepperoni.

The three women made small talk while Jo and Lynae devoured their pizza. For the first time since Mike's death, Jo found the conversation with her aunt comfortable. She was surprised at how much time had gone by when Trudy stood to leave.

Jo walked her to the door. "I appreciate you thinking of me, Aunt Trudy, I really do. But a singles cruise really isn't for me."

Trudy shook her head and waved a hand in front of her face. "I understand. We all have our own preferences. I'll see you Sunday at your mother's. Will Lynae be joining us?"

Jo frowned and looked over her shoulder at Lynae, who was busy cleaning off the table. "Oh… I don't know. I haven't asked."

"She seems nice, dear," Trudy whispered, laying a hand on Jo's arm.

Jo watched her aunt until the woman got into her car and drove away. She walked back into the kitchen, where Lynae was rinsing the plates. "Once we got past the singles cruise, that went better than usual. I think I need you around whenever I have to have a conversation with Aunt Trudy. I can't remember the last time we had a nice talk like that."

Lynae looked over her shoulder and gave Jo an evil grin. "That's because she thinks I'm your girlfriend."

Jo's mouth dropped open. "She does not."

"Oh yeah, totally. You'll be getting a call from your mom any time. You're welcome, by the way."

Jo broke into laughter. "You're brilliant!"

Lynae gave her a confused look. "What? You're the one who introduced me as your partner after I walked in half dressed."

"That explains the weird look she gave me. For the first time ever, I wish I knew what was going on in her head."

Lynae tossed the dish towel onto the counter and grabbed her beer. "I could see she was stressing you out. She obviously wasn't going to leave you alone about the singles cruise or trying to get you to find a man."

Jo raised her beer bottle in a toast. "I bet she will now."

Lynae tapped her bottle to Jo's. "Here's to me being your new escape hatch."

Jo smirked. "She likes you, by the way."

Lynae spread her arms wide and looked herself over. "What's not to like?"

Jo laughed and winked. "Couldn't agree more right at the moment. Except..."

"Except what? What's not perfect about it?"

"I don't want other people to think I'm gay."

Lynae scowled. "Why, you got something against gay people?"

"Seriously? Of course not. You know me better than that."

"Then what?"

"I don't want anyone to think that what I had with Mike wasn't real."

"Don't overthink it. It's only your busybody aunt. Neither confirm nor deny. Let her think what she wants if it will keep her off your back about dating. If and when you start dating again, she'll realize she was wrong."

Jo grinned. "It would be nice to have her off my back."

Lynae gave her a shoulder bump as they headed back to the living room. "And you could do worse than me."

CHAPTER 32

JO SETTLED BACK ON THE sofa. She patted the cushion, and Mojo jumped up and snuggled in next to her. Lynae set her beer on the end table then planted herself in the recliner. She grabbed the remote and passed it back and forth between her hands.

Jo eyeballed her. "You gonna turn on the television?"

Lynae laid the device on the arm of the chair. "No, I'm not."

Jo cocked her head. "What's wrong?"

"You asked for my help on Mike's case, but we never talk about it."

"What do you mean? You came with me to the jail, and to talk to Tonya Mereck."

Lynae shook her head. "You talk about leads and suspects, but you've never told me exactly what happened. If I'm going to help, I need you to tell me what you know. I've been waiting for you to tell me on your own, but I don't think that it's going to happen."

Even though Jo obsessed about finding Mike's killer, she never talked about it with anyone. It was so painful she couldn't bear to. But it was time. She gazed at the beer bottle in her hand while the events of that night played out in her mind. "A little over two years ago—two years, one month, and ten days, to be exact—Mike's partner, Rick Lewis, got a tip from an informant that a drug shipment of significant size would be coming into Grand Rapids and unloading at the Weston Auto body shop. The two of them went to check it out."

Lynae frowned. "Don't they usually have a team for large drug busts?"

"It was Rick's informant, and Rick said the guy was a bit hot and cold on his tips. They didn't want to set up a big operation without more information. They were just going to stake out the location, see if there was any activity, and determine what they needed from there."

Lynae nodded. "Okay, I follow."

"Mike called me about one thirty that morning and said nothing was happening. He thought the place was deserted, but Rick had a feeling and wanted to wait it out a little longer."

Jo picked at the bottle label. "According to Rick, at about ten minutes before two, a white Ford Econoline van pulled up to the warehouse loading dock and backed in. Two people got out. One entered the building, and the other stayed by the van. When the first person came back out, the pair opened the back, got out several packages, and took them into the building. Since the place had appeared to be deserted and there were only two people involved, Mike and Rick decided to go in. Rick called for backup." Her voice broke. "Mike didn't wait. He started to go in while Rick was on the call, so Rick followed him."

Jo's hand trembled as she took another drink. She buried her other hand in Mojo's soft fur. "When they went in the building, all hell broke loose. It wasn't empty like they thought. By the time backup arrived, Mike was down, and Rick was wounded... shot in the arm. And there was no one in the building except them. No white van, no drugs. They all got away."

The tears flowed unchecked as Jo stared blindly out the dark window across the room. She saw her husband lying on a cold concrete floor, bleeding to death. "Mike was alive when the ambulance got there. I got the call when the ambulance did and beat them to the hospital. But it was too late. He died on the way. The bleeding was just more than they could stop."

Lynae leaned forward and laid her hand on Jo's leg.

"The EMT told me that Mike said two things: 'Jo' and 'sit up.'"

"Sit up?"

Jo shrugged and rubbed her eyes. "I don't know. He was agitated and trying to get up. He was out of it, dying. He didn't know what he was saying."

Lynae handed her a tissue. "He thought of you. He knew what he was saying then. What about the white van? I assume they called in the plate."

Jo nodded and wiped her nose. "Yeah. It was stolen, of course. It belonged to a woman on the northwest side. She didn't even know it was missing. She had gotten groceries that morning in Standale. Someone probably took the plate in the parking lot, slapped it on the van that night, and ditched it right after."

"No security in the store parking lot?"

Jo shook her head. "Not in that part of town. No real reason for it."

"What about ballistics?"

Jo rolled her eyes. "Nine-millimeter semiautomatic. The same gun everybody else in the city carries. Needle in a haystack."

Lynae popped out of her chair and started to pace the room. "It's unusual that they would leave a witness, especially when that witness is a detective that they would assume could give a good description."

"Rick said they heard the backup coming and took off. He got lucky, and Mike didn't."

"What kind of description did Rick give? Did he see anyone?"

"He said it all happened too fast. He didn't really have anything useful on the people involved. The two from the parking lot never turned their faces toward him. He could say they were males and give their approximate heights. That's it."

"Huh."

"Huh, what?"

Lynae stopped behind the recliner and tapped a slow rhythm on the soft leather. "I don't know. It's just… two veteran narcotics officers get into a suspicious situation, and they don't see anything? Don't tell me they just burst in there and started shooting. They would have gone in quietly to assess."

"Yeah, that never added up for me, either, knowing Mike. He was very cautious and by the book." Jo looked up at Lynae. A tear slid down her cheek. "I made him promise to be careful so he would always come home."

"Tell me about Rick."

Jo shrugged. "Rick's a good guy. He and Mike were very close. In fact, he was the best man at our wedding." She hung her head. "I haven't talked to him in two years."

"You haven't questioned him? Is Madison blocking you?"

"No, Madison has been great. How do you think I got copies of the file? I read the reports and Rick's statement."

Lynae's eyes softened. "You can't make yourself talk to him."

Jo leaned her head back on the sofa and stared at the ceiling. The tears clogged her throat and made her voice guttural. "I can't look at him without wishing that he had died instead of Mike. If only Mike had called for backup, he would have been the one who was behind by a few seconds. Maybe that would have made the difference. I could have gone to *Rick's* funeral and comforted *his* wife. Then Mike and I could have moved on with our lives like Rick and his wife have." She raised her head and stared at Lynae. "God, I'm such a horrible person."

Lynae came around the chair and squatted down in front of her. "You have to know that's normal, Jo."

"I don't know what's normal. I just know that I'm not." Jo looked Lynae in the eye. "It was the same day I made Lieutenant."

"Oh, Jo..."

"Mike didn't even know. I didn't want to tell him over the phone. I had made a nice dinner, wanted to have him come home to a surprise. Even a bigger surprise than me making dinner." Jo tried to chuckle, but it came out hollow even to her own ears. "When he called to say he was gonna be late, I was a little pissed, and I got snippy with him. It wasn't fair because I did that to him all the time. I'm just glad I talked to him again later. I'm glad I told him I loved him. I just wish I had told him the rest, you know? He had helped me prepare. He was as much a part of the promotion as I was, and he never even knew."

Lynae took Jo's hand. "I'm sorry, Jo. I don't know what to say. I wish I had some great speech that would make you feel better."

"There's nothing to say. But you help more than you know."

Lynae squeezed Jo's hand. "You know I'd do anything for you."

"I know."

"Can I take the files home with me and read them over?"

"I guess you'll have to. I can't imagine that I've missed anything, as many times as I've gone over them. But I do want another set of eyes to look them over. Eyes that I completely trust."

"I'm glad that's me. And you may be too close to it."

"That I am," Jo said quietly. Her phone rang. She checked the screen and was surprised to see Isaac's name. It had to be important for him to call her at home, especially when he wasn't even supposed to be working. "Isaac, what's going on?"

"I just got a call from my friend at the hospital. Tonya Mereck is awake."

Jo raced her demons to the hospital. She parked in the visitor lot and jogged to the front desk, with Lynae on her heels. They flashed their badges and were pointed to Tonya's room.

A man sat next to Tonya's bed, holding her small hand in his. His frame was too lanky for him to sit comfortably in the small hospital chair. Blond hair, closely cropped, framed a handsome, angular face. He looked up as they entered. "Can I help you?"

"Who are you?" Jo asked.

He smiled congenially. "I'm Drevin Clayburn, Tonya's boyfriend."

Jo felt a tingling in her fingers and a sickening clenching in her stomach. *Could I really be standing in the same room as the man who killed Mike?* Tonya stared up at them, her gaze flicking between Jo, Lynae, and Drevin. Her eyes were a bit cloudy, probably from painkillers.

Lynae stepped over and shook his hand. "Detective Lynae Parker. This is my lieutenant. We'd like to ask Tonya a few questions."

He glanced at Tonya and rubbed his thumb over her still hand. "She fell down the stairs. She doesn't remember how it happened."

Jo found her voice, and it was an angry one. "We'd like to ask her, if you don't mind."

"She shouldn't be talking to anybody right now. Besides, she already talked to the police."

"We'd like her to talk again. Why don't you wait outside?"

Drevin frowned. "She's not going to tell you anything I can't hear. The other cops didn't make me wait outside."

What the hell? She'd have to have a talk with whoever had interviewed Tonya. It was standard procedure to talk to a woman alone after she "fell down the stairs."

"We're not the other cops, now, are we?" Jo felt her anger rising as she took a step closer to the guy.

Lynae moved to stand between Jo and Drevin. "If you could wait outside for a few minutes, we won't be long."

Drevin gave Jo a smug look then turned and addressed the woman in the bed. "Tonya, I'm right outside the door."

Making sure she stays in line. Jo closed the door behind him.

Lynae sat on the edge of the bed and took Tonya's hand. She had a look of such compassion and understanding that Jo waited a beat before approaching them.

Tonya's right eye was swollen completely shut, the tissue surrounding it shining deep purple in the center and easing out into a sickening blood red. Her top lip was split and swollen so that it hung over the bottom lip. Her right arm was in a cast to the elbow. When she attempted to shift positions, she sucked a quick gasp of air through her teeth and whimpered. Her gown shifted enough to reveal bandages around her ribs.

Fell down the stairs, my ass.

Lynae whispered soothing words to the woman. Tonya's only response was a single tear that rolled down her cheek.

Jo approached the bed and forced a patient tone. "Tonya, I'm sorry that this happened to you. Can you talk to us about it?"

"Fell... down... stairs." The words were slurred as she spoke through the small slit of her swollen mouth.

Jo stamped her foot. "That's bullshit, and we all know it."

Lynae scowled and shook her head at Jo. Tonya closed her eyes and turned her face away from them.

Jo sighed. "I'm sorry. It's just that we can't help you if you don't talk to us."

Tonya lay there and stared at the wall. Her hands on her hips, Jo paced the room. The silence grew heavier with each lap.

Finally, Jo couldn't take it any longer. "Everyone in this room knows what really happened to you. You can't just lie there and protect him!"

Lynae stood up and gave Jo a not-so-gentle nudge toward the door. "Why don't you wait outside? Maybe grab some coffee, and I'll stay here with Tonya for a while."

Jo stood her ground. "Tonya, I need you to tell me what you know about that police shooting that we asked you about yesterday. We can help you. We can get you into a shelter, help you get on your feet. Just help me. Damn it, I need to know what you know."

Tonya shook her head slowly. Her eyes widened when the door opened, and Drevin walked back in.

Jo whipped her head around and stood toe-to-toe with the much taller man. "Did we tell you to come back in here?"

"You got no right to keep me out of here." He looked at Tonya. "You told 'em what happened, how you fell, right?"

Tonya nodded slightly.

Drevin looked down his nose at Jo. "There's nothin' more to say, then, is there?"

Lynae stepped back to Tonya's bedside and took the woman's hand. She leaned in and whispered something. Tonya's eyes flicked toward Jo then quickly away as Drevin flopped down in the chair next to her bed and took her other hand.

Lynae put an arm around Jo's shoulders. "C'mon. We need to go."

Jo started to argue, but Lynae shook her head and gave her a push toward the door. Neither said a word as they stepped into the elevator. Two passengers already in the car jabbered on about the newborn they had just seen for the first time. Jo clenched her teeth and stared at the descending numbers. When the doors opened, she pushed past the others and marched through the lobby.

Jo held it in until they cleared the hospital doors. "Shit, shit, shit! We have him, right there in the damn room! All she has to do is say he did that to her, and I've got him in custody. That would give me a reason to question the shit out of him. That's all I need from her. Three damn words: 'He did this.' I get him locked up for that, and we have all kinds of time to get her to give us a reason for a search warrant. I need that fucker behind bars!"

"She's scared, Jo. Look what he did to her."

Jo flung her hand in the direction of the hospital. "Well, a hell of a lot of good it's going to do her to sit there and hold his hand."

Lynae shoved her hands in her pockets. "You don't understand."

"No. You're right. I don't!" Jo huffed and forced herself to bring her voice down a notch. "I'm trying like hell to understand because I love you, but it doesn't make sense. I don't understand protecting someone like that."

Lynae stared at her feet as they walked back to the parking garage. "She's not protecting him, Jo. She's scared shitless. She knows what will happen if she goes back with him, but she doesn't know what will happen if she doesn't. She'd rather stick with what she knows."

"She'd rather stick with getting the hell beat out of her whenever he chooses?"

Lynae looked up. "She believes she can survive that. She's more afraid of the unknown. She'll come around. She has it in her, I know she does. But you can't badger it out of her. Badgering is the last thing she'll respond to. She'll just shut down. You have to be patient."

Jo squeezed her eyes closed and pinched the bridge of her nose. "I can't, Nae. I've barely thought of anything else for two years. We're close. I can feel it. This doesn't feel like another wild goose chase. I know she knows something and just won't tell us."

"Give her some time." Lynae looked at Jo with pleading eyes. "Give *me* some time."

Jo opened the Ranger door and slid into the driver's seat. "I'm not sure my sanity has much more time."

Lynae smiled. "I'll keep you sane a little longer."

"What did you say to her right before we left? She gave me a strange look."

"I told her the detective was your husband."

Jo groaned. "I didn't want her to know this was personal."

"She already knew it was personal. She just didn't know *how* personal. I think it's important."

"Why?"

"If there's one thing you understand in an abusive relationship, it's loss. She's experienced the loss of herself, and she's afraid to lose what she sees as love. Sometimes when you can concentrate on someone else's loss, it helps you get over your own."

Jo raised her eyebrows. "That's deep."

Lynae smirked. "I'm a pretty deep person. Now, do you think I can go home and get a couple of hours of sleep before I have to be back at work? My boss is a bitch when I'm late."

Jo snorted. "So I've heard."

CHAPTER 33

THE NEXT MORNING, JO WANTED nothing more than a cup of coffee that didn't have the consistency of motor oil. She certainly wasn't going to get that at the station, so she made a stop at MadCap on her way in. While she was standing in line, Jack Riley walked through the door.

Shit, I'm not ready for this.

With no place to hide and no way to get out the door without walking past him, when she got to the counter, she ordered two coffees. As she turned with the cups, she caught his eye then held up the coffees and nodded at a table by the window. He gave her a little smile and stepped out of line.

At the table, she took her time adding cream and Equal then stirring as if the perfect blend could only be achieved with the utmost care. Jack sipped his black coffee and stared out the window.

Jo took a deep breath and blurted, "I'm sorry. I didn't know."

Jack pulled his eyes from the window and gave her a half smile. "It's okay."

"No, it's not. I shouldn't make assumptions about people." She nodded at his left hand. "You wear a wedding ring."

Jack cocked his head without taking his eyes from hers. "So do you."

Jo held up her hand and adjusted her ring so the diamond was centered on her finger. "Yeah, I always thought I was weird for doing that."

He shrugged. "Well, if you're weird, then I guess I am too."

"I just thought you were another good-looking guy who thought he could charm his way into cheating on his wife. I should have found out more about you before I jumped to that conclusion. I'm sorry."

Jack gave her a devilish grin, his green eyes twinkling. "You think I'm good looking?"

Jo laughed. "Out of that whole speech, that's what you took away?"

He held up his hands. "Hey, I'm a guy. You have to talk in short sentences. And once you said 'good looking,' I stopped listening."

The knot in her stomach loosened a little. "I still feel like an ass."

"Don't. I shouldn't have asked. It was impulsive." Jack rolled his eyes. "No, that's a lie. I knew your situation and thought..."

He didn't finish his sentence and didn't appear as though he was going to. Jo raised her eyebrows. "Thought what?"

On a long breath, he replied, "I thought you were probably lonely too. I'm not really looking to date. Just, you know, enjoy each other's company."

Jo had to struggle not to spit out her coffee. She set her cup down hard on the table. "Oh my God! You think I'm gonna be your hookup?"

"No, that's not what I meant!" Jack ran his hand through his unruly hair. "Man, I'm really screwing this up." Redness crept up his neck.

"Well, I owe you one foot-in-mouth moment. Why don't you try again?"

Jack looked down at his coffee and started picking apart the cup sleeve. "I don't know a lot of people in Grand Rapids. And the ones I do know are married friends that Laura and I had. It's weird to hang out with them now. They try to include me, but I'm always the odd man out. So mostly I make up a reason not to go."

Jo nodded. "Yeah, I know what you mean."

He pointed at her. "See, that's what I mean! You know where I'm coming from. I thought we could have dinner or something. You know, get to know each other, just as friends, with neither of us expecting or wanting anything different."

Jo smiled and raised her cup. She couldn't imagine going on a date, but having dinner with a male friend might be okay. "We've had coffee now, so that's a start."

Jack winked. "It's a start."

"For future reference, if you're going to ask any other women to have dinner just as friends, you may want to work on your approach."

He laughed. "I'm a bit rusty."

There's that laugh again. Jo leaned forward and wrapped her hands around her cup. "So while I have your undivided attention, how about we talk search warrant?" She quickly laid out the information she had on Steve Markham, hoping for an encouraging word to contact a judge.

He leaned back in his chair and crossed his ankle over his knee. He took a sip of his coffee then rested the cup on his lap. "So let me get this straight. You want me to get a search warrant based on taillights that a ten-year-old kid saw in the dark and a text message to a man who was forthcoming about the fact that he was counseling the victim regarding her pregnancy."

"He didn't tell us he was paying for it," Jo pointed out. She knew she sounded defensive, but she couldn't help it.

"Did you ask?"

She raised a hand. "Come on! It's one thing for him to talk to her and try to help her, but it's entirely different for him to pay for an abortion for a teenage girl, especially the daughter of one of his friends. And he didn't tell her parents, either."

He shrugged. "I agree it's odd. But it's not a crime. Maybe he's a genuinely nice guy who was trying to help out a friend's kid. You have a fingerprint from the inside of her purse that you can't verify is his and an eyewitness that saw him leave work well past the time of death. Why are you after this guy?"

"I have a forty-five-year-old guy who's paying for the abortion of his teenage babysitter. I have text messages between them, discussing the pregnancy. And he's the only person who knew she didn't have the abortion. The fingerprint didn't hit on any of the criminal databases. That just means he's never been booked."

"I understand, but as far as evidence, it doesn't help us. What about the boyfriend?"

"The message the vic sent to him said they needed to talk. It didn't say she didn't have the abortion. For all he knew, at least according to the texts, she wanted to talk because she was upset."

"She asked him for a ride home. It stands to reason he picked her up."

"He sent several messages afterward, trying to contact her. And he drives a twelve-year-old GrandAm. Not even a ten-year-old kid is going to mistake a GrandAm for a Cadillac."

He took a sip of his coffee then shook his head. "It's simply not enough, Jo. This is an upstanding man in the community. A pillar of society. We can't search his house based on very shaky circumstantial evidence. We need that smoking gun."

"What about—" She stopped when her phone rang. The screen showed the number for ShapeShifters. "I'm sorry. I have to take this." She sat back and put the phone to her ear. "Lieutenant Riskin."

"Lieutenant? This is Dan from ShapeShifters."

Jo rolled her shoulders to ease the tension. "Hi, Dan. Do you have some information for me?"

"I don't know why I didn't think of this before, but I know what that line is on the picture you showed me."

Jo's eyes snapped to Jack. "You do? What is it?"

"That isn't the *S* from MSU. It's the *S* from Stanford. Stanford has a tree in the middle of their *S*. It was a pain in the ass to make, but the guy paid a mint for it."

Stanford. That's where Dr. Markham went to school. "Are you sure?"

"I remember doing it. It's the only one I've ever done. I was so focused on MSU that it didn't hit me until now."

"Do you have the records on who you sold that to?"

"I can get 'em, but I remember the guy and the car. I don't do many Caddies."

Jo cocked her head. "You did this for a Cadillac?"

"Yeah, guy was a doctor type, maybe lawyer. You know, a

suit. Said him and his wife both graduated from Stanford and he wanted to surprise her with it for the new car he was getting her."

Jo grinned. "Dan, you may just be my new best friend. Can you e-mail a copy of the receipt to me right away?"

"You bet. I'll pull it and have Tracy send it to you immediately."

Sliding her phone back into her pocket, Jo smirked at Jack. "You can get me that warrant now. We have our smoking gun."

CHAPTER 34

WITH NO TIME FOR A trip to the cemetery, Jo did the next best thing. She sat in the quiet of her office with the door closed, her murder board in sight and Mike's picture in her hand. She laid out the whole case with every thought she had and every reservation.

When she stopped, she heard Mike ask in her head, *Why do people kill, Jo?*

Jo ticked off each motive on the fingers of her right hand. "Jealousy, money, revenge, status."

Who had one of those motives to kill Megan?

"Hunter Stone didn't want to be a dad. He didn't want to lose his chance at going to college and having a future. He had motive."

Did he have opportunity?

"Technically, but it would be very tight."

Do you think he did it?

"No, I don't. His car doesn't fit the description."

A description you got from a ten-year-old kid.

Jo ran her hand through her hair. "I think Jeron did good with the description, but I wouldn't want to have to take it to court. My gut tells me Hunter's a good kid who found himself in trouble. His text messages appear to be from a guy desperately looking for his girlfriend. I don't think he's mature enough to have planned everything out the way our perp did. It may have been a crime of passion, but after the fact, the person stayed calm and thought things through. I don't think an eighteen-year-old would think that way."

But the killer made a mistake. He threw the phone out without erasing pictures and messages.

"He didn't think someone from that neighborhood would turn it in to the police. And rightly so. We caught a huge break on that."

Someone with a disdain for the people in that neighborhood? Someone who doesn't think anyone from that area would do the right thing?

"Maybe. Or someone who understands the neighborhood and the people in it. Someone who knows how they feel about the police."

Who else has motive?

"Dr. Markham. He stood to lose a lot if she had that baby."

Like?

"His marriage, his friendship with Dr. Tillman. And probably most importantly to him, his reputation."

Do you believe he's the father?

"Why else would he pay for her abortion?"

Maybe he's exactly what he says he is.

"He has the right kind of car. It's his wife's, but spouses switch cars all the time."

What's bothering you? What do you think you're missing?

Jo peered at her murder board. "The scrapes on her face and side. They came from the dumpster postmortem. The person who put her in that dumpster had to have pushed her body up the dumpster and over the edge. Markham could have easily picked her up."

He has a shoulder injury.

"Wrong shoulder. His injury is to his left arm. If you're left handed, you're going to carry the heaviest part of the body with your left hand. The wounds on the body suggest a right-handed person. Head goes in your right hand, but you're not strong enough to lift it that high. Our killer didn't count on her being too heavy. Or maybe didn't count on the dumpster being so tall."

You're getting your warrant. Search his house and see what you can turn up.

"We should have it in our hands shortly."

Who else had motive?

"I'm thinking!" She rose to her feet and paced the small space. "Jealousy, money, revenge, status." She stopped and stared at the picture of Dr. Markham at his fiancée's funeral that hung on her murder board. "Status and influence."

What about status and influence?

"How far would someone go to attain status? To have people look at them differently, see them as something more?"

To some people, that would be everything. They would do anything.

"Especially someone who hasn't always had it. Someone who had to work for it."

The wheels are turning. That's my girl.

Jo smiled and ran her hand over the lines of Mike's face, ignoring the cold glass frame between them. "What would I do without you?" she asked quietly.

No answer from Mike. She never got an answer to that question.

CHAPTER 35

While Jo waited for Jack to come through with the warrant, she put a team together to perform the search. With that in place, she called Kent Alderink.

His soothing voice came on the line after the first ring. "Kent speaking."

"What's the word, Kent?"

Kent sighed. "Believe it or not, I haven't come up with one yet today."

Jo was flabbergasted. "I'm at a loss. Kent Alderink without a word of the day?"

"Sorry to disappoint you. I've spent my morning with the autopsy report you asked me to look over."

"I'll forgive you if you tell me you found a second smoking gun. What do you think? Did Dr. Markham's son die of SIDS?"

Kent hesitated. "Without a full autopsy, I can't say with certainty, of course."

"I'm not going to pull you into court on it right away."

"Microfibers were found in the child's lungs, which could be consistent with SIDS. However, in the pictures, I see a slight discoloration of the lips and what looks to be a broken blood vessel in the right eye."

Jo scowled. "What does that mean?"

"It means if I had done the autopsy, I would have marked it as suspicious and requested an investigation. It was done while I was on vacation."

"You take vacation?"

Kent chuckled. "I have been known to on occasion. Notes

indicate that Mrs. Markham wanted it done immediately. I think it was rushed. It's unfortunate that I wasn't able to do it myself. I don't rush."

Why would Dr. Markham kill his own son? What about his wife? How far would she go to protect their perfect family? "Unfortunate or conveniently timed that you were on vacation?"

"I just give you the facts, Lieutenant. You put them together."

"That's what I'm trying to do. Based on this, would you be willing to request that the case be reopened?"

"I called Gaint, since he did the autopsy. He said he was suspicious at the time but didn't feel he had enough evidence to make a case. Personally, I think there's enough to ask some questions. I'll talk to the primary and have it reopened for a thorough examination."

"Good idea. We'll take a look at it after we have him in the box. I'm going to tread very carefully for now. I would hate to even suggest something that heinous without solid evidence."

"Yes, it's not something to take lightly."

"Murder never is. Thanks for your help." Jo hung up and strode out into the bull pen.

Lynae held up an envelope. "We've got the search warrant. I've notified the team. They're ready to go when you are."

"Give me two minutes." Jo stepped over to Isaac's desk. "I need a quick favor from my favorite computer geek."

Isaac smiled. "I'll give it my best shot."

"I need the fingerprint from our victim's purse run through another database."

Isaac frowned. "I thought we ran them all."

"Not this one. Grand Rapids public schools fingerprint their employees. See if that extends to volunteers also. I need this yesterday. Text me the results as soon as you have them."

Isaac nodded. "I'm on it."

Jo turned and pointed at Lynae. "Let's do this."

CHAPTER 36

WARRANT IN HAND AND HER team behind her, Jo drove to the Markham residence. She followed Lynae's Mazda between brick pillars that stood on either side of the estate's entrance and parked in the circle drive in front of the house. Two forensic techs were close behind in a county van, followed by an officer in a cruiser. Jo grabbed her bag and stepped out of her vehicle.

Lynae was standing outside her car, surveying the property. "Not the kind of place we usually find our perps."

Jo eyed the sprawling brick home. "Perps come in all shapes and sizes. And tax brackets."

Lynae crossed her arms. "Seriously, though, that apartment over their garage is bigger than my whole place. Who needs four stalls in a garage?"

Jo patted her shoulder. "Keep working real hard, and you might be able to afford that four-stall-garage apartment."

Lynae huffed. "Doubt it."

The techs came around the back of their van, carrying their heavy equipment cases. They set them down next to Lynae. The older of the two said, "We're all set, Lieutenant."

Jo nodded. "All right, our warrant is for the garage and car. Start with the silver Cadillac." She pointed at Lynae. "Look for the golf clubs or anything else that has that same shape and size. Bag and tag everything."

Lynae patted the bag that hung over her shoulder. "I'm packing Luminol, and I'm not afraid to use it."

Jo snorted. "Great. Luminol the hell out of the place. And

that apartment you're so fond of would be considered part of the garage, so make sure you search it. Check in with me if you find something we can use." Jo turned to the uniformed officer. "Zimmer, you come with me. I'm going inside to show the warrant to Mrs. Markham and have a little chat."

Lynae swept her hand toward the garage. "Let's go, guys."

The techs hoisted their cases and followed her. Jo walked up the steps and knocked on the front door.

Steve Markham swung the door open. "Good afternoon, Lieutenant."

"Dr. Markham, I didn't expect to find you home at this time of day."

"I had an early surgery. I came home to..." He frowned as he scanned the driveway. "Why are there four cars in my drive?"

Paula Markham appeared in a doorway behind him. "Steve, why is there a police car out front?"

Jo held up the warrant. "I have a search warrant in connection with the murder of Megan Tillman."

Steve backed up a few inches. "A warrant? I don't—"

Paula stormed across the foyer. "Murder? How dare you walk in here with such a thing! Do you know who you're dealing with?"

Jo looked down at the other woman. "Yes, ma'am, I do."

Paula turned to her husband. "I'm going to call your father."

Steve held up his hand. "That's not necessary, Paula."

Paula grabbed his arm. "You can't let her come into our home and do this!"

Steve put his hands on his wife's shoulders. "Let them do their search. I haven't done anything wrong." He turned to Jo and held out his hand. "I'd like to see that warrant, Lieutenant."

Jo handed him the document.

He scrutinized the form for a few seconds. "This warrant is for the garage and cars only."

Jo nodded. "That's correct. My team is in your garage right now."

Paula held up her phone and started to walk toward another room. "I'm calling Jim."

Steve nodded. "That's a good idea." He handed the warrant

back to Jo. "Jim is our lawyer. I'm not going to talk to you until he gets here."

"That is your right. May I wait inside?"

Steve shifted aside and pointed to a doorway on the right. "Of course. Have a seat in the dining room."

Jo went in the direction he indicated and sat down at the polished cherrywood table. Officer Zimmer stayed in the room's entryway.

Paula walked in a few minutes later, her arms crossed tightly over her chest. She glanced at Jo then looked up at her husband. "Jim will be here in a few minutes."

Steve smiled at his wife. "It'll be okay." He pulled out a chair and sat across from Jo.

Behind him, a cathedral-style window looked out over their expansive front yard. A school bus stopped at the end of the long drive. Jo glanced at her watch. *Three o'clock. Bad timing.*

A young boy and girl hopped out of the bus. They stopped on the sidewalk in front of the house, tucked in their shirts, ran their fingers through their hair, then walked up the driveway. *What kid tucks in his shirt to come home?*

When the front door opened, Steve jolted. He looked at his watch then dropped his hand back into his lap. "The kids."

The little boy walked into the room on stocking feet, while his sister stayed in the doorway. His face lit up when he spotted his father. "Dad! What are you doing home?" He ran to Steve. "What are all the people doing here?"

Steve tousled the boy's hair, pulled him onto his lap, then pointed at Jo. "This is a detective who has some questions to ask us. I came home for a little bit to talk to her."

The little boy shrugged. "Huh, okay." He hopped down and walked toward the kitchen.

Paula stepped in his path, and the boy tensed. She straightened his hair, took him by the shoulders, and turned him around. "What do we say when we have guests in the house?"

He raised his eyes to Jo but didn't really look at her. "It's nice to meet you," he said robotically.

Jo smiled. "It's nice to meet you too."

"You two have homework to do, so off to your rooms to do it," Paula said sternly.

The girl immediately turned and ran up the stairs.

The boy hung his head. "I got my math test back today."

"And?" his mother prompted.

He shuffled his feet. "I got an A minus."

Dr. Markham held up his hand. "That's great, buddy!"

The little boy grinned and gave his dad a high five.

Paula crossed her arms. "What didn't you understand about the material?"

The boy's smile vanished. "I understood it. I just made a mistake on one of the problems."

Paula raised her eyebrows. "We'll talk about it later. For now, go to your room and get your homework done."

They have to be perfect. That's why all their photos look staged. They have to fit into this perfect world.

Steve watched his son walk up the stairs then turned back to Jo. "Is it necessary to do this while my kids are home?"

"We have to execute the search warrant now. And I assumed you would rather talk here than go down to the station."

Steve crossed his arms and looked away. Paula excused herself and went into what Jo assumed was the kitchen.

When the doorbell chimed, Steve bolted from his chair and rushed to the door. Paula came back in, folding a kitchen towel. Jo thought it odd that the woman had been cleaning with the police there ready to question her husband. Without even a glance at Jo, Paula patted her hair into place then joined her husband. Voices mumbled in the foyer.

Jo stood when the trio walked into the dining room.

A stout man in a pinstripe suit approached her and held out his hand. "Jim Gannon."

"Lieutenant Riskin," Jo said, taking his hand and giving it a brief shake.

Steve motioned toward the table. "Why don't we all sit down?"

Jo resumed her seat, and the Markhams sat down across from her.

Jim set a legal pad and pen on the table then pulled a chair close to Steve's. "Mr. and Mrs. Markham have asked me to be here as Mr. Markham's legal representative. Against my advisement, he has agreed to speak with you."

Steve huffed. "Because I have nothing to hide."

Jim held up his hand. "I will stop you if I think you're crossing a line, Lieutenant."

Jo nodded. "Understood." She turned to Steve. "I just have a few things to clear up from our previous conversation. To get your attorney up to speed, I'll remind you what we talked about."

Jim nodded curtly. "Appreciate it."

Jo pulled out her notepad and flipped to the page she had titled "Steve Markham." "When my partner and I came to your office, we talked about the fact that Megan Tillman was pregnant and was talking to you regarding her pregnancy."

Steve nodded. "I was consulting with Megan as a family friend."

"At that time, we had phone records that showed Megan contacted you shortly before her death. You were, in fact, the last person she contacted."

Steve sighed. "So you've said."

Jo leaned forward. "What you failed to mention, and what we found out through a text message, is that you were paying for Megan's abortion." Jo watched Paula out of the corner of her eye. The woman showed no reaction.

Steve crossed his arms. "I didn't think it was relevant."

Jo glared at him. "You didn't think it was relevant that a man your age was paying for the abortion of a teenage girl?"

Jim held up his hand. "You don't have to answer that."

Steve shook his head. "I can answer her because there was nothing to it. Megan didn't want to ask her parents for money. They would have wanted to know why she needed it. She said she would tell them later and asked me to loan her the money."

"Do you want that money back now that she's not going to need it?"

Steve gaped at her. "What? My God! What kind of question is that? Give it to charity or something. I don't want it."

He doesn't know that there was no money found with the body. Jo checked that off her mental list. "Do you know how we know what her text messages to you said?"

Steve folded his hands on the table. "I assume you found her cell phone with her."

He doesn't know that Megan's phone wasn't found with her. Jo flashed back to her conversation with Paula and Joyce Tillman. *Paula had said, "Someone probably wanted her phone and money."* She had stated it as a fact that the money and phone were missing.

"No, her phone was brought to us by a young man who found it."

Steve shrugged. "Okay."

Paula crossed her legs and wiped a scuff from her shoe.

"You indicated that you didn't get the text message that Megan sent you after she decided not to have her abortion."

Steve huffed. "Yes, we've been over this. I didn't get that message. Do you have any *new* questions, Lieutenant?"

"As a matter of fact, I do. Did you not get that message because you forgot your phone at home that day?"

Something flickered in the man's eyes. "I don't know why I didn't get the message, but I didn't."

Jo smiled at Paula. "Mrs. Markham, did you know your husband was paying for your teenage babysitter's abortion?"

Paula adjusted the placemat in front of her. "No. I didn't. But I trust my husband. I'm certain he was only trying to help the girl."

"Do you know if your husband forgot his phone at home that day?"

Paula reached out and adjusted the already perfect floral arrangement on the table. "He forgets it sometimes, but I can't say if he did that particular day."

Jo nodded. "Fair enough." She turned to the doctor. "Dr. Markham, you sent messages to Megan regarding the pregnancy and her abortion prior to that day. Is that right?"

"Yes, a few."

Jo turned to Paula. "Mrs. Markham, did you have occasion to see any of those messages between Megan and your husband?"

Paula pursed her lips. "I don't look at my husband's phone messages, Lieutenant."

Jo cocked her head. "Really? I used to pick up my husband's phone by accident all the time. I would hear it ring, and I would just react. You don't do that?"

Paula raised her eyebrows. "I know the difference between my husband's ringtone and mine."

Of course, because you're perfect. "Were you aware that Megan was pregnant?"

Paula nodded. "I was there when you told Joyce."

"Your friend Karen works at the clinic where Megan went for her abortion. Did she mention to you that she had met with your babysitter and possibly talked her out of having the abortion?"

Paula straightened the table runner and brushed off some invisible dust. "Karen wouldn't tell me private patient information."

Jo shook her head. "No, I'm sure she would never intentionally do that." Jo noted the fidgeting but decided to change tactics. She turned to the doctor. "Doctor, Megan Tillman sent you a message at four thirty-two on Tuesday afternoon. I'm going to read that message to you. She consulted her notes. '*Karen's right, I can't do it. I'm having the baby. I'll give your money back probably tomorrow. Gotta tell my parents. Will you help?*"

Steve took off his glasses and rubbed his eyes. "How many times are we going to go over this? I never got that message."

Jo nodded. "I believe you."

Steve dropped his hand and looked up at Jo. "You do?"

Jo glanced at Paula. "I don't think you got that message because it was erased from your phone before you ever saw it."

Steve scowled. "I don't know what you're implying, but—"

Jim laid a hand on Steve's arm. "Don't say anything else, Steve. Lieutenant, please stick to questions, not accusations."

Paula's hands trembled as she reached out again to turn the flower vase a few centimeters to center it precisely on the lace doily. She gave Jo a tight smile. Her eyes shone a little too bright. "Where are my manners? Can I get you something to drink?"

What? She's delusional. Does she think this is a social call? Jo shook her head. "No, thank you. Mrs. Markham, you drive a silver Cadillac CTS Coupe, correct?"

"Yes, I do."

Jo forced a complimentary tone. "That's a nice car."

Paula smiled proudly and laid a hand over her husband's. "It was a gift from Steve for our anniversary last year."

"That particular color and type of paint was found on the dumpster where Megan Tillman's body was found."

Jim heaved an exaggerated sigh. "I'm sure there are a lot of cars in Grand Rapids that are that color."

Jo nodded. "I'm sure there are. However, we have a witness who picked up Megan Tillman's phone after seeing it thrown out of a Cadillac."

Paula brushed back her hair. "When it's dark, you can't—"

Jim blurted, "Paula—"

Paula jerked and looked at the attorney.

Jo cocked her head. "I didn't mention that it was dark outside."

Paula straightened the front of her blouse. "Well, I just assumed."

Jo pulled some of the autopsy pictures from her bag. She never took her eyes off Paula as she laid the first one on the table in front of the couple. "This is a picture taken of the back of Megan's head. This is the only wound she sustained where the blow didn't break the skin." Jo placed two more of the photos beside the first. "Unlike these."

Dr. Markham jumped from his seat. "What is wrong with you? How can you just lay those out there and make us look at them?"

Paula remained in her chair. She glanced at the pictures then looked away. She twisted her wedding ring set so that the huge diamond glinted in the sunlight streaming from the window.

Jim looked at the pictures and blanched. "Is this necessary?"

Jo kept her eyes on Paula. "An outstanding feature of your anniversary car is the gearshift, a custom job with the logo of your beloved alma mater. That's a pretty unique shape and design." Jo slapped a fourth picture on the table. "The same unique shape and design that put that mark on Megan's head." She pointed to the mark on Megan's head where the hair had been shaved.

Paula stared at the picture for about thirty seconds before looking away.

Steve held up his hand. "Lieutenant, my wife was with me Tuesday night. I told you that two days ago."

Jo nodded. "Yes, I know you did. According to the coroner, the time that you told us you met your wife for dinner would have been approximately two hours after Megan Tillman's death."

Steve shook his head. "This is ludicrous."

Paula wiped some imaginary lint from her slacks and smoothed them over her crossed legs. She acted as if they were discussing the weather.

Jo's phone beeped. She took it from her pocket and read the text from Isaac: *Lab results back. Fingerprint on wallet positive match with school database.* She looked up. "Mrs. Markham, I'm sure you're aware that Grand Rapids Public Schools keeps fingerprints of all of their school volunteers."

Paula nodded. "Yes. I've been working there for quite some time. I really enjoy helping the kids." She beamed at Jo as if waiting for a commendation.

"Can you tell me why your fingerprint was found on the inside of Megan Tillman's wallet?"

Jim held a hand up to Paula. "Paula, I advise against answering that question."

Paula turned to Steve and touched his forearm. "You should call your father, honey."

Steve stared at her with a bewildered expression. "Why do we need my father?"

Jim glanced at Jo then turned to his clients. "Why don't we take a few minutes to step into another room and discuss this?"

Lynae appeared in the entryway to the foyer with another officer. "Lieutenant, I think you should take a look in the garage."

Jo gave the attorney a Cheshire Cat grin, closed her notebook, and stood. "Looks like you'll have a moment for that talk." On the way out, she told Officer Zimmer to wait in the foyer to give the attorney some privacy with his clients.

Jo followed Lynae to the garage. She stopped in the doorway. Bloodstains glowed blue on the floor and walls. A few drops even speckled the ceiling.

Lynae waved her hand. "There's enough blood in this garage to do a transplant. He was brutal."

"*She.*"

Lynae gaped at her. "She? Paula Markham did this?"

Jo nodded. "Yeah, the perfect Mrs. Markham did this."

"You sure?"

"Well, she didn't raise her hand and say, 'I'm your murderer,' but I have no doubt she did it. Every time I touch on a subject that makes her uncomfortable, she starts fixing things."

"Fixing things?"

"Straightens the flowers, smooths her shirt, adjusts the table runner, stuff like that. It's a nervous tell. Like she's trying to straighten her life out by making her little world perfect."

"Weird."

"It gets weirder. I don't think this is the first time she's killed. I would bet she killed her son, and maybe even her college roommate, Dr. Markham's fiancée, all those years ago."

Lynae gasped. "Seriously? Why?"

"Look at the house she lives in, the life she leads. She's the poor girl from the wrong side of the tracks who didn't want to go back."

"That could explain the fiancée, but why her son?"

"He was handicapped. To her warped brain, he wasn't perfect enough for her family. I hope I'm wrong, but I don't think I am. I think she's been shattering lives for a long time and using the pieces to build this perfect, twisted mosaic of a life for herself."

"That is messed up."

"I'm going to get the baby's case reopened. It can't hurt to take another look." Jo looked around. "Did you find golf clubs?"

Lynae nodded. "Eight iron found in a Stanford golf bag.

Luminol shows blood in the grooves. We have it bagged for evidence, along with the rest of the set."

Jo peered through the open car door, carefully keeping her ungloved hands from touching anything. Luminol glowed in a bright patch on the passenger seat. "So Mrs. Markham reads a text message from her husband's phone and finds out that Megan decided not to have the abortion. She decides to pick Megan up at the clinic and try to talk some sense into her."

"I'm sure Megan denied that Dr. Markham was the father."

Jo nodded. "And she would have been telling the truth. Unless he's a hell of an actor, I don't think he's the father."

"So Megan denies it, and they get in an argument. Paula ends up smashing Megan's head into the gear shifter." Lynae frowned. "Wait. That doesn't add up. If Paula was driving, it would be almost impossible to get that kind of leverage. And the wound is on the back of Megan's head."

Jo thought about that for a second before responding. "Megan probably got scared or was somehow tipped off that Paula was going over some edge. I bet she tried to get out of the car at a stop sign or light. Then Paula grabs Megan by the only thing she can reach, her hair, and pulls her back in. Bam! The back of Megan's head hits the shifter."

"You think she meant to kill her?"

"Probably not at first. She most likely just panicked and grabbed her. But there were three wounds of similar size and shape to the shifter. Once she started it, she tried to finish it."

"With the kind of blood you get from a head wound, Paula probably thought Megan was dead when she brought her back here."

Jo looked around the garage. Tools were lined up neatly on a pegboard. A shovel, a rake, and a branch trimmer hung on a separate rack. "So she brought her back to the house to figure out what to do with the body. Maybe she was going to get a shovel and bury her or stash the corpse in that apartment upstairs until she could dispose of her. No way to know what was going on in her head."

Lynae pointed at a thin streak of blue leading out of the car to a smeared stain on the floor. "She dragged the body out of the car and laid it there. She had already called her husband to say she would be late meeting him. She knew he was at work and wouldn't come home at that point. The kids are with Grandma. With the garage door closed, she's locked in tight."

Jo followed some blue drops to a larger colored area in front of the service entrance. Spatters glowed on the wall and door. "Megan must have regained consciousness and tried to get away. It looks like she made it all the way to the door."

"Poor kid." Lynae pointed at a streak starting at the large stain and stopping partway through the garage. "She dragged her to there."

Jo followed the trail back to the car. "To put her in the trunk. Then she scrubbed the garage, went inside and took a shower, then headed out to dinner with her husband. She would have had to hurry because she couldn't be late for dinner."

"That is one cold woman."

Jo put her hands on her hips. "After dinner, the doctor goes back to work, and Paula drives out to the Slope to dump Megan's body in the trash. She doesn't count on how heavy a lifeless body will be. She has to push the corpse up the side of the dumpster to get it in."

Lynae nodded. "She's in a hurry, maybe a little bit of a panic, and she bangs her car into the dumpster as she's leaving."

"That or she tapped it when she backed up to it." Jo walked around to the back of Paula's car and squatted down. She bent over and spotted a green scrape on the back bumper. "Hasn't had time to get that fixed."

Lynae knelt to have a look. "It's pretty minimal. She probably didn't want to have her husband ask a bunch of questions. She could wait it out and then make up some excuse to get the work done."

Jo stood up. "Did you find golf shoes?"

"Yep, they were still in the trunk. By a cursory exam, the cleats will match the marks on Megan's hip."

"Good, we'll let Kent give us a positive on that later." Jo looked around. "Where's that eight iron?"

"There's an evidence cart by the door. I'll grab it for you."

Lynae retrieved the bagged golf club and handed it to Jo. "Here you go."

"Thanks. I'm gonna go play a round." She turned and strode back into the house.

All eyes turned to Jo when she walked back into the dining room. She laid the golf club on the table and took her time sitting down and getting situated.

Steve stared at the club, clearly perplexed.

Paula smiled brightly and pushed her chair back. "I'm going to make some coffee."

Jo spoke firmly. "Please have a seat, Mrs. Markham."

Paula lowered herself back into the chair. The smile faded.

Jim leaned back and crossed his legs. "I've advised my clients against speaking any further with you."

Jo suppressed the urge to smirk. "They have the right to remain silent, but I'll just go ahead and ask the questions, anyway."

Jim inclined his head. "Go right ahead."

Jo pointed at the golf club in its plastic evidence bag. "This eight iron was found in a Stanford golf bag in your garage. By the length of it, I would guess it belongs to you, Mrs. Markham. Is that correct?"

Paula glanced at Jim, and he nodded. She responded, "Yes, that's my iron."

"Have either of you had to use this club to kill something—"

Jim slapped the table. "Lieutenant!"

Jo raised her eyebrows. "Like an animal that got in your garage?"

Steve frowned and shook his head.

Paula fidgeted with her necklace. "I would call an exterminator."

Jo picked the club up and examined it. "That's interesting because, although it appears clean, if you look close, you'll see a blue stain in the grooves. That's Luminol. It's a chemical that reacts to the presence of blood. If you were to walk into the garage right now, you would see this same color emblazoned across the floor, in the car, and even on the walls."

Steve swallowed hard. "I don't understand."

"Your garage has been cleaned up pretty well, but bloodstains can't just be washed away. And there are a lot of them in there. My techs are taking samples, which will be taken back to the lab and compared to Megan Tillman's."

The color drained from his face. "There has to be some mistake. Are you saying there's blood in my garage?"

Jim shook his head and put a hand on Steve's arm. "Steve, don't—"

Steve shook off the attorney. "Why? I haven't done anything!"

Jo nodded. "And in the silver Cadillac."

Jim placed his hands on the table. "I'm advising both of you not to say anything else."

Jo leaned forward and met Paula's eyes. "At what point did you decide that your husband was the baby's father?"

Jim said, "Paula, you don't have to answer that."

Paula crossed her arms. Her foot bounced nervously.

Confusion and fear played out in a sad dance on the doctor's face as he searched his wife's eyes. "Paula?"

Paula grabbed her husband's hand. "It's okay. I forgive you. It doesn't mean anything."

He pulled his hand away. "Paula, my God! Megan's baby wasn't mine. She was a child!"

Paula frowned in confusion. "It wasn't?"

Steve's face crumpled. "I was counseling her. She was fifteen, Paula. After all these years, how could you think that of me?"

"What was I supposed to think? You were paying for her abortion."

Steve leaned on the table and covered his face with both hands. "I paid for it because Dan's my friend. I was just helping his daughter."

Jo laid the club back on the table. "Megan decided not to have that abortion after all. Mrs. Markham, did you kill Megan Tillman because you thought Steve was her baby's father?"

Jim held up both hands. "Mrs. Markham won't be answering any more questions at this time."

Paula reached out and adjusted the centerpiece.

Jo stood up. "That's fine. I don't need any more at this time. Paula Markham, I am placing you under arrest for the murder of Megan Tillman."

Paula's face turned white. "Steve—"

Jo walked around the table and pulled Paula to her feet. "You have the right to remain silent."

Jo pulled the woman's hands behind her back and snapped the cuffs on as tightly as she could without bruising her. "Anything you say can and will be used against you in a court of law."

"I just wanted to talk to her—"

Jim slapped the table. "Paula, stop talking."

Jo glanced at Jim. "You have the right to speak to an attorney."

Paula raised her chin and looked down at her husband, who was still seated and looking stunned. "Steve, call your father. We can fix this." Her husband didn't even look up at her.

"If you cannot afford an attorney, one will be appointed to you."

Paula's eyes were wild. "Don't let this woman take all of this away. Do something!"

"Do you understand these rights as they have been said to you?"

Paula lunged toward her husband, and Jo had to hold her back. "The kids. Steve, our kids. What will people think?"

What will people think? Jo held firmly to Paula's cuffed hands and spoke directly into her ear. "Mrs. Markham, do you understand your rights?"

Dr. Markham remained silent. He sat with his head in his hands, his fingers in his hair. He never looked up at his wife.

"Yes, I understand," Paula finally murmured.

Jo pulled her out toward the doorway. Paula turned to look one last time at her perfect home before Jo led her out the door and to the waiting car.

CHAPTER 37

JO GATHERED HER TEAM IN a conference room where she had doughnuts and a fresh pot of coffee. Her Megan Tillman murder board stood front and center. "We just booked Paula Markham on the murder of Megan Tillman. Kent will also ask to have the case of Joseph Markham, her son, reopened."

Isaac slouched in his chair and rolled his pencil between his fingers. "You think she killed her son too?"

"I believe she wanted a perfect life and wasn't afraid to remove the obstacles that got in her way. Even if one of those obstacles was her own son." Jo seethed over the loss of Megan Tillman's young life, but the thought of a mother killing her child was unfathomable. "We'll see where that goes. It may lead to a further look at her old college roommate."

Lynae sipped her coffee and stared longingly at the doughnuts. "If you're right, she got away with it for a long time. Her roommate died twenty-three years ago. No one even looked at Paula for that, or for her son."

Charles spoke around the doughnut in his mouth. "A drunk coed and an infant with SIDS—no one looks at anyone else in either of those cases. Paula was even in the limelight a bit, which someone like her would get off on. Her best friend dies in a tragic accident. *How sad, you poor thing.* Her baby dies? There's nothing worse. No one wants to look at the parents. No one is going to when they're the perfect family."

Jo stared at the board where she had placed Paula Markham's picture. "She acted on impulse with Megan. She saw the text message, and instead of asking her husband about it, or at least doing some kind of checking, she just went after her. She's been playing this perfect role for so long I think she finally snapped and lost control. It was impulsive, and impulse always leaves a trail. I don't think this would have been the end for her. There's always another obstacle to get in the way." She looked around at her team. "Good job putting this away quickly, everyone. Grab another doughnut on your way out. I don't want any left."

After grabbing their doughnuts, the detectives noisily filed out of the room, arguing over which flavors were best. Lynae stood by the table, practically drooling over the remaining sweets.

Jo rolled her eyes. "Just take a damn doughnut, Nae. Life's too short."

"Easy for your skinny butt to say." Lynae sighed and grabbed a Long John. She took a bite and groaned. "Okay, totally worth the workout I'll have to do later."

Jo picked up a black permanent marker and put an *X* over Paula Markham's face. "God, I hate this woman."

Lynae smirked. "I'm just glad we nailed the bitch. Even though she'll probably get an insanity plea, we can still chalk it up to a victory for the good guys."

Jo pulled the picture off the board and stared at it. "Yeah, some fucking victory."

"We nailed her. How's that not a victory?"

"How is any of this good? How do you call it a victory? Is anyone any less dead because of what we do?"

Lynae took a sip of coffee and motioned at the board. "We at least get some justice for the victim and her family."

"Justice, my ass. There's no justice for murder. Does it really help the families? So they know who did it. Great. Now they know that their so-called friend killed their daughter. I'm sure they feel so much better." Jo ripped Paula Markham's picture in half and threw the pieces in the trash. She stormed out of the conference room.

In her office, Jo flopped into her chair and turned on the television. *Damn, missed the monologue.*

Lynae appeared in the doorway. "I think it does help. It can at least give them some closure."

"This isn't the time, Nae. *Ellen*'s on."

Lynae stepped in and closed the door. "What the hell is it with you and that show? I'm trying to talk to you, and you would rather watch a damn TV show. It's not normal, Jo. Do you see anyone else around here with a television in their office?"

"I don't give a rat's ass what anyone else has in their office. Now if you don't mind, I said this isn't a good time."

"Then I'll wait for a commercial." Lynae sighed and leaned against the doorframe.

Jo pointed at Lynae. "You wanna know why I watch *Ellen* every day? You want to know why it's so important to me to get back here to see that show, why I have a television in my office? Because she's my friend."

"Wait. What? You know Ellen?"

Jo rolled her eyes. "No, I don't know Ellen." She leaned back in her chair. "But watching her show is like having coffee with a friend. For one hour, I can just laugh with a friend and forget my life. I can forget that everything else about it sucks. I can forget that my husband is dead and after over two years I don't have a clue how to live without him. And I can forget that everyone here thinks I'm crazy because I talk to my dead husband."

Lynae grabbed the visitor chair and pulled it around to the side of the desk before taking a seat. "No one thinks you're crazy."

Jo closed her eyes for a moment. "It's not just that. I can block out that I spend my days trudging through the blood that someone has spilled for no good reason. I can block out that I have to tell parents that their daughter is dead because she made a tough decision and someone else didn't like it, that someone killed their little girl to keep a social status intact. I can forget for one damned hour that I had to break the news to a man that his wife killed a teenager because she was afraid of losing her perfect life. How fucked up is that?"

Lynae sat with her elbows on her knees, leaning in close to Jo. She nodded and spoke softly. "A lot of what we see is fucked up."

Jo blinked back the tears that threatened to spill. "And I can forget that I know what it feels like to have someone come to your door and tell you that your life will never be the same and there's not a damn thing you can do about it. I can forget that I have to be that someone for people like the Tillmans. For that one hour, I'm just spending time with my friend, and the world has some laughter, some kindness, and maybe even some hope." She shrugged and rubbed her eyes. "Then at five o'clock, I turn it off and have to face reality again. But I have that one hour. And every day, that one hour helps me get to the next."

Lynae took Jo's hand. "You have to remember that you have real friends, Jo. You have friends like me who care and want to know how you're really doing. I care, and I can help. Ellen can't help. She doesn't know you or care about your life."

"Don't you see that's what makes it work? I don't want to face how I'm doing because reality sucks. You're the best, Nae. I told you more the other night than I've ever told anyone. But if you and I sat down for an hour every day just to talk, you would ask me how I'm doing without Mike, and..."

"Of course. I—"

Jo held up her hand. "I know it's because you care. I know you want to help. But if you ask, I either have to lie and say I'm fine or tell you the truth and probably have a breakdown. If I talk about it, I'll just cry."

Lynae squeezed Jo's hand. "So you cry. I can deal with that."

"I can't. When I start crying, I never know if I'll be able to stop."

"You have to let yourself grieve, and you don't have to do it alone."

Jo stared blindly at the television. She worked her jaw to push down the tears. "I can't... I can't deal with any of it right now. I'm just going through the motions, trying to put one foot in front of the other. I get out of bed in the morning and try to pretend my life is normal when all I really want to do is pull the covers over my head and stay in the dream where Mike is still alive and my life is great. Because I have that same dream every night. But I can't stay in bed. I can't stop living, stop working, stop putting that one foot in front of the other because then I'll break. And what good am I to anyone if I break?"

"If you don't talk about it and you keep trying to face it alone, you're going to break anyway. I know you have a hard time dealing with some things on the job that you didn't before. I can see it on your face. I'm not a counselor, but I am your friend. I can help. Please. I don't want to lose my partner."

Jo snorted and reached for a tissue. "You're not going to lose me. I'm too stubborn to go anywhere. I promise I'll talk to you before I go completely over the edge."

"Stubborn doesn't even begin to describe you. You're a mule." Lynae sat back and crossed her arms.

Jo shrugged. "Yeah, well, what can I say? I know it's messed up, but I'm going to keep talking to Mike and thinking I'm handling life just fine. Maybe someday it will be true."

"You're crazy, Jo, but I love you anyway."

Jo lowered her head and watched her hands pull apart the tissue as if they belonged to someone else. She whispered, "I'm not crazy."

"Geez. I didn't mean it like that."

Jo shrugged. "Maybe not, but I know some people around here think it. I know Mike's not really talking to me. I know what I hear is in my head, my subconscious, whatever. I don't see him. I'm not crazy. It just helps."

Lynae searched Jo's eyes for a moment then gave her hand a squeeze and got to her feet. "Okay, I'll leave you alone about it for now. But not forever."

"And Ellen would totally care if she knew me," Jo said, glaring at her friend.

Lynae cocked an eyebrow. "I already care, but whatever."

Jo smiled the first smile she had genuinely felt all day. "I know you do. Hey, how about lunch at my parents' tomorrow?"

"Really? Yeah, that sounds like fun."

Jo grinned. "Aunt Trudy is expecting you. We wouldn't want to let down good ol' Aunt Trudy, would we?"

"Of course not. What kind of girlfriend would that make me? And don't worry, I'll try to keep my hands off you as best I can."

"Please do. Mom thought it was brilliant, by the way."

"I love your mom."

"How could you not? I don't know what she's making for lunch, but I know it will be better than anything I've eaten since the last time I was there."

"If I don't have to poke plastic with a fork, it will definitely be better than what I had planned."

Jo laughed. "I promise no plastic poking will be involved."

"Then I'm in."

CHAPTER 38

JO KNOCKED ON THE DOOR of the two-story home a couple of doors down from the pharmacy where Megan Tillman's body had been found. The roof of the small house sagged dangerously, and the paint on the wooden frames around the old windows was peeled and chipped. Chances were good the windows hadn't been able to open for decades. It would be stifling hot in the summer, and the cold air would blast through the old frames in the winter.

"Who is it?"

"Detective Riskin, Mrs. Heard. I'd like to talk to Jeron."

Two dead bolts clanked, and the door opened a fraction on its chain. Jo positioned herself so the other woman could see her face and badge.

Mrs. Heard pushed on the door, released the chain, then opened the door all the way. She wore a simple blue dress with a light jacket. "What's this about, Detective? My boy didn't do anything wrong."

Jo grinned. "No, ma'am, he didn't. He did something very right, and I'm here to thank him."

Mrs. Heard looked surprised as she stepped aside for Jo to enter. Jeron peered around the corner from the next room. His mother motioned for him to join them. He was dressed in black dress pants slightly worn at the knees and a button-down shirt.

Jo smiled. "I'm sorry to come unannounced on a Sunday morning. It looks like you're heading somewhere."

Jeron sighed. "We got church."

"We *have* church," his mother corrected.

Jo nodded. "So do I. I won't keep you." She turned to Jeron. "I just wanted to stop in and tell you that we caught the person who killed Megan Tillman, and the phone you brought us was a huge help. We couldn't have done it without you, kid."

Jeron looked at her skeptically. "For real?"

"For real. You did a really good thing, and I want you to know we appreciate it."

Jeron shrugged and became very interested in his shoes.

"I know you could have made some money from that phone, but I hope it makes you feel good that you did the right thing."

"Yeah, it kinda does."

"Maybe you'll be a police officer when you grow up."

Jeron looked up at Jo and scowled. "You gotta go to college for that. My friends say college is for chumps."

Jo cocked her head. "And what do you say?"

He shrugged again.

"Well, what do your friends think is the cool thing to do?"

Jeron took a step back and posed gangsta style with his arms crossed. "Join up with the WidowMakers, if you can get in. Or another gang if you can't."

Jo shook her head. "Why would they want to do that?"

Jeron held out his hand and rubbed his fingers against his thumb. "Money. It's all about the money."

Jo nodded and pursed her lips. "Probably. Until you get caught and end up in jail, or worse, dead. Have you ever seen the inside of a jail, Jeron?"

He shook his head. "Uh-uh."

"It's a terrible place to be. You ask anybody who's there, and they'll tell you to stay out of the gangs. Maybe I can arrange to bring you to the jail and show you around." Jo looked up at Mrs. Heard and got the nod. She decided she would make that happen. She put a hand on the boy's shoulder. "You're a good kid, Jeron. You did the right thing where a lot of people wouldn't have. They would have sold that phone or kept it for themselves, and we might not have caught the person who killed Megan. The person who threw it out the window didn't count on a person like you finding it. That should make you feel good."

"Yeah, I guess it does."

"I'm glad." Jo was excited to give him the gift she had picked up that morning. She didn't mind spending a bit of her paycheck if it meant making an impression on the kid. She pulled the present from her coat pocket. "I have something for you."

Jeron gaped at her. "Really? What?"

She handed him the box and laughed as he jumped up and down and screamed.

"Mom, it's a iPod! Oh, man, this is awesome!"

Jo pulled an iTunes gift card out of her pocket. "You can use this to download some music."

He threw his arms around her waist and gave her a hug. "Thank you!"

Her heart melted a little bit. "You're welcome. Who's the chump now?"

He looked up at her with a smile, still hugging her waist. "Okay, I guess the police ain't so bad."

Jo hugged him back. "Remember that, kid."

CHAPTER 39

DINNER WITH JO'S FAMILY WAS always a party. Loud conversations, punctuated by frequent bursts of laughter, made the eight-person gathering sound more like twenty. Her mom's meals were feasts that could feed at least twice as many people.

After gorging herself on pork roast, mashed potatoes, glazed carrots, and a fresh fruit salad, Jo finally pushed her plate away. *If I don't stop now, how will I have room for apple pie?*

Lynae's phone rang, and she glanced at the display. With a puzzled expression, she answered with "Parker" as she made an apologetic gesture and stood. She suddenly turned and gave Jo a wide-eyed look. "What can I do for you, Tonya?"

Jo jumped up, her full stomach forgotten, and reached Lynae in two long-legged strides. All conversation at the table stopped. Lynae held up her hand and motioned for Jo to follow her. They moved into the foyer, where Lynae stood against the wall, listening to Tonya, and Jo paced in front of her. Time seemed to stand still while Jo waited.

Lynae checked her watch then said into the phone, "I can be there in thirty minutes."

Jo ran to the closet and grabbed their coats. She threw on hers as she jogged back to Lynae, who was sliding the phone back into her pocket. "I'll drive."

Lynae took her coat. "Jo, you can't go with me."

"Like hell!"

"She wants to talk to me. Just me."

Jo grabbed Lynae's arm. "I need to be there."

"She doesn't trust you. You don't understand. I do."

"This is my case, Nae. And don't forget that I'm your lieutenant."

Lynae pulled Jo's hand from her arm and held it firmly. "This isn't your case, and you're not my lieutenant right now. You're my friend, and you have to let me do this alone."

"Not my case? It's my life!"

"Then trust me with it," Lynae said gently.

Jo rolled her shoulders. "Shit, Nae, don't put it that way."

"You scare her. That won't get us anywhere. She trusts me, and that's what we need right now."

"I won't push her. I just need to be there."

"You've been pushing the limits on this case, and I've kept my mouth shut. But I think we have a chance that she'll talk. If you're there, it could be used against us in court. It could be seen as coercion."

Jo threw her hands up. "I'm not going to do anything to jeopardize the case. I know how to talk to a witness."

"Just you *being* there jeopardizes the case. You know that, Jo. You're just not seeing it because you're too close."

"How am I supposed to sit here and act like everything's fine while you're with her?"

Lynae opened the door. "I'll call you the second I know anything. I have to go now. Even if nothing pans out today, she has to know she can trust me to be there when she calls. Nancy was always there for me. I'm her Nancy."

Jo ran her hand through her hair. She knew she didn't really have any options. "Better not keep her waiting."

Lynae bolted out the door. Jo watched her drive away and sent up a silent prayer that they could finally get the break she needed to put the case, and Mike, to rest.

She walked back to the table, where her family sat quietly. As close as she was to her family, she had hidden her pain and obsession as well as she could. She didn't need more people worrying about her or questioning her sanity. They knew she grieved, but none of them knew the extent of it.

Her mom slapped a hand on the table. "Quit the bullshit,

Joellen." Every head turned her way. When Mom swore, she meant business. "You jumped out of your chair like it was on fire. What's going on?"

Jo looked around the table at the people she loved most, even crazy Aunt Trudy. She took a deep breath and... dissolved into tears. Her brother's crushing hug only caused a deeper crack in the dam that had finally burst.

"It's about time," he mumbled. He held her tightly and rubbed her back until her sobs quieted to hiccupping sniffles.

"Okay, so maybe I'm not dealing with Mike's death quite as well as I've let on." Jo studied the faces of her family and knew that she hadn't been fooling anyone. They had just been letting her deal in her own way, waiting for the moment they all had known would come.

Her mom came over and gave her a gentle hug, the kind only a mom knew how to give. "You're so stubborn, Jo."

I'm not ready to give up watching Ellen *or chatting with Mike, but maybe there's something to this talking to real people.* Jo laid her head on her mom's shoulder and took comfort in the familiar scent of her perfume. "You called me Jo."

"Just this once. Now are you going to tell us what's going on with Lynae?"

Trudy cleared her throat. "Who is this Tonya? Is she someone from Lynae's past?"

Jo snorted. Mom's shoulder shook a little, and Dad rolled his eyes. Brian winked at his wife. Jo knew her mom must have passed along their "neither confirm nor deny" ploy to keep Aunt Trudy off her back.

Jo scrubbed at her face and rubbed her temples in an attempt to stave off the building headache. "No, this is about Mike's case."

Dad set down his coffee cup. "What do you have going on?"

It was time to talk about the elephant that had been in the room for so long, the one she hadn't even realized was sitting there. She told them everything, even the most painful parts that she had buried deep.

When Jo finally ran out of steam, Mom put an arm around

her shoulders. "I sit in the cemetery sometimes and talk to your grandpa."

Jo wiped her nose with a tissue Aunt Trudy passed her. "You do?"

Mom nodded. "It's healing, and it's okay. Just make sure you talk to living people too."

"So I'm not crazy?"

Mom smiled and motioned around the room. "Not any crazier than the rest of us."

Jo laughed. "Is that supposed to make me feel better?"

Mom elbowed her and grinned. "Why don't we cut that apple pie?"

Jo followed her mom into the kitchen. "I'm not sure I can eat, but for your pie, I'll give it my best shot."

They cut the pie and brought plates back to the table for the others. Jo picked at her piece while her family peppered her with questions about Tonya, Drevin, and Treybro. When her phone rang, the conversation screeched to a halt.

Jo snatched her phone off the table and hustled into the kitchen. She needed to be alone. "Lynae?"

"Get ahold of Madison. Tonya's ready to talk."

Can this really be happening? Jo's heart thundered in her chest. "You're sure?"

"She's tired and hurt and scared to death, but she's ready to get out. She has a sister who lives out of state, and she's already called her. She's moving there to get away from him, and I'm going to help her."

"So will I. But she can't leave until we put this guy away."

"I know. We've talked about it. I'm hoping her statement will be enough, but she's ready to testify if it comes to that."

Jo dropped her head back to stare at the ceiling. "Oh, Nae, I could kiss you."

"Let's save that for never. Just get to the station."

Jo hung up the phone. She needed to go, but she couldn't seem to get her feet to move. Brian walked into the kitchen. "Are you okay?"

Jo looked up at her brother. She had shut him out for too long. "The witness Lynae went to see is ready to talk. This could be the break we've been waiting for." It all came out in one gush.

"Why are you standing here, then?"

Jo gripped the countertop, breathing in short, ragged spurts. In the back of her mind, she wondered if she was having a panic attack. "I can't move. What if she's wrong? What if this is just another dead end?"

Brian took her by the shoulders and gently turned her to him. He put his finger under her chin and lifted her face to his. "Then you'll move on. You'll keep looking until you find the road that isn't a dead end. And hopefully, you'll talk about it with us. I don't want to be visiting my baby sister in the nut house."

Jo snorted and wiped a tear. "We crazy people prefer you to call it our vacation home." She gave her brother a quick hug. "You're right. I have to do this. I don't want to stop to explain. Can you tell the family where I've gone and why?"

"You got it. Go. Call me later, though, and let me know."

She only barely heard the last part as she ran for the front door. Outside, she hopped into her Ranger, hit the Bluetooth, and dialed Kirk Madison's number.

"Hello?"

"Kirk, this is Jo Riskin."

"Jo, what's going on?"

Jo laid a path in the gravel as she spun out of her parents' driveway. "We got him, Kirk. I have a witness ready to finger our killer."

Kirk didn't even ask what killer she was talking about. "Tell me you haven't talked to this witness."

Jo chose not to mention the earlier visit in the hospital. "Lynae talked to her. She's ready to give a statement."

"Damn it, Jo! You should have called me. You can't be pursuing leads on this case."

"She hasn't given a statement. Lynae is there as a friend."

Kirk sighed. "I hope that flies."

"I'm sorry, I should have called you. I've just had so many dead ends. I didn't want to waste your time until I knew for sure. This one is legit, though, Kirk. We're going to nail the son of a bitch."

"How did you find this witness?"

Jo zipped into the left lane to pass a tractor. "I got her name from an inmate at Ottawa County."

Kirk's sigh came through loud and clear. "So you interviewed this guy without me present?"

"I got a call from a detective saying this guy asked for me specifically. No way I could have known what it was about."

"And you didn't think you should call me when you did know?"

Jo huffed. "I'm sorry, Kirk. Can we just concentrate on getting the witness statement and putting the bastard behind bars?"

"I'll need you to fill me in on everything before I talk to this witness. I can be at the station in twenty minutes."

Jo sped down the county road. "I'll be there."

CHAPTER 40

JO SAT IN HER RANGER in the parking lot of Drevin Clayburn's apartment complex. She watched Kirk talk with the building super outside the main entrance while his team milled around in the yard. The two-way police radio sat on the seat next to her. She was fuming. "I can't believe he's making me wait out here!"

Lynae turned in her seat. "He had to, Jo. Any second-year law student could blow holes in a case if the victim's wife was involved in the search."

"I would never taint evidence. I want to know I put the right guy behind bars."

Lynae nodded. "I know that, but the eight members of a jury don't know you. Would you allow it if this was your case and someone else's spouse?"

Jo leaned her head on the window. "No. I know this is necessary. It just sucks."

"As it is, Kirk's going to have to do some fancy footwork to get around what we've already done."

"Kirk said Tonya's statement was solid. She had details that only someone involved in the shooting would have known. The judge had no problem signing the search warrant. We'll be okay on that."

Kirk shook the super's hand and walked into the building with him. His team gathered their gear and followed. Jo kept her eyes trained on the door as the time ticked away in her head like a bomb.

The radio crackled. "Drevin isn't here. The super let us in."

Jo put the radio to her mouth. "Shit. Well, we know who he is.

We get the gun, then we'll stake out the place and grab him when he comes back."

"Gee, thanks, Jo. I wasn't sure how this procedure worked."

Jo rubbed her forehead. "Sorry, Kirk. It's hard to sit out here."

The radio sputtered. "Just giving you a hard time. I'll let you know when we find something." Jo heard the smile in Kirk's voice.

Jo squeezed the radio button. "Thanks." She laid the device on the dashboard and slouched in her seat.

A couple walked to the front entrance, laughing as they juggled grocery bags while trying to get the key fob raised to the security box. A woman came out a few minutes later with a dachshund on a leash. She popped earbuds in and took off on a jog. The little dog scrambled to keep up on his miniature legs. Two kids rode through the parking lot on bikes, too young, in Jo's opinion, to be by themselves. But then again, she had seen too much.

Jo groaned. "What's taking them so long?"

Lynae checked her watch. "It's only been a few minutes. It seems longer since we're just sitting here."

Three teenage boys sauntered out of the building. One casually dribbled a basketball, bouncing it around and between his legs.

Jo watched them pass in front of the vehicle. "Busy place."

"I was just thinking the same thing."

The radio crackled. "We found the gun."

Jo and Lynae let out a whoop and high-fived.

Jo spoke into the radio. "That's fantastic! You coming out with it?"

"I'm going to finish searching this closet. It's chock full of boxes. Dude's got a bit of an obsession with shoes. The gun is bagged and tagged. I want to take it to ballistics myself to keep the chain of custody minimal."

"It's Sunday. Is anyone in to run ballistics?"

"I got that covered. I called Canfield before I left the station. He's standing by to come in to run the ballistics when I call."

Jo smiled. "You thought of everything, didn't you?"

"This isn't my first rodeo. Why don't you head out and meet me at the station? There's nothing you can do here."

"On my way." Jo dropped her head onto the steering wheel. "I can't believe this is actually happening."

Lynae put her arm around Jo's shoulders and gave her a squeeze. "You did it."

Jo rolled her head to the side to look at Lynae. "I couldn't have done it without you."

Lynae winked. "Oh yeah, you totally owe me for the rest of your life. We'll hash out the details later."

Jo sat up and started the Ranger. "Let's get to the station. We'll draw the contract up there."

As she turned the wheel to pull out of her parking space, she spotted a familiar face. The suspect was climbing out of a car a few rows over. He strolled through the parking lot, apparently heading for home.

She hit the brakes and grabbed the radio. "Kirk, Drevin Clayburn is coming up the walk right now."

"Perfect timing. We'll grab him on the way in."

Jo and Lynae hunched down in their seats. The last thing they needed was for Drevin to see and recognize the two cops sitting in a car in his parking lot. Jo held her breath as he got closer to the building.

A few feet away from the door, Drevin stopped. Jo turned her head to see what he was looking at and saw the white county van parked a few spaces behind her.

Jo smacked the steering wheel with the palm of her hand. "Why did they drive a county vehicle? Sticks out like a sore thumb."

Drevin turned and jogged back to his car.

Jo yelled into the radio. "He's bolting!" She tossed the radio onto the dashboard and popped her vehicle into drive.

Drevin hopped into his car and started to pull out of his parking space. Jo swung her car around and blocked his exit. Drevin looked up and locked eyes with her then jumped out of his car and ran.

"Shit!" Jo shoved the car door open with one hand while unbuckling her seat belt with the other. She sprang out of the car and took off after him. She could hear Lynae's feet pounding the pavement right behind her.

Drevin sprinted behind a building. His long legs ate up the ground at a breakneck pace. Jo poured everything she had into the pursuit. Her mind raced with thoughts of Mike: his smile, his laughter, their long talks and debates, the love and security she had felt with him. She thought of the baby that she would never know. The only piece of Mike that she had had left, and that had been taken from her too.

All of the anger and pain, the sleepless nights, and the frustration of hitting dead end after dead end came rushing at her. Her focus zeroed in on the cause of that pain. She could see nothing but the killer, hear nothing but the sound of her heart racing and her own ragged breathing.

Drevin darted left then scrambled back when Lynae came around that side of the building. The hesitation was all Jo needed. She launched herself at him. Her teeth clamped together on impact with him, and they both fell to the ground. Lynae trotted over with her hand on her gun. Drevin gave Jo a shove, trying to get her off of him.

Jo rolled away and pulled her gun out of the back of her jeans. Lynae drew her gun and trained it on him. They both yelled, "Freeze! Police!"

He held up his hands. "Whoa, chill! I didn't do anything wrong."

Jo was panting from the exertion. "Why did you run when you saw me, then?"

He shrugged. "I don't like cops."

"I got a feeling you're gonna like us even less very soon. There's a whole team from the county searching your apartment right now. They've already recovered a gun."

He frowned then regained his composure and gave his customary smirk. "So I got a gun, so what?"

"Maybe you don't want to be quite so cocky. We have reason to believe, and a witness to testify, that the gun was used in the shooting and murder of a police detective."

Drevin licked his lips. His eyes rapidly darted between Jo and Lynae. "Who told you that bullshit?"

"You wanna just save us some time and confess right now?"

"I ain't confessin' to nothin'. You got nothin' on me."

"We have a gun from your apartment. We're going to take that gun back to the station and run it through a ballistics test. You know what that is? That's going to tell us if it's the same gun that killed Detective Riskin."

"Riskin? Ain't that *your* name?"

Jo gritted her teeth. "Yeah. Yeah, it is."

Drevin's eyes flicked to the gun. "What, you gonna shoot me?"

Jo's hand shook as she fought to hold the gun steady. Drevin's wild eyes shot to Lynae. Beads of sweat dripped from his temples. "Hey, get this crazy bitch away from me!"

Lynae took a step toward them. "Jo…"

Jo glared at Drevin. She knew he was guilty. She felt it. In her gut, she knew she was looking at the man who had blown her world apart. But she needed the proof. She needed to know she had put the *right* man behind bars. She heard Mike's voice. *You're a cop, and you believe in the system. Take him down, lock down the case against him, and throw him in a cage. That's the way Lieutenant Riskin does things.*

"I'm not going to shoot him, Nae," Jo whispered. "He's unarmed."

Drevin swallowed hard. "Then maybe you should point that gun somewhere else."

"Get down on the ground. I'm sure you know what to do."

Drevin dropped down and spread his hands and legs. Trying to calm down, Jo holstered her gun, pulled out her cuffs, and slapped them on his wrists.

As she pulled him to his feet and started patting him down, she began reading his rights. "You have the right to remain silent…"

Kirk Madison trotted around the corner of the building. "I couldn't find you."

"You're just in time." Jo handed the suspect over to him.

She was done. She had finally found the man who killed her

husband, and she would make sure he paid. But she would do it the right way, the way Mike would want. She would make sure Drevin Clayburn would never live outside of a cage, and that was going to have to be good enough.

CHAPTER 41

JO LEANED AGAINST THE COLD tombstone, her head back, soaking up the warmth of the late-fall sun. "Why 'sit up,' Mike? The paramedic said you kept repeating it. Why?"

I also said, 'Jo.' I was thinking of you.

Jo smiled. It was comforting to know he had been thinking of her, that her name had been the last word on his lips. His last words haunted her, but she knew she would never get an answer to what they meant. After all, Mike lived only in her head.

Let it go, Jo. You got your man. It's time to move on.

She felt torn. She had finally found Mike's killer. Tonya had signed a statement and was willing to testify. With the gun being a match, they had enough evidence to put Clayburn away for good. And she knew they would. There was no mercy or second chance for a cop killer. But she had been so focused on finding the killer for so long that now that she had, she didn't know how to move on.

"What am I supposed to do now?"

Now you live your life.

"I don't know how."

You'll figure it out. You just have to let yourself.

"I loved my life with you. I was okay being half of a whole. I don't know who I am anymore."

You're Jo Riskin. Kick-ass homicide lieutenant.

"Yeah, I guess I am."

And don't let anyone forget it.

"How could they?"

That's my girl.

Jo closed her eyes and smiled. Maybe she would be okay after all.

ACKNOWLEDGMENTS

If it takes a village to raise a child, then it takes a metropolis to publish a book. So many people have helped me with support and encouragement along this journey that I can't possibly make a complete list. I sincerely appreciate each and every one of you.

Special thanks goes to:

The amazing team at Red Adept Publishing, especially my editors, Lynn McNamee and Angela McRae, for taking my story to the next level. I humbly bow to your knowledge, expertise, and incredible eye for detail.

The artists at Streetlight Graphics for creating my stunning book cover.

Bill Jack, a fellow writer, who was instrumental in getting me started on this journey. Thanks for your beta read, your encouragement, and for making me think, "Hey, if this guy can write a book, anybody can."

Stacy Hubert (wielder of the red pen), for your honest input, subject expertise, and most importantly, your friendship.

My sisters for your constant support, love, and insane sense of humor. Without your late-night texting-me-off-the-ledge sessions, unwavering belief in me, and an occasional kick in the pants, this book would never have made it outside my computer. No one makes me laugh harder or gets me like you do!

My parents, my role models, who believed in me long before anyone else. Thanks for encouraging my wild imagination and for supporting every dream I've ever had. If I could have one wish granted for this crazy world, it would be that every child could grow up with parents like you. I'm thankful to be one of the lucky ones.

My kids, my reason for everything. I am able to follow my dreams, because my greatest dream—you—has already come true. I love you beyond measure.

Finally, to my husband, John. You are my constant, my rock, my strongest supporter, and the love of my life. Thank you for never allowing me to give up and for giving me a gentle nudge when I needed it. Without you beside me, this dream would not be complete. I love you so.

ABOUT THE AUTHOR

Debbie TenBrink grew up on a farm in West Michigan, where her family has lived for over 150 years. She still lives within five miles of her childhood home with her husband, four children, and dog, Mojo (who is the only real-life character in her book). She has a master's degree in career and technical education, and she taught computer classes in two local colleges before beginning her current career as a software specialist for a law firm.

In her free time, Debbie enjoys camping, hiking, sports, and any other activity she can use as an excuse to spend time in the great outdoors. Other hobbies include reading (of course), having long conversations with the characters living in her head, and an almost frightening interest in true crime TV shows.

Her passion for writing began in childhood with short stories and poetry, and she can't remember a time when she didn't know that she would someday write a novel.

39478089R00150

Made in the USA
Middletown, DE
19 January 2017